Two-Star Hotel

(Where the Stars Don't Mean Anything)

By Mike Avitabile

For Jake, Dave, Cory, Erin, and Matt

"The act of painting is about one heart
telling another heart where he found salvation."

– Francisco de Goya

Prologue

Sofia always says that I'm too fixated on boats. But what does she know? She was never trained in the arts. She wouldn't know art if it hit her in the face. If it paid for her dinner, her wardrobe, this villa. Sometimes she's just so inconsiderate. She doesn't realize all that I do. All that I *am*.

My brush is flitting across the canvas, my palette knife slashing away at the globs of paint and chopping them into sliced smudges. I'm making choppy waves at the expense of the boat. When I think of Sofia, I make them choppier. That poor ship; it is really in rough water. The sailors—I don't paint the people on the boats, that's bad luck—they are probably below deck, holding back their nausea. Puking on each other. Making a mess of the whole cabin. Making everyone else who wasn't nauseous begin to feel it as well. The vomit sloshing across the creaky oak floors, seeping into their pores, the smell never able to be fully expunged. All because of the waves. All because of Sofia.

"Antonio!" she yells out, her voice echoing down the empty hall.

The poor sailors, trapped in a stench-ridden galley, miles from land. Their clothes are probably reeking of the whole awful mess. I'm in there somewhere. Maybe I'm the captain. Maybe I'm someone else. A part of me is always in each of my creations. It just is that way.

Sofia's footsteps approach me—*pitter-patter, pitter-patter*—until she's practically on top of me. I don't turn around. She knows that I can hear her. The rest of the place is as silent as a tomb.

"Antonio," she repeats. "What did you say?"

I shake my head.

"I was creating," I try to tell her. "I need space. Can't you see? I need space to create. This is what I do. I am a *creator*."

"You have space," she tells me. "You have all this space!"

She flings her arms wildly around, as though the air a meter above the ground is the space I'm concerned about.

"No," I tell her. "I don't. This room—it's practically bursting with all these paintings. I can barely walk from one side to the other without tripping!"

I stand up from my stool to show her exactly how crowded it is. She's making it worse by just being in here.

"Then let me help you with that," she purrs.

She grabs the canvas closest to her and drags it across the floor to the other side of the room. I let out a deep sigh as I sit back down.

She continues dragging, canvas by canvas, until the area beneath my feet is clear. I stare straight ahead at the easel, still holding my brush.

"Another boat?" she asks, leaning her bony forearms on my shoulder blades.

"Yes, another boat," I tell her. "I did a bus too. Do you want to see?"

"No," she says.

So I sit, dumbly, and I don't move until eventually she steps back and her hands slip away from my shoulders. I set the palette down on the floor, sighing as I turn back to look at the mess she's created.

"Shit!" I yell, springing from my stool and pushing her out of my way as I drop frantically to my knees. "These are oil paintings! You can't just rest them against each other!"

She has stacked two of the canvases face-to-face. I can't tell which ones they are, but that's irrelevant. I slowly start to peel the pair apart from each other. The corners—they're sticking, and I can't separate them without a level of force that I don't want to use.

"How can you be so careless?!" I scream. "So selfish! You're insane! Insane! You know how important these are, and you probably just ruined them!"

My eyes are tearing up. She just keeps staring at me, unfazed. I slide and twist the frames, and I eventually separate the two canvases from each other. The paint in the corners—it's all muddied and smashed together, one transferring to another and transferring back to the other until it's impossible to tell which paint was from what canvas. These two paintings will never be the same. Their worlds, their characters...it's all just one big mess now.

I flop my body against the wall behind me and throw my hands up to my face to catch my head as it falls. Through my bent fingers, I peek out at the canvases, hoping that maybe I saw it all wrong and they were fine, that nothing had happened.

"Why?" I ask her. "Why couldn't you have just left them alone?"

She turns and stares at the painting closest to her.

"Tell me about *this* boat," she sneers. "How's it any different than the other dozen boats you've already painted?"

"It's not the boat, Sofia. It's the *people* in there."

"I don't see any people," she remarks.

"Just because you don't see them doesn't mean they aren't in there," I sigh. "We've been through this how many times? I create these worlds so that these people have some place to *be*. A place to find their salvation."

"That's right," she murmurs and then slowly turns away from the painting to face me directly again. "You and your perfect little sinners."

I shake my head.

"They are what they are. You know, I didn't choose any of this," I remind her. "This is just what I'm here to do."

"It'll be fine, Antonio...you can still sell them. I'm sure no one will even notice the difference."

"It doesn't matter if anyone wants them. Selling them is beside the point," I tell her. "What matters is that they're ruined!"

Her arms are folded as she shrugs. She knows exactly who I am and how important this all is, but she doesn't give the slightest shit. To Sofia, I'm just another painter, and these are just paintings.

She rolls her eyes and then turns her back to me, whispering as she strolls out the door: "You know what they say, Antonio...one man's trash is another man's treasure."

— Excerpt from the journal of Antonio Palmieri
Fontainebleau, 2013

Grant

(GREED)

My quads are burning. Glutes too. Why don't they have escalators here? It's not quaint. It's inconvenient. I can't stop counting the steps as we continue ascending…72, 73—I look at my watch but get dizzy and look away—76, 77.

"How much longer?" Piper asks.

I crane my neck up, and all I see is a winding staircase, walls covered in grimy, white subway tile. There is no end. I shrug.

"Can't be much longer. It's already been like eighty stairs."

It's not *like* 80. It's 84, 85, 86. I just don't want her to know that I've been counting.

"Hope so."

The burning turns into tingling. My legs might be falling asleep. How is that even possible? I'm *walking* up stairs. I'm using the damned things. A tiny bit of pressure pokes against my rear right pocket, and I spin around out of instinct. A little girl, maybe eleven or twelve years old, stares back at me with a scowl.

"What are you, crazy man?" she snarls.

Her French accent would be cute if she didn't look downright mean, her furrowed brow defined by years of mistreatment, no doubt. How does a kid get to be so tough at such a young age? I reach back and pat my pocket, feeling for my wallet.

"The fuck..."

I turn around and keep climbing, feeling stupid... 102, 103, 104. Then, finally, daylight: 110. We're above ground now. Poor kid. I probably scared the shit out of her.

I'm breathing hard. The cold gust of air that runs over my face reminds me that it's November. My lungs fill with icy bursts of vapor. Paris is nothing like L.A. Sam told me that it was eighty-five degrees the other day. Everybody went to the beach, drinking rum and diets in unsuspicious twenty-ounce bottles while the lifeguards sat in their aging towers, distracted, swiping left like there's an endless line of people and none of them actually matter. I'm so glad I don't have to participate in that shit anymore. It feels good to be *committed*.

Wendy's sweet face appears somewhere in my conscious mind. I love the way she stares at me when it's just the two of us. When we're apart, I yearn for the chemistry between us. It's like nothing I've ever felt. It wasn't even that long ago that I realized I wanted to be with her. What's it been...half a year now? Before that, I chased her for a solid month, hoping she'd eventually break down and give in, finally deciding that there could be worse things than dating me. Sometimes I wonder if I forced her into something she didn't even want. I know I can make her happy, but we're not always happy...

Wendy fades from my mind, and Sam and the beach reappear. Supposedly there was some kind of Regatta that started in the Marina, and there were sailboats all up and down the coast; but this is Sam's account of the events, and I don't even know if he knows what a Regatta is. Now Sam and the beach fade, and all that's left is me and the busy Parisian street. I'm in a jacket and a scarf. As soon as I realize it, I take the jacket off. It's making me sweaty.

A long thread from my scarf gets stuck on the zipper, and the whole thing wraps itself around my head. I'm temporarily mummified. Piper helps me get out of it.

"What was that back there? You make a new friend?"

"I don't know. I thought someone was grabbing my wallet. But it was just that little girl behind me."

"She's probably a thief."

I look around to find her, but I can't.

"The girl? No. She's like ten years old."

"That's a thing, you know. That's a thing here."

"What's a thing?"

"They get these kids to pick people's pockets, and then they split what they earn with their handlers. Like, these older criminal guys that know they look too suspicious to lurk behind regular people on the stairs. But nobody's going to suspect a little girl." Piper pauses, then nods knowingly. "Yeah. I'm telling you. She's a thief."

"Really?"

"Definitely."

"Where'd she go?"

"How about you put that thing in your front pocket, hmm?"

She has a good point. I switch it to the front, and immediately it's not as comfortable. These are new jeans, and the front pockets are tight. No one makes stylish pants with even semi-deep pockets anymore. If we've got any more stairs ahead of us, my wallet's probably going to burst through the intentional thigh rip in these jeans and make John Varvatos a little richer when I get back home.

"You think a girl that young could be a thief? Really?"

Piper shrugs. The sign over the stairs says *METROPOLITAIN*. I can't remember if that's the English way of spelling that word too. I pull out my map.

"What station is this again?"

"Abbesses."

"What kind of name is that?"

She ignores me.

"I think we go that way."

Piper points north, or maybe northwest. I follow her as we start to walk away from the station, a merry-go-around spinning quietly behind us, a few kids clinging to the poles like their lives depend on it.

Piper

(PRIDE)

I love it here. It's so romantic, but all I can do is think about Sam. I hate myself for it, but I'm wondering what he's doing right now. Maybe he's still lying in bed. Alone. I hope he's alone.

Grant's fidgeting with his wallet, trying to adjust it in his front pocket, so I walk ahead of him. He's not going to make me miss my chance to see the Sacre-Coeur before it closes. I don't even know if it closes. I've got to keep the pace here either way. It's already 16:30, and the sun sets at 17:13 today. I've been practicing saying times the European way. I barely had to practice, and it's already starting to set in. I could totally live here.

"Come on, man."

"Do you really think she was a thief? I've never had someone try to pickpocket me before. Definitely not a little girl."

"God. Who cares, Grant? Nothing happened. Let's go."

"How does that make it any better?" he mutters as he trails behind me.

Grant

More stairs. Great. This city and the fucking stairs. This time there's fifty-four and then another landing. Then another fifty-two. I may as well be at the damned gym, all this climbing. I didn't sign up for this. Who the hell builds a church all the way on the top of a giant hill anyway? How are all the disadvantaged people—because let's face it, that's the majority of the church population no matter where you are—how are they going to make it all the way up there?

"What's so great about this place?"

Vapor huffs out of my mouth as I'm talking. I purse my lips and try to blow a smoke ring, but that doesn't work with vapor, and I think I already knew that. I just got caught up in the moment.

"Just...come on. It's historical. And beautiful."

There are a few cafés to the left, and people are sitting down at a cluster of tables that line the sidewalk, all crammed in and surrounded by a bluish haze of cigarette smoke. It's all so Parisian—the cobblestone streets and sidewalk vendors and people drinking wine against the slants of light from the late afternoon sun. I thought that was all just cliché. I didn't realize until now that Paris was *actually* like this.

More stairs.

"You've got to be kidding me."

"Come on," Piper moans.

I'm walking behind her, and I can't help it—like, I literally can't help it—but I'm staring at her ass. It's not bad, not from this angle, though I'm pretty sure it's just that her jeans are doing their job very well. I doubt her ass is that great when you get past the jeans. I turn my eyes to the ground.

Sam

(SLOTH)

I hate these sheets. Wait, are these my sheets? Why are they wet? Is this my bed? Am I in my house?

Look around. See the tiger poster on the wall by the door. See my neon alarm clock.

"Where...?"

My back is damp, and I'm hoping it's just sweat, so I roll over to my stomach and lie on the other side of the bed, examining the wet stain on my sheets. It looks like a reverse snow angel, the shape of my torso and arms pressed into the fabric and exposed in a slightly darker shade of red. I really hate these sheets. They were hand-me-downs. Who even buys red sheets? I press my nose up against them and reluctantly sniff.

It's been hot. I think when I got back last night after the bar shut down and they kicked us out and we walked through Thai Town and got some curry at a place that shouldn't have even been open that late, I think I forgot to turn the A/C on before I fell asleep. So now, this. A sweat angel.

Head is pounding, look for some Tylenol, can't find any. Look at my phone, have a few messages from Grant:

> *You'd like Paris. Gotta take you here next time borth!*
> *I tried to order an Americano at a Starbucks. Thought you'd appreciate that*
> *Btw Piper says hi*

Piper

We pass by an outdoor craft fair. There are local painters sitting down at their easels, some of them brushing faint strokes across what can only be previously completed pieces, pretending that they are *just* putting on the finishing touches. Some of them are sketching caricatures of willing tourists, plopped dumbly in front of the back of a stretched canvas. All the subjects are ugly, but their painting-selves are gorgeous. Imagine what they could do for me? I'm already at least an L.A. eight. Maybe a Parisian seven. Some painters are just sitting there wearing berets, staring down at their phones. My ankles roll slightly in their joints as we meander along the cobblestone plaza.

Paris is everything I thought it would be. We keep walking. Grant tries stopping a few times, but I'll be damned if we miss the sunset, so I leave him behind. The sunset is the whole reason we waited this long to come up here in the first place. He catches up soon enough.

"We almost there?" he moans.

God. It's like he's never walked before. The guy goes to the gym every fucking day, but he can't handle a couple hours of casual strolling?

"I think it's right over here," I tell him, though I have no idea. I'm just walking in the general direction that I glimpsed from the map. I haven't looked at it in a few minutes.

We turn a corner, and I see, peeking through some clumsily strewn-together trees, a sliver of the skyline of the city beneath us. I turn to the left, and then I see it.

"Sacre-Coeur," I whisper under my breath.

Grant trots alongside me.

"This it?"

I nod.

"Let's go around to the front."

Grant

Wow. A big church. Never seen that before. And a sunset too? Jeez. Can't believe it. I just can't believe it. They have these in Paris? Unbelievable.

"It's nice," I say.

Piper is marveling; her mouth is gaping open. She's taking a hundred pictures, though this time I'm not counting. But it's probably a hundred. A huge smile is beaming across her face, and I can't help but smile too. She looks so happy. I don't know if this trek was worth it, but I'm sure she thinks it is, so I don't say anything negative to avoid ruining the moment.

"Can we go inside?"

"You don't even believe in God," she reminds me.

"I believe in architecture though. Does it cost anything?"

"No, I don't think so."

"Then yeah. I want to go in."

"You're not going to make fun of everything once you get in there, are you?"

"Piper, what kind of asshole do you think I am? Just because I don't believe in God doesn't mean that I shit all over people who do! I just want to see the inside of the damned thing. We walked all the way up here, after all. Might as well see what it's all about."

"All right."

"Who knows. Maybe this will convert me."

She's already ahead of me again, shaking her head. Sometimes I just say stuff to piss her off. I consider it the give and take of opposite-sex friendships. Or maybe it's just because I think of her like my little sister. I listen to all her girly shit and problems and whatever, and in return she has to deal with my sarcastic, never-ending cynicism. If we didn't have this between us, we'd probably have fucked around and ruined the whole thing. It's better this way.

We walk inside, and there are signs in multiple languages that all convey the same general message: when you walk in here, shut the fuck up. I guess it makes sense. House of the Lord and all that. We slowly shuffle along the guided path that circles the pews and wraps around behind the altar. Little tea lights are strewn across wide, stacked plates, flickering without rhythm. Easels are presenting unremarkable photos of patrons who have seemingly come and gone. An occasional clergyman stands off to the side, enraptured in deep, ecclesiastic thought. A dozen or so people are crouched on kneelers, huddled near the middle of the left row of benches. Praying in the middle of the afternoon on a Saturday. Damn if I'll ever do that.

Piper

He touches me, and I feel his power, his strength. I feel loved unconditionally. He speaks to me when I'm in here, and he says words to me that only I can hear. I'm in his house now, so I listen. I should always listen, but sometimes I forget to.

"This cool or what?" Grant whispers.

Someone shushes him. That was fast, but I'm relieved. It saved me from doing it.

We keep walking along the path, and we're almost all the way out now. It's still dark, and the smell of wood furniture polish is wafting through the air. Or maybe it's someone's aftershave, I don't know. Grant bumps into me from behind, and I laugh. He's such an idiot sometimes. And he's the smarter one of the two of them.

The light from the main exit door guides us outside again to the steps in front of the basilica. Hundreds of tourists and locals are mixed together on the larger staircase below. Everyone's using selfie sticks. I want to add this to my story, but the data charges will kill me, so I just stand still for a bit and watch the setting sun. It's pretty, but I'm twitchy. I need to capture this moment somehow.

"Should we have someone take our picture?"

Grant scowls and then tries to hide it. He hates pictures.

"Sure."

He reaches over to a guy next to him and asks. The guy declines, but the girl he's with says yes. Grant hands the girl his phone from his pocket.

"No! Use mine!"

He looks at me with an impatient smile. We swap phones, and the girl stands in front of us, the church directly to my back. Grant walks over and puts his arm around my shoulder. His hand is warm and heavy. I try to ignore it and smile. The girl taps the screen a few times, smiles, and hands it back to me. They wait the few-second courtesy wait, and when I nod, they go back to whatever it was that they were doing.

"Any good?" Grant asks.

I'm swiping back and forth between them.

"I look like an elephant," I say, even though I look cute in all of them.

"Of course you do," he says.

Grant

The train station looks different than when we left it earlier in the afternoon. The people are less amused and joyful. It feels like a commuter crowd, but it's a Saturday, and I know the French don't like working too hard.

We're waiting in line to buy our return tickets.

"Oh my God, Grant! Look!"

Piper grabs my arm and points toward the bottom of the staircase.

"Is that her?"

I slide to the left to get a better view.

"Yeah."

That little French thief, she's back at the bottom of the stairs! She's got a cigarette resting on her lip, looking like a defeated waitress at the end of a long shift and nothing like the child that she, in fact, is. I grab my wallet to make sure that it's still there. A tingle of adrenaline courses through my veins. My hands are shaking.

"Look!" Piper blurts again, even though I'm already looking.

The girl puts her cigarette out and trains her eyes on a naïve-looking older man. I lean my head to the side and spot a bulge in his back pocket. The girl begins to slowly follow up the stairs behind him.

"Fucking scam artist!" I whisper, grabbing my wallet again, just in case.

"Should we stop her?"

"What? No! You said it yourself. She has *handlers*. I'm not getting myself wrapped up in any of that shit!"

"But that poor guy. She's going to steal his wallet!"

"Poor guy," I repeat.

"Could have been you."

"Yeah. But wasn't."

Laurent

(LUST)

Tumbles of strawberry blonde hair cascade over her face like a waterfall, the late morning sun twinkling in through a crack in the thick, room-darkening curtains. I run my finger down her jawline and stop at her lower lip, pressing against it slightly and watching as it puckers ever so slightly under the pressure. Patrice smiles.

"I could lay here all morning," I whisper.

Tenderness. I can't speak at full volume, or I'll ruin the tranquility that encapsulates us. I can only whisper.

"But you can't," she says.

"Pssh. Says who? *Je vais bien.*"

She raises one eyebrow.

"Come on, Laurent. You know we can't. Besides, I'm hungry."

"Food can wait, my love."

She shakes her head. "We can either lay here all morning, or we can go get something to eat. Let's go get waffles!"

"No."

"Crêpes?"

"No."

"Parfait?"

"Possibly."

"Come on. Let's go out."

"We can't," I remind her, and I ruin the mood.

She sighs.

"Well, I want waffles."

This is a negotiation, and I've just lost the upper hand.

"A waffle, my love. Absolutely. I'll call down to the front desk and have them fetch one for you."

"S. Plural."

I'm on the other side of the room, pulling my pants over my naked ass.

"*Excusez-moi?*"

"Waffles with an S. I'm *hungry.*"

Sam

"Venti iced coffee with an added shot, light cream, and sugar."

Every day. I can't stop ordering it. I hold my phone out and scan it with the barcode reader. The barista smiles at me.

"We call that a redeye, you know."

"I know."

"Sam, right?"

I nod.

"Thanks."

I walk over and stand in the area where all the other people are waiting. I don't know if this is where we're supposed to wait, but it's where we always do wait.

In the back corner of the coffee shop is a guy with an elaborate workstation set up at one of the tables. There's no overstating the elaborateness of this thing. Two monitors, a mixing board, five full speakers, and a few other things that have a bunch of wires coming out of them. It's like the guy moved here and has to make an entire album before he goes home again.

"Hipsters," I mutter under my breath.

"Sam!" someone yells from behind the counter.

Too quick. Must be another Sam. I look at the counter, and some other Sam is inspecting his coffee and croissant like he forgot what he ordered. My stomach rumbles. Shit. I should have ordered a croissant too. Other Sam had the right idea.

Wendy

(WRATH)

"Granted, it's only like ten here, but he hasn't even tried to text me yet today."

Kana has a tight look on her face. It's not anger, but it's definitely disapproval, I think. I can't always tell with her.

"He's probably doing who-the-freak-knows-what with who-the-freak-cares," I continue. "I told him it'd be fine if he went. I didn't make a big deal about it, not at all."

"That's good."

"Right? I feel like I'm being a good girlfriend, letting him travel where he wants—freaking Europe, whatever—with another girl. Aren't I? I mean, isn't that pretty generous of me?"

Kana nods.

"Oh yeah. Yeah."

Exactly. Kana gets it. That's why we're friends.

"Anyway, what's up with you? How's Bertrand?"

"He's the same," she shrugs. "Nothing new."

"See? That's nice. I think that's nice."

"What's nice?"

"Nothing. Just...nothing." I pause. "It must be nice."

Kana shrugs, and a waiter comes over to our table. I didn't even know this place had waiters.

"Can I get you two anything else?"

We both shake our heads, and he walks away. Kana laughs.

"Waiter at a boba shop?"

"Boba at 10 a.m.?" I return.

Grant

Piper takes for-fucking-ever to get ready, so when we get back to the hotel, I take another walk. It's even colder now that the sun has fully set. My breath is leaking out of my nostrils in plumes. The front buttons on my jacket are all fastened.

I don't know the name of the area we're staying in Paris, but it's north of the river. A girl from London that I dated for a little while last year told me that St. Germain is the only place in Paris that she would stay. She was a bitch, though, so I didn't listen to her. I look up at the street sign above me. RUE PASQUIER.

A taxi speeds across the street in front of me, and I stop walking, realizing that I have no idea where I'm planning on going. I take out my phone. It's only been fifteen minutes. Piper needs at least an hour.

I let out a deep breath and look over to a small gallery perched on the corner, walls of glass windows revealing a slew of paintings. I walk slowly along the edge of the window, inspecting each painting carefully. We didn't go in the Louvre; we only walked by and took pictures of the glass pyramid. This is going to have to be my dose of culture for the trip.

I turn the corner and stop walking. Directly in front of me is a large canvas. It's taking over most of the window. Or maybe I'm just hyper-focused on it, because I can't see anything else. It's a palette knife painting, the vibrant colors slicing and smudging across the canvas haphazardly. At the center of the frame is a city bus, seemingly in the rain, a handful of potential passengers surrounding it with umbrellas high above their heads. I think I'm looking at the back of the bus, because there are streaks of tire marks leading up to it; but there are also wipers on the windshield, and that makes me change my mind.

Is it coming or is it going? Why is everybody just standing around? Why don't they get on it? It's raining, for God's sake. Don't they want to stay dry and warm? I rub my hands together, reminded of my own coldness, but I can't stop staring at this painting. I'm drawn to it, like there's something about it that just speaks to me, like it's a world unto itself that I've somehow been afforded the ability to glimpse from the surface.

My mind wanders toward an existential ravine, and if I'm not careful, I may fall in. Is *this* world even real? Are we in a simulation? I don't know why I'm thinking this. Even as I'm thinking it, I'm questioning myself. Once I get on this thought tangent—which happens often enough that I can identify it—it usually fucks up the rest of my day. Sometimes in a positive way. But often in an oh-shit-nothing-matters-what-is-life kind of way. Inevitably, this leads me to determine, if ever so briefly, that all the things I want in life are somehow within my reach. I just need to try harder, I tell myself. I can have everything I want, since the obstacles in front of me might just be part of a fabricated reality anyway.

Wendy hates it when I broach this topic. She thinks it defies God. Most other people simply roll their eyes or, at best, politely smile and nod. But I can't help myself. I read one article, and the concept has been rooted in my brain ever since.

My breath is disintegrating into the night air in front of me, clouding the path between me and the gallery window. The painting hangs there in its awesome glory. I get lost in my thoughts. I may not find myself out of this one for a while. I touch my gloved hand up to the glass, a reminder of the separation between me and this other, elusive world.

A middle-aged man and a young, blonde woman clinging to his side turn the corner from Rue Pasquier and nearly stumble into me. I can't blame them; I'm the one stopped lifelessly in my tracks. I turn and look at the man. Our eyes lock, and I shiver.

"*Bonsoir*," he emits in a surprisingly velvety, rich voice.

"Hi," I say, unsure what else to respond with.

The man looks away from me and stares ahead down the sidewalk. Then he looks back at me and smiles.

"Fancy something you see?"

I look back at the painting, but before I can respond, the woman glued to his side lets out a shriek.

"Oh, chérie! Regardez ce tableau *merveilleux!*"

He smiles, still staring at me, but then turns to face the gallery window.

"Ce? C'est d'accord," he states coolly.

"Non, c'est *extraordinaire*. Oh, chérie, qu'est-ce que tu penses?"

I'm beginning to feel a bit like an intruder into their conversation, but since I don't even know what they're saying, I'm okay waiting it out a little while longer.

"Qu'est-ce que je pense? Je viens de te dire. C'est d'accord."

"Non," she whispers, and then nudges him sharply. "Que penses-tu de cet *achat* pour moi?"

The man laughs, but then as he sees the seriousness on her face, he tones it down a bit.

"What do *you* think?" he asks, looking again in my direction.

"Me?"

"Yes, you. Who else?"

"What do I think about what?"

He nods, realizing I definitively do not understand French.

"What do you think about me buying this painting for her?"

I think about it, but it doesn't take long.

"I say you should always go for what you want. Even if everyone thinks you're crazy. You should always take what you want from the universe. That's why it's there in front of you."

The man nods.

"Words to live by, young man."

I shrug.

"Well," he continues, now addressing the girl. "Le galerie est fermée maintenant de toute façon. Peut-être quand ils sont ouverts…"

This response is apparently enough to put her back at ease as she smiles and nuzzles her face into the thick scarf wrapped around his neck. He looks at me again, and as our eyes lock, I feel the same feeling that caused me to shiver the first time.

"What brings you to this part of town?" he inquires.

I point down the street.

"I'm staying just down there," I tell him.

"Which hotel?"

"Uh, the Madeleine Haussmann."

"Is that right? And, are you enjoying your stay?" he asks as he smiles.

I look deep into his eyes, trying to suss out the duality of his remarkable voice and his polished demeanor. He's an attractive man, no doubt, with an indescribable French quality to his looks that I don't think anyone would disagree with. There's something alluring about him, even I can see this. I take a breath and let it exhale fully before speaking.

"Sure. It's all right."

He raises his eyebrows.

"All right?" he returns.

I search my memory and recall a scant few details: the hotel's tattered wallpaper, the worn-down wood surrounding the doorways, the general lack of upkeep in what is an otherwise unremarkable establishment.

"I mean...I've stayed at better."

Whatever remained of his smile has now faded, and a puzzled look has spread across his face.

"I own that hotel," he says, rather smugly. "I'm sorry you feel that way. Is there anything in particular that is not to your liking?"

I feel my face flush as I look down toward my shoes. I don't have an adequate response, so instinctively I let out a nervous laugh. When I look up, he's smiling.

"Ha! It is somewhat of a dump, yes?"

"I didn't mean to—"

"Nonsense!" he shouts. "I'm well-aware of its condition, just as you are. I see what you see. I'm not oblivious. It's a two-star hotel, at best. The reviewer said as much, the only time they came out. They wouldn't even bother after the first time."

I smile, reminded of a lyric I could never get out of my head. "*The stars don't mean anything*," I recite in my head. I shove my hands in my pockets and step backward off the sidewalk, attempting to signal my impending departure.

"It was nice to meet you, but I should get going."

"Of course," the man replies. "We're on our way as well. Have a lovely rest of your evening."

"Thank you. And really...forget what I said. The hotel is just fine. Who cares what a reviewer says?"

He smiles as he nods, and then they slowly continue their walk down the sidewalk and eventually out of my sight. I look back at the painting and I sigh, and then I get caught up in it all over again.

Eventually, motivated by a force that I can't recognize, I begin to carry the shell of my body back to the hotel. My soul remains at the gallery...or at least that's how it feels. In front of the hotel, the sliding glass doors part as I stand in front of the entrance, the overzealous sensor anticipating my arrival like my mom on prom night. *Are you here yet? Are you here yet?* Inside, the lobby is desolate, and it smells of a deep must infused with an underwhelming cleaning product.

Etienne

(ENVY)

"Have you seen a tall man, this high?" I motion to the bartender, my hand a few inches above my own head.

"Tonight?"

"Yes, tonight. Here."

I point at the ground, even though I really just mean in the bar somewhere. The bartender shakes his head. Dammit. Armond said he would meet me at 19:30, and it's 19:30. Maybe he's just running late.

"Fetch you a drink?" he asks.

"Sure. Champagne."

The bartender laughs and pulls out a bottle, pours some bubbles into a flute, and slides it over to me.

"What's funny?" I ask.

"Champagne for one," he chuckles.

I turn my nose up at him and then look away. I take a sip of the champagne and sigh, then I look at my watch. 19:35. Armond is never this late.

I consider calling him, but instead, tap my fingers in a rhythm on the bar top. Then I take out my phone from my jacket pocket and actually do call him. It rings a few times. No answer. I wiggle my foot impatiently and think about calling him again. I look at my watch, and it's 19:37. Dammit.

Some guy I've never seen here before is walking toward me. I pull the phone up to my ear to show him that I'm in the middle of a conversation, so he doesn't try to...

"Excuse me, sir."

He's staring down at the ground. I roll my eyes and look away from the fake bit of nothing that I was staring off into.

"What is it?"

"Sir, I believe that..."

Then the fire alarm starts shrieking. It's loud as hell. I look around, startled, and there's smoke coming out from the kitchen door.

"*Merde!*" I mutter. I take a sip of my champagne, set it back down on the bar, and walk out to the street.

Fire engines come after a few minutes. The bar is filling with smoke. I can see it through the big window panes that line the front of the building. Fifty-something people are standing outside on the curb, most smoking cigarettes and mumbling quietly. The air feels like it might snow. It has a wetness to it that reminds me of snow. I look around the crowd for Armond, but he's not here.

"Excuse me," I ask the fire marshal as he walks by. "How long until we get to go back inside?"

He has a gruff laugh, but he answers me politely.

"At least thirty minutes until we're cleared. Usually takes more like forty-five."

"Thanks," I reply, disappointed.

I call Armond again. No answer. Then I walk down the sidewalk and head back to Pyramides. It's not that late, but I'm tired. I'm going home. We can try again tomorrow. I have a few left, at any rate.

Piper

I'm sitting on the bed, swiping through the pictures of Grant and me on the stairs. I look great in all of them. I delete all but the best one, and I lock my phone. Grant's getting ready in the tiny bathroom. I appreciate that he let me go first because I know that I take a long time, but now I just want to get out of this room.

It's comically small. You can barely walk around the bed without bumping into it. We had asked for a room with two twin beds. We ended up with a room with two twin beds that were sewn together at some point in their individual lives. Now they're just one shitty king bed, and we have no choice other than to sleep in it together. I think about Sam. Then I wonder what Wendy will think if Grant tells her. I don't think he will though. I mean, why would he? It's no big deal.

He walks out of the bathroom with his jeans on, no belt, his bath towel wrapped around his neck. Steam billows out into the room, and he's looking over his shoulder at the shower. I look down at the bed.

"That thing produces a lot of steam," he comments, then sits down next to me on the bed.

"You gonna finish getting dressed, or what?"

He shrugs.

"I'm hungry."

"Relax. I just want to sit for a bit. I've been on my feet all day."

"You should have sat while I was getting ready."

He laughs.

"I don't need *that* much rest. Just a couple minutes, okay, *sis?*"

"Don't 'sis' me."

He shrugs and takes the towel off his shoulders. We're just sitting here on this awkward, conjoined-twin monstrosity of a bed, Grant with only a pair of pants on and me dressed up and ready to go out. We don't say anything for a little while. I'm tempted to turn my phone back on and look at the pictures again, but I just sit in silence and hope that it makes him so uncomfortable he finishes getting ready.

"You look nice," he comments, though it sounds empty and forced.

"Thanks. You look half-dressed."

He gets up and starts pacing.

"I saw this painting on my walk. At a gallery just down the street, like two blocks away."

Here we go.

"Yeah? And?"

"I think I stared at it for like twenty minutes."

"Oh yeah? Was it life-changing?" I snort.

I'm immediately embarrassed at my indignation, but I try to pretend like it was justified, even though I know it wasn't. My skin turns red. Grant doesn't pick up on it.

"There was something about it. I couldn't stop staring at it. It's like it was made for me...or something."

Oh, Grant. Please.

"Was it for sale?"

He nods.

"So, go buy it."

"The gallery wasn't open. Also, it was nine hundred fifty euros."

"Never mind then. That's way too much for a painting."

"Is it?" he asks. "I paid five hundred dollars for that green painting from my Boston friend, the one with the bombs exploding over the desert."

"I could paint that thing for you for forty dollars."

I don't know why I'm being such a bitch. Maybe it's because I look good tonight. My makeup turned out almost perfect, and I love this shirt. I wore these jeans all day, and even though my ass got a little sweaty when we were walking up all those hills, they feel nice and broken-in, so I put them back on after my shower. I look good. And here I am, wasting it all with *Grant* in this stupid hotel room.

"Is nine hundred fifty euros really a lot?" he asks.

"Well, you make a lot more than me. So I don't know. It is to me. That's like...rent and groceries for a month."

"I don't know what it is about it. It just captivated me."

"So buy it. And then we can go out. And have fun. And do something. Instead of *this*."

"Yeah...but then I'd have to lug it around with me on the train to London and then on the flight back to L.A. Doesn't that seem like a pain in the ass?"

"Well, yeah. But you're the one who wants it. I wouldn't do any of that for a painting."

"You have posters of Disney characters in frames on your walls," he lobs at me with a smile. "What do you know about art?"

"Dude, just buy it or don't. Don't try to deflect your shit on me. I don't care. Can you get dressed?"

He gets up and walks over to his suitcase, looking back at the shower again as he leans down.

"What are you looking at?" I ask.

"Don't you think that thing produces a lot of steam?"

Grant

The night air is colder than when I was staring at the painting for who-knows-how-long, but I guess that's what happens to air at night on the verge of winter. It gets colder.

I'm just glad to be out and about. I felt like we were never going to get out of that tiny-ass hotel room. All Piper wanted to do was sit on the bed and talk. So typical.

"It's pretty cold," I state so blandly I almost laugh.

"Where are we going?" she asks.

"Dinner."

Whatever. She knows where we're going. We already picked the place back at the hotel.

At the restaurant, there are a couple of fully set tables right on the sidewalk, no heat lamps or plastic enclosures anywhere in sight. The tables are, of course, empty. It's practically freezing out. Nobody is going to eat dinner outside in this weather, not even in Paris.

I open the door for Piper, and she walks inside. I take my time following her, knowing that it's going to be stuffy and hot once I get inside. I want to get as many gasps of the cold air as I can.

"*Deux?*" she asks the host, then looks back at me.

"Inside or out?"

She laughs.

"Inside."

"Very well. This way then, madam."

I'm still halfway in the door, and the host looks at me with disgust. But then he nods and shows me to the table anyway. Dick. We sit down at the table and order a bottle of wine and some oysters, because fuck it.

"Foie gras too!" I yell out, but the waiter pretends like he doesn't hear me. All the assholes in Paris pretend like they don't hear you whenever they're not feeling it. The wine comes, and we down our glasses before the oysters come out. We get drunk, and it doesn't take that long. The walls are dancing and swaying. All that walking earlier was dehydrating.

"I've got to have that painting," I tell her again. "There's something about it..."

Piper shakes her head.

"Should we steal these napkins?"

"What?"

"Look!" she shouts.

A couple at a table next to us sighs. I give them a look, and they stare back down at their plates. I feel tough for a moment.

"Look at what?"

She waves a napkin in front of my face, a monogrammed P square in the front center panel.

"I see."

"Should we?"

I shrug as I look around.

"I don't think anyone will notice either way. So, sure. Go for it."

Her face lights up as she starts to devise a plan to stuff a few of them down into her purse. I don't know why this gets her off. Stealing is so middle school.

The meal is forgettable, and they've cleared our plates before I realize it.

"Dessert?" the waiter asks.

Napkins are billowing out of Piper's bag. I don't know how he doesn't see them.

"*No, merci. L'addition, s'il vous plaît?*"

It's the only French I know. The St. Germain girl taught me this. The waiter leaves, and Piper continues stuffing the napkins further into her purse.

"I don't really get what this accomplishes."

She gives me a fuck-you face and keeps on stuffing them further and further into her purse. *You can take the girl out of Ohio*...I think to myself.

When we've finished our meal, I pay in cash and stumble out the door. Now that I'm upright, I realize that I'm more drunk than I expected to be. The bell on the door goes *clink-clink* as Piper walks back out into the chilly night. I'm following a few steps behind her. As I near the door, I look over at the host and wink. His eyes are trained on the white linens puffing out of Piper's purse as she steps onto the sidewalk and turns out of sight.

Piper

"Why don't we just pick another one?"

Oh. God. I'm slurring so much. Focus, focus. Hocus pocus.

"Because, look at all these people!" he exclaims. "If they're all outside waiting to get in, it's got to be good in there."

"Or maybe they all just came out to have a cigarette."

Grant shakes his head, but he doesn't know that I'm wrong. They could all just be smokers, coincidentally out at the same time. The door to the bar swings open, and a guy dressed up like some sort of Euro fireman walks out and waves his hand in the air. People start herding back into the bar.

"Told you," Grant sings, putting his arm around my shoulder and dragging me in toward the scuttling group of people. I try to wriggle out from under his arm, but I can't, so in we go. Everyone shuffles over to the bar.

"This is going to take forever," I moan.

Not that I need another drink. I can barely see straight. Grant still has his arm around me, and I finally shrug it off with a heave of my shoulder. He steps back.

"You all right?"

"Sorry," I mumble.

"All good. What do you want? I'll squeeze in up there."

"Whatever you're having."

I find a high-top table and sink down onto one of the two stools tucked underneath. The air smells like burnt toast, but I'm so full from dinner that it almost smells good. Grant spends a few minutes trying to wiggle his way in to order a drink, but the bar is slammed. I prop my chin up on my hand and look down at the table. I think about my mom, wondering if I should text her and tell her how beautiful it is here, just like she told me it would be.

A guy wanders over to my table and tries to sit down on the other stool. I shake my head.

"My friend. Big guy."

I nod over to the bar. There are a bunch of big guys, so that works. He walks away. A few minutes pass, probably. I don't know.

"Finally," Grant announces, slamming a glass down on the table.

"Vodka soda?"

"Yup. For you."

Grant sits down, and we both just stare at the table for a while. The crowd around the bar starts to thin out and disperse throughout the room. Our table, previously a lone island with a distant view of the crowd, is now surrounded by chirpy, bumbling Parisians. They all smell like smoke, but then again, so does the rest of the room. It's loud, and I'm feeling claustrophobic.

"Can we go sit at the bar? I can't breathe."

Grant gets up and picks up my drink, then his drink. There are two stools at the left corner of the bar, and I sit on the one on the very edge. Grant stands alongside me.

"Better?"

"It was just too crowded over there."

"All good. And look!" he shouts. "You get a free drink out of it."

He nods to the bar at a spot right behind my arm. There's a mostly full glass of champagne. No one else is around it, so I take a sip. Grant laughs. I did it for the laugh. I don't even like champagne, not really. He grabs the glass and takes a sip as well.

Times like these, I wish he isn't who he actually is. I wish he were someone else.

"You know I don't even like champagne," I mutter.

"You're a good sport. How drunk are you?"

I raise my eyebrows and smile, nodding.

"Me too," he says.

He looks down at his feet and is quiet for a moment. Then he looks back up at me with a dead-serious look on his face, like he has something super meaningful to tell me.

Please don't ruin the moment. Please.

"What?" I ask.

"Uhh, if I told you that we had to leave, like right now, would you get up and go? If I told you that, would you...would you trust me?"

I grab my vodka and soda, and I pull it up to my lips, chug the whole thing in two gulps, then gently but quickly set it down on the bar. I don't say another word, but my answer to his question is a resounding *yes*. I bundle my jacket up and walk quickly toward the door. A stream of bubbles is traveling down my esophagus and into my gut and it tickles me to the point of near-laughter. I don't know exactly what he's doing, but Grant leans down and grabs something by his foot and then follows me out the door. It's not snowing outside, but it feels like it's about to.

Grant

As soon as we step outside, a huge gust of wind almost pushes us right back in. I put my hands behind Piper and start pushing her down the sidewalk quickly.

"What's going on?" she asks.

She's wobbly, and I feel bad, but I know I have to keep pushing her, just for a little bit longer. I say nothing until we get to the end of the block and turn the corner. Then I pull out a small fold of money from my coat pocket. There's a fifty-euro bill wrapped around the outside of the stack.

"Found this on the ground," I whisper, and then my eyes dart around the dimly lit street behind us.

"How much is it?"

I start to unfold it slowly. My hands are too cold to move any faster.

"Fifty-something," I laugh. "Can you believe that?"

I look up at her face, and she's smiling. Everybody likes free shit, but Piper likes free shit more than anyone I know. The heap of monogrammed napkins still stuffed in her purse is a clear testament.

"Looks like more than that," she says.

I look down at the wad of money again. Inside the fifty-euro bill is another fifty euros, and then it's followed by one hundred euros. And another hundred. And then two more hundred euros.

"Holy shit!" I yell.

Piper grabs the cash and rifles through it quickly, probably trying to make sure we're not so drunk that we both miscounted. Or maybe she thinks that it's just monopoly money, because that's how all these damned euros look anyway. But it's not. It's real. Five hundred euros worth of real. I throw my arms out and wrap them around her shoulders. I'm not much for hugging, but this occasion seems fitting. Her cheek presses up against mine, and we stand here for a couple of seconds. It's awkward, but I initiated it, so I can't pull away too quickly, lest it make it even more awkward.

"I can't believe it," she mumbles. "Can't believe it! Are we *that* drunk? Did this just happen?"

"I think it's real. Hey...let's get out of here, huh? I don't want whoever's this is to come out and ruin it for us."

"But, Grant..." she slowly hesitates. "This is wrong. This is someone's money."

"Yeah," I say, emotionless. "It's *our* money."

"No. It *was* someone's. It didn't just appear there out of nowhere. Should we go back and return it?"

I look around the empty street for an answer. I shake my head.

"Trust me...if we bring this back to the bar, the bartender is going home with an extra five hundred euros. There's no way it makes it back to whosever it was."

Piper nods solemnly. I'm just speaking the truth here. That is exactly what will happen. We may as well keep it. We're certainly more deserving than that bartender. He wasn't even that good, and his pour was weak. I nudge Piper, and she begins walking.

We haven't exactly sobered up, because it's only been two minutes since we left the bar, but we are walking with more focus and pep than we had earlier. It must be the adrenaline. This must be what it feels like to have great shit happen to you. I've never found more than twenty dollars before. And just earlier in the day, I almost had my damned wallet snatched away from me. Life's a fucking rollercoaster sometimes.

"What should we spend it on? We have to spend it here. Okay? We have to spend it here."

Piper nods in agreement.

"Yeah, we can't bring it back to London and exchange it either. It's got to be in Paris."

"Should we get a table at a club or something?" I ask.

"Blech. A club?"

"Okay, some very expensive bar that meets your personal music and vibe and décor standards? Some place so expensive, we would never normally go there?"

We're walking by restaurants, and all of them still have the little, white linen-covered tables out on the sidewalks, like anyone is going to sit down at one. The permanent optimism of these Parisian restaurant managers is frightening.

"I'm too drunk," she counters after we walk for a little while. "Let's just go back to the hotel and figure out how to spend it tomorrow."

"It's not even that late yet!" I yell. "What are we gonna do, roll around on the bed with all the money?" She looks at me weird, like I actually meant it, so I keep talking. "Come on! Let's spend it now! Let's go crazy!"

"I'm too drunk," she repeats.

"One more drink," I beg.

She relents, and we walk into the next brasserie we see. It doesn't hurt my case that there's practically a brasserie on every block. Piper leans on the door with her shoulder and slides into the entrance.

"Inside or outside?" the hostess asks, her face buried in a paperback. She seems slightly alarmed but mostly blasé. I'm guessing that's just how her face looks most of the time.

"Inside, for God's sake," I practically yell.

"Right this way," she says, not missing a beat.

We sit down at a small table in the back. It's so dim that I can't even see the lines in my palms as I hold them out in front of me. I'm not sure why I'm doing this, and when Piper catches me, I pull my hands under the table and onto my lap. I order a bottle of wine, and Piper shakes her head. Whatever. I'll have the whole thing if I have to. It's barely eleven o'clock.

"Should we split it fifty fifty?" I ask, though I don't mean it. "Or should we buy something together? That could be pretty cool. Like a shared...thing."

"Like what?"

Her face is scrunched up against her palm as she leans her head heavily toward the table. Her eyelids must weigh a pound each; they're barely fluttering enough to be considered open.

"Yeah, I don't know. That's a dumb idea. And I feel like an even split just seems so formal, you know? Like, this was a total surprise, and now we're already dissecting it."

We both take turns shrugging. The wine comes. I down my first glass before Piper has her second sip. The only reason she even has the first sip is because I forced her to cheers me.

"You can have it all," she offers.

"Me? Why?"

"You found it."

"No. How about I give it to you? An early birthday present."

"You're buying me a real birthday present this year, asshole. I'm not taking some money you found on the floor of a bar."

I look around the brasserie just in case the guy who lost it is prowling around scanning each table for the new owner of his cash. Everyone is focused on their conversations or their booze.

"All right, then what do we do with it?"

We're quiet for a while, and I pour myself another glass. I'm really starting to feel it. This is exactly what I wanted. I don't want to be sober any night, let alone a Saturday night in Paris.

"I've got it," she says, her eyelids now fully closed, her lips pursed up toward her nose. "Now you can go buy that fucking painting."

Wendy

I've got all these deals that I need to close by the end of next week. It just passed 2 a.m. It's Sunday. My laptop screen is searing my retinas, but the work has to get done. So, I rub my eyes, feeling the dryness of my contacts through my eyelids. They're about ready to quit on me.

Throughout the night, I've been kicking myself for not having made plans when I knew that Grant was going to be in Europe. Sometimes I depend on him too much already, this early in our relationship. I even slept at his apartment the first night he left because I was too lazy to pack up my things and bring them home. It's bad.

I'm redlining the crap out of this one. Gosh, it's bad. A message pops up on my screen. It's Sam.

Hey, hope I'm not waking you up, but do you remember Grant's Netflix password?

Come on, man. It's 2 a.m. As if there's anything I'm going to be doing right now other than pretending that I'm asleep. Besides, I don't know Grant's password. He's secretive like that. Sometimes I think he's leading a separate life, but then I think about *how much* he's into me, and I realize that he can't be. But what if he is? And if he's that way with *her* too? And if she's wondering the same thing about me?

He still hasn't called me, but I did get a check-in text to let me know that he was having fun and still safe. He mentioned something about almost getting his wallet stolen.

Okay, deals. Deals. I have to stop thinking about him. Deals. He pisses me off too much. Deals. I might have to break up with him when he gets back if he doesn't start calling me more often.

Piper

Orange juice in Paris costs six euros. Coke costs about the same. Wine, however, is something like three-fifty for a carafe. National priorities are in order here. At breakfast, I order two glasses of orange juice, and the waiter gives me a look like I'm some sort of a plutocrat.

"Any better?" Grant asks.

I'm slumped back in my chair, wishing it was a booth.

"*So* hungover. I told you I was too drunk," I grumble.

"Eating didn't help at all? Your omelet, no good? *Oeufs. Oeufs?* Yeah, *oeufs.* They good?"

They're fine. I'm just not in the mood. And it's so hot in here, I'm solidly regretting this stupid turtleneck that I thought looked cute when I packed it.

"*Oeufs,*" I repeat after him.

"Should we get the bill? *L'addition?*"

"If you're done, I'm done."

"Can we stop by the gallery now?"

I regret giving him the idea last night. It's the last actual, tangible thing that I can even remember about last night, and it's a memory all wrapped up in regret. Who cares about the fucking painting? It's just a painting. What did he say it was of? A subway car? How trash is that?

"Sure."

The bill comes, and Grant motions that he's got it. He pulls out a fifty and smiles at me when he sets it down on the table.

"Keep the change," he states coolly, though not as cool as he probably thinks he sounds.

I glance at the bill, and it's forty-four and thirty euros. That's not exactly worth gloating about—five bucks and change for a tip. But whatever. It's free money. Free breakfast. I'm not complaining.

The sidewalks are relatively empty as we're walking down the street. It's around ten thirty.

"Where is everybody?" I ask aloud, hoping that some Disney character will pop out from behind a wall and sing me an answer. Maybe the

Hunchback of Notre Dame; that would be nice. He's from here. But no one pops out. It's just me and Grant and a bunch of randomly strewn litter. Up ahead is a discarded umbrella, the metal arms crumpled into something resembling a mechanical squid, resting against a huge, blue door with the handle in the middle.

"Church, probably."

He's craning his neck and checking out the tops of buildings like there's something happening up there, but there isn't. He does weird shit like this sometimes. I think he does it to try to seem interesting. I don't think he even knows why he's doing what he's doing sometimes. But as it goes in his life, nobody really questions him about it…about anything.

"How far away is the gallery?" I ask.

I kind of have to poop, but I don't want to tell him. He always makes fun of me for how much I talk about going to the bathroom.

"Just a few blocks. And then it's just a couple more away from the hotel, so after I buy it, we can drop it off in the room and then go out and do the rest of whatever it is we're going to do. What is it that we're going to do, by the way?"

"Fuck, man, I don't know. I'd like to sleep another three hours. Can we do that?"

"In the city of lights, you want to sleep," he deadpans.

"Fine."

We turn a corner, and Grant stops in front of a window. I assume, correctly, that it's the gallery. Hanging right in the middle of the window is a large painting. There's a bus in the middle. That's right. A bus. Not a subway car. Whatever. Same difference.

"That's the one?" I ask.

Grant nods, and I lean in to inspect the painting through the glass. The characters are all smeared, as is the entire canvas, but even still, none of them look all that attractive. Maybe that's what the artist was going for…or maybe that's just because I'm comparing them to what I'd look like if someone painted me.

Grant rubs his hands together, not because it's cold, but in that appetizing kind of way. Then I look over at the door to the gallery and at the sign that says *FERMÉ*.

"What's that mean?" I ask.

Grant tries the door, and it doesn't budge.

"Shit."

"What?"

"It means they're not open."

"What time is it?" I ask.

"I don't think that's it," he sighs. "Didn't you notice all the shops on the street we were just walking down?"

Notice them? I'm still drunk.

"Yeah. So?"

"I was thinking it was weird that they're all closed. I mean, maybe it's like London. Maybe they don't open until noon on Sunday."

"Oh, or maybe they don't open at all on Sunday. They're pretty religious here, you know."

"Son of a bitch! I should have bought it yesterday when I had the chance!"

"Relax, dude," I tell him, knowing very well that telling an angry person to relax is like kicking a bee's nest. "Just buy it tomorrow."

"But we leave tomorrow in the morning!"

"So come over before we leave. What's the big deal?"

"I guess."

He sits down on the curb, like that's going to do anything to improve the situation. He props his elbows up on his knees and stares down at the gutter underneath his bent legs. Another squid-looking umbrella carcass is a few feet away. The city is lousy with them.

"Come on. It's not even that good of a painting. I mean, look at it. Who cares?"

Grant jolts up and shoves his arm out as far as he can, his index finger missing the window by no more than an inch. He's pointing adamantly but saying nothing.

"Yes?" I ask aloud, hoping he'll realize how stupid he looks right now.

"Look at it!" he shouts, and a nearby pigeon takes off in startled flight. "You can't tell me that this is not just...the most captivating thing you've seen in years. You can't!"

He's so dramatic. I shrug, intentionally visible enough for him to see in his peripheral vision as he continues to stare straight ahead.

"I actually prefer that green bombs painting you have back home. That at least has character. This one? Forgettable. It looks like it would be on the wall in an executive conference room."

"You don't know what you're talking about," he mutters, sitting back down on the curb again.

"Look, let's get back to the hotel. I'll change, maybe go to the bathroom, or whatever, and then we can head out. You can buy it tomorrow, okay? It'll be fine."

He looks up at me, and he looks sad as hell.

"What? It'll be fine," I repeat.

"Bathroom, again?" he asks with a faint smile.

Grant

My legs are sore from all the walking. It's been two days in a row of at least six, seven miles. Probably more like ten each day. It's a different kind of exercise than anything that I do at the gym. This shit really takes it out of me.

We walk all along Champs-Élysées, and almost all the stores are closed. So then we climb up the winding staircase to the top of the Arc de Triomphe and take pictures of the cars below us as they try to merge and exit the traffic circle. What a disaster. After the Arc, we cross the river and head to St. Germain to have lunch. I talk a little too much about the girl who brought me here the first time. Piper just listens. She's a good listener when she wants to be. Then we head further east and stumble upon some stores that are actually open, so Piper shops for a while, but comes out empty-handed. I insist on beginning to drink again at three; Piper relents and joins me at maybe five or six. By dinnertime, we're not even hungry, but we go into a brasserie and order eggs and burgers and wine. By nine, I'm ready to call it a night, but Piper seems to have a burst of energy now that she's drunk.

"Let's do something crazy," she spurts. "Like, anything!"

"My turn to be lame. I'd rather just go back to the room and crash."

"Sure. Crash. Like...crash a party! Let's...let's follow those people right there!"

She points across the street at two people walking down the sidewalk with a bottle in each hand. I think maybe she had spotted them a while ago and was just waiting for the right time to make the suggestion.

"Follow them and then what?"

"Crash their party!"

"Why?"

Honestly, sometimes this girl is so in her own head, I have to ask these kinds of questions to make sure it's not for something even dumber than it sounds.

"Come on," she yells, dragging me behind her.

We cross the street, and as the couple enters a glass door that leads into an apartment building, she runs ahead and motions for them to hold the door open for her. They oblige, and we're in the lobby now. The couple heads to a corner and disappears out of sight, though I hear footsteps ascending stairs, so I have a pretty good guess as to what they're doing.

"Now what?" I ask her.

Again, I have to ask. I love the girl like a sister, but...dumb as rocks. That's why I thought she and Sam should have tried to work it out longer. Two dumb peas in a pod.

"Now we go up to the *party*!"

She walks toward the corner where the couple disappeared, and I follow her, because what the hell else am I going to do? We go up a few flights of stairs and start to hear music playing from down a hallway somewhere. We follow the sound until we're outside of a door to an apartment that's clearly having a party.

"And again...now what?" I ask.

Piper opens the door and walks in. I cringe and stand behind, not sure if I should follow or run or grab her or just stick my head in the sand. This is stupid. I'm drunk, but I'm not *this* drunk. This is some college-level bullshit, and I'm a (mostly) grown-ass man now. I decide to just wait in the hallway. Piper looks back at me and motions for me to come in, but I don't budge, so she turns away and walks farther into the apartment.

"Jesus," I mutter.

I take my phone out and think about texting Wendy. It should be afternoon there. She's probably free. I decide to just call her instead. She'll probably wish I just text her, but it's all the same anyway. The phone rings a few times—that strange European ring that doesn't at all sound like the American ring—then she picks up.

"Hey, babe," I start. "How's it going?"

She says something, but it's muffled, and I can't hear it.

"What's that? Hello?"

There's a shuffling sound over the phone speaker, and then her voice becomes much clearer.

"Hello? Grant?"

"Hey, babe," I try again. "How's it going?"

Then she proceeds to tell me how it's going because, well, I asked. Blah blah blah. Working on some deals. Blah blah blah. Up until 3 a.m. Blah blah blah. Man, the girl loves to work. It's a wonder she's even with me. I like work but only because I like money.

"Well, take some time off then," I finally weigh in. "Enjoy the afternoon. What time is it there?"

She tells me, but I don't listen. I'm wondering what Piper is doing in there. She still hasn't come out. Maybe it's an amazing party. Or maybe they've tied her up and are holding her hostage. I don't know what I would do in that situation. I care for the girl, but not enough to risk my own damned life for her, especially if it's because of some stupid decision to run into a stranger's apartment uninvited. I don't know if I want that scrawled on my headstone.

I tell Wendy some more of the details of the trip, like how we found the money and what we've been doing so far. I tell her mostly the fun stuff. I'm trying to keep it light. Then Piper bursts out the door, though she doesn't look rushed or alarmed. She waves to someone inside as she shuts the door behind her. I gesture *WTF?*

"Party was lame," she mouths, then nods toward the stairs. "Let's go."

Sam

For the past week, I feel like my body hasn't taken a break from sweating. This heat wave is supposed to taper off soon, I heard, but I heard it from a very unreliable source in an elevator conversation, so I don't trust it. My body definitely doesn't trust it. It just keeps sweating like it's the only thing it knows how to do.

I'm sunk into my couch, feeling guilty, knowing that all my sweat and odor is seeping into the fabric in the most vulnerable of places. I want to get up, but I'm too lazy, plus I don't know if I've seen this episode of *Fresh Prince*. I need to wait until I find out.

I look down at the remote, see the Netflix button, wonder what company prints out the buttons on the remotes. How many Netflix buttons have they made, and what do they do with the extra ones? You can't use them for anything else. They probably just melt them down and make other red buttons. I wonder if Grant knows. I wonder what Grant's password is. Is this the episode where Will's dad shows up out of the blue? I've seen that one a few times.

Bertrand walks in, smiles, walks to his room, says nothing. Probably just got laid. Good for him, the bastard. It seems like he and Kana have a good thing going. I'm guessing he's going to move out soon, move in with her, leave me stranded, make me have to find another roommate. I hate having to find roommates. It's too much work. I wish Grant had just kept the house. That was so much easier.

I look back at the Netflix button. I wish I remembered his password, wish it was easier to remember in the first place. He's the kind of guy to have one of those elaborate passwords for no reason, like sharing a Netflix account is something that anyone cares about. Just make it something like *hambone123* and be done with it.

This is definitely the one where Will's dad comes to town. I sigh. Time to get up.

Wendy

"Are you sure he said, 'one bed'?"

"One hundred percent."

"Maybe he was joking."

"Grant is sarcastic about basically everything, but he wouldn't joke about this. It's too weird. And he was so nonchalant about it too."

"Tell me exactly what he said again."

This is why I like Kana. She's an *active* listener.

"He said, 'blah blah, we got to the hotel, and they didn't have any rooms with two beds, so we had to share a bed, can you believe it?'"

"That's it?"

"Yeah! That's it!"

"That doesn't seem like Grant. Really?"

This is what I don't like about Kana. She always sides with the wrong person. Grant is the wrong person in this situation.

"Really."

"Do you think they're...doing anything?" she asks.

I shrug. He seems like the type to cheat, but I don't know. He never has, at least not that I know of.

"No. I don't. But it's still shady."

"It is shady," she agrees.

Plus one for Kana. Siding with the present company. That's the right way to be.

Guy

(GLUTTONY)

Marion's face is as round and cherubic as the day we met, as the day we married. Her rosy cheeks are exceptionally rosy when winter comes to visit. I melt every time I see them. When I look into her eyes, I fall in love again and again, every time. And I know she feels the same way about me.

"Is the table set?" she asks from the kitchen.

I nod, then remember that she can't see me.

"*Oui, mon cher.*"

She leans back from the stove and looks in through the doorway, smiling at me. I smile back. Thirty-three years, and she's still smiling at me. I'm the luckiest man in all of France.

"It'll just be a few minutes more," she adds. "Call the kids?"

I walk over to the stairs and knock on the wall a few times. They come out of their rooms, and I nod.

"Two minutes. Come down."

Marion has made cassoulet, my favorite. She spoons heaping portions into each of our bowls and serves herself last. Outside the window, the faintest hint of snow is falling from the sky. Or it might just be ash from the chimney.

"Remember when you used to work on Sundays?" she asks me, and the kids chuckle. "And you missed out on *cassoulet*?"

"It was not the same reheated. It never is."

"How long has it been?"

I think back. I don't know.

"Two years, maybe."

The meat in the cassoulet is so tender, I can barely think about anything else. The tastes that are filling my mouth are overwhelming. And it's like this every time I eat it; I don't understand.

"You should have never been open on a Sunday in the first place," she reminds me, and I nod.

"That's all in the past now. Now I spend my Sundays with *ma famille*."

"Old man, finally choosing his family over his shop!"

The kids chuckle. They don't talk much. They're good kids.

Piper

I'm sick of the damned orange juice here; it's too expensive, and the oranges taste like they were a day from being moldy when they got squeezed. I'm sick of Grant's heavy breathing while he's asleep next to me. It's 7:10 a.m. I shouldn't be awake yet. He's not. He's just breathing over there, loud as hell, the same as he did for the entire trip thus far. It's not loud enough to call it a snore, but it's not quiet enough to ignore. I get out of bed, deciding to skip the continental breakfast and shower instead.

He's right: this thing does produce a lot of steam. It's borderline absurd. I wrap my body in a towel before I wipe the fog from the mirror. When I look at my face, it looks better than it has in a while. As I walk out into the room, Grant is lying on the bed in the same pair of yellow running shorts that he wore to sleep, but the covers are all shoved to the foot of the bed, and the rest of his bare body is exposed. His hands are behind his head, and he's staring up at the ceiling.

"Good morning," he mumbles, then smiles.

I tighten the towel around my chest, looking down to make sure that everything is tucked in where it's supposed to be. The last thing I want to do is walk out into a room with a tit out.

"You need the bathroom?"

He shakes his head. I look at him.

"What?"

"What do you mean, *what?* I need to change."

"Oh."

He props himself up on the bed, then he slowly gets up and walks toward the bathroom. I'm not looking, but I think he has a hard-on. The bathroom door closes, and I sigh, then I tighten the towel again out of habit.

I'm wearing just my underwear when he opens the door and asks, *can I come out?* I'm facing away from the door, my top exposed, but facing away so he can't see anything. *No,* I tell him. I cover my chest with the towel and turn around. He's in the doorway, his hand over his eyes. I'm not sure how long he had his hand there though.

"What do you need?"

"Just a pair of boxers. You can pick them out. Any pair in there is fine."

I go over to his suitcase and pull out the first pair that I see. The towel slides down my shoulder, and I feel the cold air from a draft by the window blow down into the gap between the towel and my skin, and it slightly grazes my nipple. I pull the towel back up and toss the boxers across the room to Grant, whose hand is still over his eyes. It lands with a soft thud at his feet.

"There," I announce.

I look down at his shorts, and if he had a hard-on, it's gone now. I look away. Why did I look in the first place?

He picks up the boxers and closes the bathroom door behind him. I can hear him singing as he showers. Steam seeps out into the room from the crack at the bottom of the door. I pick out a bra and shudder as I slide the straps over my shoulders, pressing the underwire firmly up against my breasts.

Grant

We're out on Rue Pasquier again, and it's a few minutes past nine. The gallery still isn't open.

"Fuck!"

"Who cares," Piper says, like that's going to help at all.

"I care!" I shout, almost emphatically. I'm never emphatic. This must mean something to me.

"So what do you want to do, miss the train?"

I shake my head. No, of course not. We have to fucking work. We have to get there right after lunchtime, or everyone will think we're just fucking around in Paris, maybe fucking around with each other. God, I don't want that to be the thing everyone is thinking. Anything but that, really.

"I don't know," I say. "Let's just check out and catch the stupid fucking train."

Laurent

The air is always crisp on Armistice Day, though I pause and consider that perhaps I only feel this way because my heart is full of the arresting sensations gifted to me by my seductress. Everything around me, even an asexual thing like the weather, feels romantic. Is it the holiday, or Patrice? This *is* usually what happens during bank holidays. They have a mysterious way of making everything in the city feel magical, like a giant buried treasure is being unearthed somewhere and all the rays of positivity are beaming out from the ground and out into the atmosphere.

My mind swings back to Patrice. It must be her. I try to recall the last Armistice Day, but it conjures no memories.

I walk past a market and stop in to pick up a few things. First, I browse the bakery. Baguettes everywhere, but that's possibly all. *Dieu.* Where is the ciabatta? The olive loaf? The pumpernickel? Why is it always baguettes? Despite my reluctance, I pick one up and drop it into my basket.

I move over to the fresh produce. Lots of squashes, some green, leafy things, some radishes. Lots of potatoes. Nothing exciting, and I blame November. I pick up something green and drop it onto the baguette. The fruit selection is abysmal, so I jaunt over to the butcher counter. The butcher is stocking the display case with fresh, blood-red ribeyes, as thick as my forearm and with stunning marbling. They're so fresh, I can smell them from here, all the way on the other side of the glass.

"How much for a ribeye?"

The butcher looks up from stacking the steaks onto the white butcher paper, and without any expression, he looks back down. I wait.

"Forty-three per kilogram," he mumbles from behind the counter.

I shrug.

"Give me two of your best," I say.

He takes his time unloading the remainder of the tray in his hand, then he brings it out back. He emerges through a set of swinging double doors a few moments later, and then he takes even longer changing his gloves and setting the brown paper out to wrap up my two steaks. He hands me the package and looks away, then sighs heavily.

"Thank you," I say. He doesn't say anything back.

At the checkout stand, the cashier is flirting with me, but she is too young, maybe nineteen, so I don't overindulge. I pay my bill and walk out, the air still cold, still romantic. The baguette is poking out awkwardly from my bag, and I look at the next few people to leave the market. I don't know any of them. I didn't think I would, but it's always best to check just in case.

Piper

Grant's been sulking for, like, the entire train ride. We've barely said more than two sentences to each other, and it's been over an hour already. I'm staring out the window at the countryside as it zips by: blurs of color, blobs that are probably trees, errant wires. I can't believe how fast we're going, and we're not even in a plane. The little monitor above the passageway between this train car and the next keeps teetering between 300 and 310 kilometers per hour.

"Are we going five hundred miles per hour?" I ask him, and then I regret it. I did it backwards. It doesn't matter. He doesn't say anything.

Grant's hair is disheveled, and his eyes are sunken into their sockets. Faint lines that will eventually become crow's feet are slowly forming, and they're especially noticeable today. He looks exhausted, but I don't know why. He was sleeping up a storm last night. We got back early too. I feel fine. He's getting old.

We go under the channel (the chunnel?) and my ears pop, instantly bringing me back, if only for a second, to the scuba trip Katelyn and I went on during spring break, when I got the ear infection. I close my eyes, take a little nap. The train hisses loudly as we pull into the station at—where are we—St. Pancras, says my map. It's eleven thirty, right when we were scheduled to arrive. That's the thing about these superfast trains, I suppose. They've taken the guesswork out of the arrival time.

Even the tube stations here are cute. Little tile mosaics on the walls, musicians playing with their instrument cases open, full of money. The people walking on the wrong side of the walkways, standing on the wrong side of the escalators. Lovely.

As we climb above ground, the air's a little warmer here than it was when we left. I almost regret wearing such a heavy jacket, but then I remember that it's the only jacket I have with me. Grant's still quiet. I jab him in the ribs, I think. His jacket is bunched up from his backpack, so I may have just hit a wad of fabric.

"What?" he asks, not even turning around.

"Just hey," I say, you asshole. I'm just trying to be nice.

"You want lunch?" he grumbles, hardly even a question.

I tell him no. He says he's going to Leon. I say I'm going to the office, but I know I'll just be waiting in the lobby because I don't know how to get up to the first floor. The glass wall that leads into the lobby is covered in an advertisement for the latest game we're selling. I don't recognize it. It's just a job.

There are turnstiles for employees, like there's a Disneyland ride on the other side. But it's just open floor seating plans and some boringly named conference rooms like *Orange* and *Blue* and *Yellow*, named after—I couldn't believe it at first—the colors of the walls of the rooms. For all the money we roll into our marketing, telling the world that we are a superbly creative company, this seems like the worst.

Grant walks in through the revolving door. It's been maybe fifteen minutes. He's not holding anything other than his rolling suitcase. I give him a puzzled look.

"Ate it there," he mumbles, then walks up to the front desk. The guy sitting behind it had a stone face when I walked up earlier. Now he's practically jumping out of his seat without moving.

"Grant, bruv! How you doing? Back so soon?"

"Always coming back," Grant coos. "Love it here. How've you been?"

"Good, bruv, good. You here all week?"

"Indeed."

"Need a loaner pass?"

Grant shakes his head, then flips his backpack around to the front of his body and unzips a small pouch no larger than a credit card. His head is down, eyes fixated on his bag for a moment. Then his hand emerges with a little key card.

"Got my permanent one last time I was here!"

"Oh, so you don't need me for anything then, innit?"

"Not so fast. I need a loaner still. Just not for me. For her," he says, looking back and pointing at me. Grant's smiling, finally, and it makes me smile back. "Colleague from the U.S., out here with me for the week."

I walk up, and the guy behind the counter, he's smiling less already. Maybe he just doesn't like me. Maybe I have something on my face. Do I have something on my face? Oh no. I need a mirror.

"Just fill this out, miss. And I need to see your U.S. badge."

We do all that and then walk upstairs. Raji sees me first and comes office-running toward us, throws her arms around me, squeezes tight.

"Welcome back, Piper!" she shrieks. She motions to the top of a filing cabinet next to her desk. "As you can see, I still have the infamous teapot."

I glance over, and there it is. The teapot. I shrug and smile. Then we spend the rest of the afternoon catching up, in *Orange* for a while, then in

White after someone knocked on the glass and pointed at their watch. *White* is the worst of them all. How is that a conference room name? Of all the possible names, just, *White?*

Grant's sitting out with the rest of the team, not talking, just poring over email. Every now and then, I glance out at him to see if his disposition has changed, but it never does. He's always just half-hunched over his laptop, eyes glaring at the screen, fingers furiously typing away. He told me to take as much time as I needed to talk to Raji, so I'm going to take him up on it. It's one of the perks of being good friends with your boss. You can kind of do whatever the hell you want, for the most part.

"How's Fraser?" I ask, interrupting the silence that suddenly fell upon us.

Guy

Wednesdays are the slowest day at the gallery, but I don't mind. I've got John Coltrane on the turntable and a meat pie that I picked up at the patisserie. A couple of passersby stopped in earlier in the morning. Otherwise, it's just been me. I walk around and straighten all the frames, even though I did it maybe thirty minutes ago. It's always good to make sure things are in order.

I'm sitting on a stool behind the counter, eating the meat pie, but thinking about Marion's cassoulet when the phone in the back office rings quietly. Remy must have turned the ringer down when he was watching for me the other day. The phone here never rings, so for all I know, it could have been this quiet for days, weeks even. I wouldn't even know. I can barely hear it. By the time I get back to the office, the ringing has stopped. I shrug.

"If it's good, they'll call back."

A middle-aged gentleman slows down in front of the north window, then comes to a stop. Hands on his hips, he's looking at the Palmieri. I can see it from behind. I smile. That crazy Italian. But what a genius.

The phone rings again, and this time, I spring back to the office fast enough to answer it. The old bones still have some juice left in them. I smile, huffing a little before I speak into the receiver.

"Allo?" There's a pause, so I repeat it again. "Allo?"

There's a man on the other end, but he's speaking fast, and I can't understand him. He's only speaking in English.

"*Pardonne-moi? Parlez-vous Français?*"

More English. I know a few words, but this man, he's speaking too quickly. I can't understand him, so I hang up.

"If it's good, they'll call back," I say again to myself.

When I get back to the counter, the man in the street that was admiring the Palmieri is gone.

Grant

"Hey, Sophie?" I ask, spinning around in my chair.

She looks up at me and squints from behind her thick glasses. Her hair is like Cathy from the cartoon *Cathy*.

"Yes?"

"Are you busy?"

"Just running some VLOOKUPs on these avails. Why? Do you need something? Did you forget the secret maneuver on the controller?"

Her French accent is very nice, much nicer than the French people in Paris. I don't understand why they can't all sound like this.

"No, it's not about the controller. I think I remember that now."

I actually don't even know what she's referring to.

"What is it then?"

Her hand moves away from the mouse, and I glance at her screen. An obscene number of rows of a colorfully formatted Excel doc stare back at me. She's clearly in the middle of something. But, I am her manager. Actually, her manager's manager.

"Do you...uh. Hmm. How do I ask this?" I pause. "Would you be able to make a phone call for me?"

"Sure, I can do that. To someone French?"

"Yes."

"Someone at Canal Plus?"

I smile when she says the plus in Canal+. *Plooos.* I shake my head.

"No, not Canal Plus."

"eOne?"

"No."

"Universum?"

"No. It's not someone at a studio."

"Oh," she smiles. "Hotel?"

Oh my God, enough with the guessing. Each attempt is making me feel guiltier about even asking her in the first place.

"No. Actually, you know what? Never mind. Don't worry about it."

She looks puzzled, afraid that she did something wrong.

"Don't worry about it," I repeat. "So, those avails..."

Then I start telling her some story about a time I...who cares. I'm not even listening to myself. This is my life.

After I finish, I go back to my desk and sit down in front of my computer. Google Maps is open, the gallery still selected, the pixels of the address and phone number searing into my screen. I look back at Sophie, and she's already plugging away at the Excel doc again. I let out a deep sigh, deciding to just try again later.

"Raji," I call out before looking up to see her seated at her desk a few feet behind me. "Want to watch me try to order an iced coffee from Starbucks?"

Piper

The restaurants in London are so small, they have no problem cramming you into the tiniest corners you wouldn't ever even imagine putting someone in back home. I mean, *maybe* in New York. But not in L.A. And definitely not in Cleveland.

We're at this place near our hotel, Café Zoe. There are eight tables and two waitresses, and I think one of them is the owner or manager, or maybe both. The kitchen is approximately the size of a decent walk-in closet. The tables can barely fit our plates. They have to take the salt-and-pepper shakers and move them to a portable side table. I look at Grant, and he's smirking as they set it up.

"Really?" he asks, after the waitress leaves. "The condiments get their own table?"

"Salt and pepper aren't *condiments*," I tell him. "Ketchup, mustard, relish...those are condiments."

He rolls his eyes.

"You excited to go home?" he asks.

"What? No! I love it here. You know that. I wish I could just stay for like a month or something. I feel like every time I get to come here, it's always over so fast."

He shrugs.

"It gets old after a little while."

"You're a dick," I remind him. "You have the best job, and you just take it for granted. You do realize that, right?"

He shrugs again. Then our entrees come out. His chicken is sitting on top of a blob of pureed squash. It looks like a blind man's Thanksgiving dinner. I don't remember what I ordered, but a bowl of pasta is in front of me.

We eat. We don't talk much. He's probably thinking about work, or about going home, or about Wendy. I'm just trying to live in the moment. The pasta was good, but not good enough for me to feel like the carbs were worth it.

Grant pays the bill, and we walk back to the hotel. It's our last night, and he wants to go out, get drunk. I tell him that I'm tired, that I want to stay awake during the flight and watch as many of the free movies and drink as many of the free drinks as I can. He tells me to act like I've been there before. I tell him to fuck off.

I walk into the hotel. He stands outside and starts texting someone. Then he walks down the street and into the cold night. Inside, the concierge smiles at me as I walk across the lobby.

"No friend tonight?" he asks, smiling.

"He went somewhere. I don't know."

The elevator doors open, and I walk in.

"Goodnight, miss!" I hear him call out as the doors pull shut and the elevator car jerks upward.

"Goodnight, lobby guy," I mumble to the empty elevator car.

Wendy

He's coming home tomorrow, but I don't even know if I want to see him. I might break up with him. This week—actually, it's been nine days— it's been eye-opening for me. I don't need him. I don't even miss him. I think I've just gotten used to him in my life, and this is how I am now. But after some time apart, everything is clearer. My head, my heart, my gut.

We just aren't meant for each other. Wesley said this about Grant when we first started dating, but I ignored him at the time. Maybe he was right. Maybe Grant and I aren't a good match. After all, he doesn't believe in God. And honestly, I could deal with that if I had to. But he's still got that single guy party streak in him too. I know how he can get. I know what he likes. It's only a matter of time that it all catches up to him. And to me.

Before I know it, he'll be kicking *me* to the curb. And I'll be so embarrassed, so ashamed that I let *him* do that. No, no. This is why I have to break up with him. He can't do that to me. He can't run me through that. I'm too strong for that. He can't.

But then I think about his face and the way that he stares at me when we're fighting. Those big, blue eyes. He's like a lost little dog. Blink, blink. Ahh...it melts my heart. Why does he have this effect on me? Hot and cold. Up and down. One minute I'm ready to leave him. The next, I'm falling head over heels. I told him that I love him when we were in Porto, but I don't know if I know what that means. I don't think I've ever loved anyone before, so I don't know. And we were both so drunk. Everything with us is just so volatile and unpredictable. I'm not normally like this. I don't get why he brings this out in me. It's him, that's for sure. It's definitely not me.

Piper

Grant leans forward and taps on the driver's headrest.

"What route is this?"

"Accident on the M4," the driver responds, his eyes focused ahead. "Big pileup. No good. So we go this way."

Grant looks down at his watch and sighs. The radio starts playing some '80s song that I'd forgotten about or maybe I have never heard in the first place. It sounds familiar, but the lyrics haven't started yet, so I can't tell if it's the former or the latter.

"You look stressed," I tell him. "Or maybe not. Are you just hungover?"

He looks over at me and doesn't say a word. I look out the window.

She was working as a waitress in a cocktail bar...

"I'm not hungover. I just...these car rides to Heathrow, they're kind of my favorite thing. I know it sounds stupid. But they are."

"Well," I laugh. "You sure don't look like it's your *favorite* thing. You look miserable."

He lowers his voice.

"This guy is taking us on some crazy route. It's throwing me off. And then—I mean, no offense—but, like, you're here. That's throwing me off too."

"What is your ride usually like? On a different road...and silent?"

He looks out the window and sighs.

"Exactly."

Grant

The flight attendant that's helping set up the bed for the old man across from me has a great ass. So does the other one with the tray of champagne. They all have nice asses in Upper Class, even the guys.

"Another champagne?"

I shrug, mostly using my face.

"Sure."

She smiles and selects a glass from the tray, then sets it down on my little glass holder. She stays leaned in for just a fraction of a second too long. I blush, out of sheer instinct.

"Dessert? Newspaper?"

"No, thanks. I'm fine."

She smiles and walks down the aisle to the next seat. I never understood the newspaper-on-the-plane thing. Is that really a thing? You board a plane with the expectation that someone will provide you with timely reading material? What if they're all out? Do you just stare at the ceiling and think of what the news could have been?

We're somewhere over the Atlantic, I don't know. It's been a few hours. Piper is in economy. A small part of me feels bad for not sitting with her, but the larger part of me is glad that I have a fully lie-flat bed and great asses to browse. The asses in the economy cabin are not nearly as good, this much I know. I *earned* this status. I saw those economy cabin asses for *years*.

When the cabin lights dim, I get up to go to the bathroom even though I don't really have to go. I just want to empty out before I take a nap. While I'm washing my hands, I decide to go visit Piper for a moment, see how she's doing. It's the least I can do...and it is probably the most I will do too.

I walk back, and she's asleep, her knee slightly bowed and angled out toward the aisle. I look down the aisle for the food cart, but it's heading the other direction. Her knee will be fine. I don't say anything and walk away.

Back at my seat, my empty champagne glass has been replaced with another one, but I don't want it, so I ring for the girl to take it away. She smiles as she leans over me again. She turns away slowly and lingers for just long enough that I feel like she's doing it on purpose. Her ass looks even better than it did before. Then again, maybe any ass looks better at 37,000 feet than at sea level. It's something about the air pressure. I feel like I'm always half-hard when I fly. The girl turns around, now a few seats up the aisle, and smiles back at me again.

"Meet me in the bathroom in ten..." I whisper, the steady hum of the Rolls-Royce Trent 1000 engines drowning out my words before they even reach my ears.

Laurent

The ribeyes are so thick, I have to cut them into two pieces each. The blood is running down the blade of the knife, dripping onto the wood chopping block when I lift it up. The pan is starting to smoke. I pour olive oil onto the large side of each steak and then rub salt and pepper into the flesh, working in a circular motion until the grains are fully adhered. Then I flip them over and do the same thing before tossing them onto the pan.

The hiss of the meat as it meets the pan is loud enough to startle Claude. Poor dog. I laugh, and he just looks at me like I did it on purpose.

"Just cooking here, old friend. I meant no offense."

I wash the greens and grab the baguette from the other counter, cutting it into one-inch pieces and dropping them into a towel-lined basket. I flip the steaks. The hiss isn't as startling this time, and Claude doesn't even flinch; he just lies there in his bed, staring across the floor.

The oven beeps, and I smile at my perfect timing. I slide the pan off the stovetop and place it onto the center oven rack. Then I open a bottle of red and sit down by the fireplace. I wish there was a fire right now, but alas, that's too much work. I lean back in the armchair and think about Patrice. About her face, her lower back, her jawline, her warm, inviting smile. She is, in all her ways, a true beauty.

The front door opens, and with it comes a gust of cold wind.

"Smells good," Jacques chirps, hidden behind the foyer wall. I hear him taking off his shoes.

"It'll be ready in ten minutes. Tell your sister, will you?"

"Okay. She's in her room?"

"Last I checked."

He walks by and smiles as he climbs the stairs. His hair is getting long, longer than a boy his age should wear his hair, if you ask me. But, what do I know? Maybe that's the style today. I just know that it wasn't in vogue when I was in school. The door opens again, and in walks Margot. She's carrying a couple of paper bags in one arm, the other dangling a set of keys from her gloved hand. She smiles as she walks over to me and looks down at my glass.

"Starting already?"

"I just opened it."

"What's cooking?"

"Ribeyes. They looked marvelous."

The paper bags still in her arm, she leans down and kisses me.

"Pour me one too, love?"

Etienne

It's cold. My breath is steaming out from my lips. Even when I try holding it in, it still seeps out as little white clouds that float past my nose. The flower bed in the garden is beyond wilted. It's turning brown and curling in on itself. No one blames the flowers. They aren't meant to survive these conditions. I told Simone, but she insisted we plant them last spring anyway.

I hear the rear slider open over at Laurent's. Then I hear it slide shut. A couple of quiet footsteps follow, then the creaking of aged wood as he sits down on the bench, or maybe the chair. They both creak, so it's impossible to tell.

"After-dinner cigarette?" I ask, my voice lobbing over the wall between us.

"Indeed. You?"

"You know I love it out here. It's my favorite room in the house."

"That's a shame," he says.

I make a face knowing that he can't see me.

"How's the family?" I ask, though I just saw Margot and the boy a couple of hours earlier as they came home.

"Great. How's Simone?"

"Usual. Hey, have you heard from Armond lately?"

"No."

"I was supposed to see him the other night, but he never showed up. I haven't been able to get a hold of him since. When was the last time you spoke to him?"

Laurent walks over to the wall and steps up on the ledge. His eyes peer over the top row of bricks.

"Weeks, maybe. I haven't needed to."

He's looking down on me with judgment. I can feel it.

"You're working fine now?"

"Like I'm eighteen again."

"After how many years? How do you do it?"

His eyes widen, then he looks over his shoulder. He doesn't need to say anything else, but he carries on regardless.

"This new one, she's just incredible."

"A new one?"

"I met her at yoga."

"You do yoga?"

"I do now," he laughs.

"Well, I still need Armond. I'm not stepping out of my house. I can't do that to Simone. I've got to have reinforcements over here."

"Even at that price?"

I can feel my blood begin to boil as I remember how I not only walked out of that bar empty-handed, but I also lost the goddamned money I brought to pay Armond. I can't tell Laurent; he'll never let me hear the end of it.

"Yes. Even at that price. I just can't do that to Simone. I don't know how you do it, to be honest."

"*C'est la vie.* Anyway, if I hear from him, I'll let you know. In the meantime, you're welcome to borrow from me until he re-ups you."

Smug bastard. Now he's just gloating.

"Thanks. Hey, I've got to get back inside. Say 'hi' to your *wife*, yeah?"

Grant

"I didn't choose the room! It was the last one they had. What was I supposed to do?"

She's so scary when she's mad. For such a tiny girl, it really doesn't make any sense.

"Why did you put yourself in that situation to begin with?"

"What situation? She's *Sam's* ex-girlfriend. I'd never."

She's fuming. I don't know how to put this fire out. I take a sip of my water; wish it were gin.

"Grant, I...I just can't. Not anymore."

"Can't what? Don't do this. Come on...not now! I just got back! I missed you so much!"

"You should have thought of that before you left me for nine days then."

"I had to *work*! What am I supposed to do? Just not go? I manage a team out there, Wendy. It's my job."

"It's your job to go to Paris for a three-day weekend before, with another girl? Really?"

"We were already there! I mean, I asked you if you wanted to come too, remember? You said *no*. You said it was fine. Why are you getting mad at me now when you said it was fine?"

She doesn't reply, just shakes her head. She's fishing in her purse for her keys. This is usually what she does when I make a good point. She leaves.

"Honestly, Grant...I don't care anymore. You do whatever you want to do, okay? It's obvious that's what you're going to do anyway. You don't give a shit about me, or my feelings, or anything other than yourself. Don't even bother trying to pretend like you do."

"That's so unfair."

"I'm leaving."

I shrug. Sometimes I just have to let her go. I can't tell if this is going to be a real one or not. I know I didn't do anything wrong, not really, so I can't bring myself to apologize. I just did what I told her I was going to do. *She* should be apologizing for not being clearer with me.

Her eyes are bulging out of her sockets as she stares at me. I think she wants me to tell her to stay, but I don't. She whips her head around and storms toward the stairs. Her heels *clap-clap-clap* down the stairs as she heads outside and slams the door. I'll have to apologize to Phil or Luna if I see them tomorrow.

Piper

Cars whiz by as I sip on my latté at the little table on the sidewalk. The air's dry today, and my skin is tight. I don't know why, but it makes me miss Paris. L.A. is not the same, not even close. Paris is even better than London. It was so magical.

"Need a napkin?" Sam asks with a grin as he walks toward me, his hand stuffed with what looks like thirty brown paper blobs.

"What the hell is all that?"

"Girl behind the counter went a little H.A.M. on the napkins."

"Ham?"

He shakes his head.

"Seriously, do you need a napkin? I don't know what else to do with these."

"Just throw them out."

"No way! That's a waste."

"Is someone else going to want to use your used, wadded-up napkins? No. I don't think so. Just throw them out."

"They're not used," he explains, placing the heap in the center of the small table.

There's a classic-looking car stopped at the light. The table is just a few feet from the corner of the intersection, and the air around us reeks from the chug of its tailpipe. I cover my nose.

"We can go. We don't have to sit here," he tells me.

"In Paris, there were old cars everywhere, but none of them emitted pollution like the cars here."

"Oh yeah?"

"It's like they've got it all figured out. Everything was so orderly and perfect."

"I thought Paris has pretty poor air quality, don't they? They have days where you can't drive if your license plate ends in an even number. Right? Isn't that Paris? I think I saw that somewhere."

"It was perfect."

"That doesn't sound perfect."

"What do you know?" I hiss.

The light turns green, and cars start to zip by again, the hum of their tires rolling across the pavement, drowning out a potentially awkward silence between us.

"You miss it, huh?"

He's right. I do. I mean, I know I do, but when he says it, it makes me realize how much I miss it.

"You should have gone with me," I tell him, then I regret it as his face lights up.

"Yeah?"

"I mean, do you even want to go to Europe?"

"Sure. Who doesn't?"

"Why haven't you gone with Grant then? He's been there like thirty times already. He could just use his miles to take you one of these days."

"Yeah, maybe. But then I'd have to get a passport. I should look into that..."

Here we go. Sam and the *looking into that*. It'll never happen, I know it.

"Let's go," I declare, standing up with my latté gripped tightly in my hand.

"Where? Europe?"

"No, you idiot. To the theater. The movie starts in twenty minutes."

We get up and walk to the crosswalk, and one of the wadded-up napkins gets caught in a breeze and tumbles alongside us. Neither of us bend to pick it up. The theater is just a few blocks away, but we don't have time. Sam's walking slowly, and I keep looking over my shoulder impatiently.

"Hey, I forgot to ask you," he begins. "Can you fit these in your purse?"

I look back, and he's holding a giant box of Mike and Ikes.

"Seriously?"

Wendy

"Does this mean we're back together?"

Beads of sweat dot his brow, his shoulders, his lower back. It makes sense. He was the one doing all the work. I just lay there. And it's been that dry, hot heat lately, the Santa Anas whipping down from the desert and dragging all the hot air with them. It's completely acceptable to be sweaty, but dangit, it's not acceptable to ruin the moment with *this* conversation.

"We didn't ever break up," I tell him.

He gives me that look. That *ohmygosh you're crazy, but I'm stuck with you* look. That *you just broke up with me yesterday and then today you slept with me* look. That *what did I get myself into* look. He does these judgmental things all the time.

"Okay."

"Okay."

We lie here, just looking at each other for a while. Then he takes out his phone, starts swiping through some things.

"Work," he explains.

It's quiet for a while. I stare at the ceiling.

"Should we go somewhere for Thanksgiving?"

He sets his phone down on his chest, and I imagine the sweat marks that'll be on the glass after he picks it back up.

"You don't do Thanksgiving with your family?" he asks.

"They don't really do Thanksgiving. We never did. It's a white-people holiday."

"It's an American holiday. You're American."

I shake my head.

"You don't get it. Anyway, let's go somewhere."

"I could do that. Where do you want to go?"

"Kana's got that trip to Hawaii, and now she has no one to go with."

"Why? What's wrong with Bertrand? They break up?"

Gosh, Grant. Pay attention.

"This was the trip she booked with *Daniel*."

"Oh."

"Yeah."

"So, you want to go to Hawaii with Kana? Just...the three of us?"

"Yeah, why not?"

He shrugs.

"Can't Bertrand go?"

"He has to work. If we don't go, she'll probably just cancel and call it a wash. But if we want, we can go and make it a little trip."

"I could do that. What island? I've never been. Have you been?"

"I went to Oahu once when I was a kid, but I don't really remember it."

"Where's she going?"

"Honolulu."

"That's on Oahu? Or the big island?"

"Oahu. I think."

He picks his phone up off his chest and wipes it on the sheets. Gross.

"Okay. I'll look up tickets."

"Just like that?"

This was a test, and he just passed it. He didn't even hesitate. He didn't say, *hey, what if you break up with me before we go?* He didn't say anything. He just marched straight ahead. I smile, continuing to stare into the ceiling. A police siren wails in the distance somewhere, but it blends in with the ambient traffic noise that emanates up from the street and in through his windows.

"Six hundred ninety-eight dollars round trip. Leaves Wednesday, comes back Saturday."

"Can we do Sunday?"

"More expensive," he explains. "But we can if you want. It's..." He trails off as he swipes around for a few seconds, then taps the screen. "Eight hundred fifty-eight dollars."

"I'll ask Kana. Do you care either way?"

"No. Either is fine. She has a hotel?"

"Yep."

He sits up.

"Hawaii."

"Yeah."

"All right. Yeah. I could do Hawaii!"

"Even with me?" I ask him, trying to be cute.

Laurent

I'm wearing one of my favorite scarves, but alas, I am full of regret. It's not that it doesn't match. It does. I looked fantastic in the mirror on my way out. I'd make love to me if I weren't me. No. It's not that. It's that it's warmer than usual today down in the Metro, and the clogged and stuffy air is pushing its way through the tunnels and into all the train cars. I take the scarf off, but it isn't helping. I've already overheated. I can't take it any longer. I look up at the display above the door.

MADELEINE

The doors open, and I squeeze my way out, shoulders rubbing against the others all trying to cram inside before the doors shut them out. If we all cooperated, we could probably get everywhere faster. All of us. But we don't.

I rush to the stairs and take them two at a time. Outside, the air isn't as refreshing as I was hoping for, but it'll have to do. I bury the scarf inside one of my pockets, and I look up at the sky. No clouds, not even one. It's not particularly warm out, but the sun is mercilessly beaming down on all of us like the city's turned into an urban version of the beach scene from *L'Etranger*.

"*Journal?*" a young child shouts in my direction. I wave him off. I'm too hot to read. And I don't want to know the news anyway. It's probably about global warming, climate change, this, that. They just held the summit here not long ago. Didn't everybody agree to something? Then why am I so hot in November?

"*Journal?*" the child yells again, but now I'm walking away, his voice trailing off into the sounds of the city.

I walk down the small side street a block over from the hotel. I pass the patisserie, the tailor shop, the toy store. A taxi zips by me, going much too fast for the width of the road. I give his registration plate a dirty look and a squint, but I can't make out the letters and numbers. I turn the corner, and an unmistakable feeling stops me dead in my steps. Déjà vu, perhaps. It feels as though I've been in this moment before.

The feeling enters me like my lungs are filling with smoke from the slow drag of a cigarette. What happened here? My head spins, and I stop to brace myself against the wall. I look down. Then I look up. And then I see it. There we are.

I walk in the door, swinging it wide behind me, and I march over to the fat man behind the counter. His glasses are dangling from his face, a sheen of sweat glistening from his forehead. The air smells like a meat pie.

"How much for the one in the window?" I ask him, straight to business.

"*Bonjour,*" he replies, sliding his glasses up the bridge of his nose. "Which one?"

He smiles, and I smile back.

"Pardon?"

"Which one in the window? They're...all in the window, Monsieur."

"Oh, right." I swivel around and point to the right of the door. "That one."

"The Palmieri?"

"Sure."

"You do know him, *oui?* Antonio Palmieri?"

"I'm afraid not, no. What? Is he famous? Is it expensive? I asked you, *how much is it?* I'd like to buy it."

"Nine hundred fifty euros."

I shrug.

"He can't be that famous. Nine hundred fifty euros, you say? What if I pay cash?"

"I only accept cash."

"Eight hundred euros, and you've got a deal."

"I don't negotiate here, Monsieur. Sorry."

"Eight hundred fifty," I try.

He shakes his head.

"You know I own the hotel just down the block, right? How about a neighbor discount?"

"Sorry, I can't."

"It's for my girlfriend," I add.

He shrugs and says nothing.

"What's your floor then?"

"Nine hundred fifty."

"Nine hundred. And I'll take it right now."

He looks down at the newspaper he was reading as though it contains the answers he's looking for. The answer is yes, fat man. It's *yes*. Find it in there somewhere.

"Nine hundred euros," I repeat.

"Okay then."

"I'll find a cash machine," I tell him. "And then I'll be right back. Can you take it down from the window so that no one else comes by and tries to take it?"

He chuckles.

"You're a possessive one, aren't you?"

"I just don't want anyone else to have it. My girl, she saw it the other day...if you were open, she would have insisted we buy it right then."

"What day? We have quite fair hours, you know."

"Last week or so. It was at night. I saw it from outside. And I had forgotten all about it until just now as I walked past your gallery on my way back to the hotel."

I tuck my hand into the pocket of my coat and fondle the ends of the scarf.

"You don't know Palmieri, do you?" he asks again.

I shake my head.

"I'll be right back. Please take it down from the window."

Guy

The kitchen smells like roasted duck, but Marion never makes duck during the week. But what else could it be? I sniff around the kitchen, searching for clues. A whiff of pomegranate fills my nose. That's not right. It was definitely duck a moment ago. Now it's fruit.

"Guy? Is that you?"

I spin around, and there's Marion—her perfect, cherubic face staring in my direction.

"Hello, my love. It is me."

"I see this now."

I kiss her on the forehead, then the cheek.

"What's in the oven?"

"Chicken."

"Not duck?"

"Chicken."

Hmm.

"Kids home?"

She nods upstairs.

"What time will it be ready?"

"Twenty minutes. Just enough time to freshen up."

"Indeed."

I walk into the other room and ease into the recliner.

"Good day at the gallery today?"

"Made one sale. A Palmieri."

"Oh?"

"Yeah. Some guy. Said he owned the hotel just down the block. *Had to have it.*"

Marion laughs. I do too.

"How much?"

"Nine hundred fifty euros," I lie.

"That's wonderful! We could have had duck tonight after all!"

"Maybe tomorrow," I suggest.

"Maybe."

Etienne

The sound this wet mound of leaves makes as it falls and lands in the trash bin below is a lot like when a racehorse takes a shit in the stable. I reach up to the gutter and scoop out another handful.

"*Merde!*"

That's for all my neighbors who paid that guy to clean their gutters while we were in the countryside for the weekend. Laurent, Sebastian, all of them. Bastards. And now no one will even return my calls. *It's too small of a job*, one guy said. *You clean leaves out of gutters*, I reminded him. I was trying to put him in his place, but he didn't waver.

At least this old ladder is getting some use. Up here, I can see most of the street as it empties out into the boulevard. It's a nice street, despite the selfish neighbors.

A pair of headlights turn onto the road, and only now am I realizing that the sun has already set and it's quite late in the day. Certainly too late to continue fishing leaves out of a rain gutter. As the headlights get larger and the car approaches, I recognize Sebastian's wife, though I forget her name. I wave from atop the ladder. I can't tell if she sees me.

Laurent is walking down the sidewalk, carrying something large and rectangular wrapped in brown paper underneath one of his arms.

I wave at him until he sees me.

"Etienne, my friend!" he shouts. "What are you doing up there? Our guy didn't do a good enough job for you?"

"*Our guy* didn't touch my gutters."

"Why not? He did everybody's."

I shake my head.

"What's that there?" I ask, sore, changing the subject.

He smiles.

"New painting I bought."

"I didn't figure you for a collector."

"I'm not. But I had to have this one. It spoke to me."

"Is that right?"

He lowers his voice.

"It's for the girl, but keep that between you and me."

"Mmhmm. Can I see it?"

He pulls the rectangle in front of his body as he stands in the center of the walkway that leads up to his front door. It shifts around in his hands as he rotates it from side to side.

"I was planning on keeping it wrapped until I give it to her. But...I could open it up and show you tonight. Come over for an aperitif?"

"I can't tonight," I explain.

"Oh well, then. Soon, it'll be hers. Besides...it's nothing remarkable. I don't even know what she sees in it, if I'm being honest."

"Where did you find it?"

"At a gallery right by the hotel. It's been there for years—the gallery, that is—but I've never paid it much attention until just last week. When we saw this one, she insisted I buy it."

"If you bought it near the hotel, why didn't you just leave it there?"

"It would be too easy for someone to walk away with it if it's not secured, and my office doesn't have a closet with a proper lock. You know how the staff can be."

I nod, even though I have no idea how staff can be.

"Can't I just see it now?"

He laughs.

"What's the fun in that?"

Grant

Honolulu is basically like California but with the ocean all around you instead of just to the west. I don't see any difference.

"Do you think it was worth the flight here?" I ask, my mouth full of Pad Thai noodles.

"You're such a *good* complainer."

"No," I blurt, a noodle slipping from my tongue and almost unraveling back down to the plate. "It's nice here. I'm having a good time and all. I get it. But, like, is it really *that* much better than L.A.?"

Kana and Wendy look at each other.

"Yes," they say in unison. I can't argue against that, so I just slurp up the remaining noodles in my mouth and set my chopsticks down.

"I was just expecting better. But maybe I'm missing something."

"Tomorrow we're going to the North Shore. Maybe that'll change your mind."

The bill comes, and I pause, waiting to see if anyone else is going to reach for it. The girls are busy in conversation, so I pull my wallet out from my pocket and place my card inside the flap of the bill holder.

"I'll get this," I say quietly.

Kalakaua Avenue is bustling with people. It seems we're not the only tourists that came to Hawaii for Thanksgiving. The sun set a few hours ago, and the sky is very dark, but surprisingly the air is still warm. I'll give Hawaii credit where it's due. It is warmer here, and I'm certainly thankful there's a bit more humidity.

We turn down a smaller street, and the crowd thins out.

"Can we go in here?" Kana asks.

"What's an ABC store? It looks like a convenience store."

"It is," Kana explains. "But I need sunscreen."

"Ooh, me too!" Wendy chimes in.

"Okay. I'll just hang out here."

They walk in, and I slowly stroll back and forth in front of the store for a little while. Kana and Wendy are looking at souvenirs. I'm getting bored, so I walk down the sidewalk. Stuck right in between a pair of clothing stores is a small art gallery. It seems like a peculiar place to set up shop.

I walk inside and start browsing the paintings on the right wall. The most eye-catching of them all is a vibrant, splashy rendition of the Waikiki shoreline, the tall buildings looming alongside an almost equally tall wave. It almost looks like a tidal wave, but that doesn't fit the vibe of this piece. Not at all. It's happy and cheerful. It's whimsical. Meanwhile, tidal waves are, well, basically death. Something about the morbidity and the painting and the bright colors make me think back to the painting in Paris. My heart gets tight.

"Goddammit," I mumble.

"Not finding something you like?"

There's a young girl behind a little desk, standing there without anything to do.

"No. These are nice."

"You sounded concerned."

"Thanks. No, never mind. Have a nice night."

Fuck this. I sit down on a bench outside of the ABC store, and while I'm waiting for Wendy and Kana to come out, I tap the photos app on my phone and scroll back until I see images I recognize from Paris.

Traffic from atop the Arc de Triomphe.

A phone booth.

Piper standing in front of two giant doors.

The river.

Me, in front of the river.

The painting.

I let out a loud sigh before turning the brightness on my phone all the way up. The painting looks even more vibrant than I remember it. My heart begins to ache in that uncomfortable, there's-nothing-I-can-do-about-it kind of way. I zoom in and focus on the bus window. I still can't tell if it's the front or the back, if it's coming or going.

Am I coming or going? I don't know. If I'm being honest with myself, I don't know where I'm going with my life. I've just been marching forward, head down, for as long as I can remember. I don't even know what I'm doing here in Hawaii. Kana and Wendy would be having more fun without me here, I think. And I'd be having more fun...

I don't know.

Wendy walks out of the store first. Kana follows behind her. The girls are smiling, but when they see me, their smiles fade and turn into something that looks like disgust.

"Finally," I moan.

"What's up your ass?"

"Fucking paintings. I don't know."

"Paintings?"

"I'm just...do you remember that painting I told you about? The one in Paris?"

Wendy looks at Kana and then blankly looks back at me.

"No?" I ask.

She still doesn't say anything.

"What? What is it?"

We all just stare at each other for a while. Finally, Wendy breaks the silence.

"Who cares about the painting, Grant?"

"Hang on," I tell her, pulling my phone from my pocket. "Have I even shown it to you?"

I hold my phone up at arm's length and away from my body. Kana squints and shifts her weight forward on the balls of her feet as she leans in to get a closer look. Wendy simply stands in position and furrows her brow.

"A bus in the rain?" Kana asks.

"It's more than that, but yes."

I look up at Wendy, and I recognize the anger as it's creeping into her eyes.

"What's the matter?" I ask her.

"I don't know!" she snaps. "It just pisses me off. Stupid freaking painting..."

She crosses her arms and begins walking briskly down the sidewalk. I look over at Kana, and she shrugs.

"Look what you did..." she scolds me.

Laurent

"*Bonjour*, my love."

"Hi, Laurent."

"I miss your face."

"It's been a while. Why haven't I heard from you?"

"Oh, busy. Busy here, busy there. *C'est la vie*."

"It's nice of you to call me."

Nice? It's for a reason. I'm not calling to chat. Doesn't she know what this is all about?

"It's nice to hear your voice. What are you doing?"

"Drawing a bath."

"Now? But it's barely sixteen hundred!"

"I had a long day already. And when I got home, and my flat was nearly frozen because the heater failed to turn on, and I had to call the serviceman, and he told me that he can't make it out today, I thought to myself, *what haven't you done for yourself lately?* And then I thought of a bath. So I figured, what the hell, why not treat myself? It's the least I could do to keep warm. Mid-afternoon or not."

"I could keep you warm," I offer.

"So can the bath, Laurent."

"Can I see you tonight?"

There. More to the point. She can't escape that one.

"I don't know. *Can you?*"

Jesus, this woman. She drives me crazy. I feel the seam of my pants rise away from my body.

"Eighteen hundred?"

"But my bath..." she whines.

"Name the time."

"Can you stay the night?"

I look up at the clock on the wall.

"I don't know, my love. Probably not tonight. I have...a lot of hotel business early tomorrow. I'll need all my things. You know how it is."

"Nineteen thirty," she replies, less of an offer and more of a declaration.

"I have a gift for you," I divulge.

"Yes, Laurent. I know about your *gift*. It's possibly the only reason I tolerate you."

"My love, not *that* gift."

"Okay, honey. Whatever you say."

"Nineteen thirty?"

"Nineteen thirty."

"Okay. I'll be there."

"*Ciao*."

She hangs up.

"*Ciao?*"

How tacky. I look back at the clock, then out the window. Margot is usually home by around 18:00. The kids come home at around the same time. I just need to be out of the house before then, and I'll be fine. I lean back in the recliner and look down at the crotch of my pants.

"Soon, old boy. Soon."

I walk over to the kitchen and open the pantry, taking out a package of crackers inside a plastic bag. I slide a few into my mouth and chew quietly as I stand at the island in the center of the room. The sun has just sunk behind the roofline out the window, and I know that soon the heat will kick on. I worry about how cold it'll be at Patrice's if she truly has no heat. Or maybe she was just flirting with me.

I look over at the clock, then back to the living room. The painting is leaning up against the wall, still wrapped in brown paper. I look back at the clock again, even though I just looked at it. 16:25. Hmm. I have a few things to take care of at the hotel, and I've got time to kill...

I grab my keys and my wallet, and then I snatch the painting up with my free hand. I dash out to the car, and in no time, I'm headed off to the hotel with the painting in tow in the rear seat. The traffic will be a mess, but I'd rather not carry this thing all the way out there on the metro. And besides, I've got the time.

When I arrive at the hotel, the single parking spot around the corner is free, so I back in slowly and lift the emergency brake. The front doors whoosh as I enter, a gust of wind from the circulating air catching the broad side of the painting and staggering me back a half step.

"Back again, Mr. Dubois?" the front desk clerk asks.

I nod, and then I gesture to the painting in my hands without saying any words to her. I follow my usual path behind the front desk, around the corner, through the manager's office, and then finally to my personal office. It's not in the most convenient location, but I like it here. No one can bother me. I set the painting down behind my desk and ask the clerk at the front to call the shift manager to come see me.

As I wait, I pick the painting up and peel back the pieces of tape. The paper is dimpled and folds very easily. That fat man might have given me used paper. I don't know how I feel about this.

As I'm uncovering the layers of paper, my heart starts to race. It's that déjà vu feeling again. What is it about this painting? I know I haven't been here, in my office, with this painting. Not before. This is absolutely the first time. My head spins a little as I pull back the rest of the paper. The umbrellas reveal themselves first, the splashes of blood red oil dotting the center of the frame, the dull strokes dazzling and blurring the lines into each other. My knees get weak, and I see my hands tremble, though I can't feel them. Everything is blurry. All my feelings have escaped my body. I'm just a shell, not a human. Just a vessel. My eyes shut, I think, or everything otherwise just goes dark.

"*Dieu!*"

Wendy

Kana's taking a shower, and I just finished giving Grant a blowjob. I don't know why. *Dangit.*

"Where am I gonna spit it out?" I asked him before.

"Wherever," was all he said back, clearly focused on one thing and one thing only.

Kana takes long showers, but we didn't need that much time. He's fast.

"Thank you," he whispers.

He's got that stupid look on his face. That *nothing is going to hurt me, everything is awesome* look. I look over in the mirror, and I don't have the same carefree look. I just look like a frustrated woman.

"So, how far away is the North Shore?" he asks as he lies back on the unmade bed and kicks his feet up on the footboard.

On to the next thing. Of course he is. What about me? I don't do these things for free, do I?

"I don't know. An hour maybe."

"How much is it to swim with the dolphins?"

"Two hundred twenty dollars."

"Each?"

"Yeah. Dolphins aren't cheap."

"Jesus. I guess not."

My phone lights up with the reminder to check into our flight tomorrow. We only have twenty-four hours left in paradise. I think I'll break up with Grant when we get back.

Sam

"What's your ETA?" Grant asks, impatient as he ever is.

"I dunno. I mean, I was going to leave soon, but first I have to go to Starbucks because I didn't eat anything yet, and I was, well, I was asleep until, I dunno, maybe an hour ago or something."

"You said you were going to be here by two. It's already three thirty."

"Oh. Yeah. Okay. I can hurry up. My alarm just didn't go off before..."

He sighs heavily.

"I have to return the truck by six o'clock. We're not going to make it back in time unless I leave right now."

"Oh. Well, um...I mean, can you do that? Like, do you need me there to help you?"

"Jesus, Sam. It's a *free* fucking couch. Now I have to drive it over to you too?"

"No, I'll come there. I mean, you said six?"

"Yeah. *O'clock.* By the time you get here, and then we load it in, and then we drive all the way back to your place, and then we drive all the way back here..."

I tune him out as I look down at my bare feet on the floor. It hasn't been swept in a while, maybe a month, and there are cracker crumbs and little hairs clinging to the corners of the hallway. I just bought the paper towels too, so it's got to be Bertrand's turn to clean.

"Sorry. You can just leave it there. I can get a truck later or something."

"Leave it here? I have a new one coming tomorrow! I don't have the room! Besides, I, what? Rented this truck for absolutely nothing? No. Fuck that. I'll find someone to load it in with me."

"Who?"

"Fuck it. I'll do it myself if I have to."

"No way. You have so many stairs. And that right angle?"

"I'll call you when I'm fifteen minutes away. Does that work?"

"Sure."

"Yeah? Your schedule will permit me to drop it off for you? Don't pencil me in if you can't make it. Fucking Sam, I swear..."

Then he hangs up. Grant never was a patient guy. Not as kids, not now. He's always got something he has to do. Something he has to get or make or buy or be. Always something.

I mean, I feel bad. I didn't want to be this late. It all just kind of happened like it usually does. I swear, I have the worst luck when it comes to getting ready. There's always something that gets in the way. I look down at my watch. Now there's plenty of time for me to take a shower *and* go to Starbucks.

Wendy

"This time I mean it."

He looks so sad, I have to look away.

"I thought we were past this," he says quietly. "I had such a good trip. Everything was great. Wasn't it? What did I do? What went wrong?"

"You didn't do anything, Grant. Okay? It just...this just isn't going to work. It's obvious. We just aren't meant to be together. It's not what God wants or, you know, it would just be a lot easier."

He frowns.

"I don't think that's how God works. Doesn't he make things challenging so that you *have to* overcome them? Like, that's all part of the great journey of life. Struggle turns into success. We're just in the struggle right now. But there is success in the future. I can see it. Can't you?"

"Can't I what?" I ask, looking out the window and acting like I was barely paying attention to what he was saying.

"See our future. Can't you?"

I turn away from the window and look back into the room. It's empty where the couch used to be. All that's left is a patch of lighter-colored wood, hidden from the sun's rays for however long Grant's been living here now.

"I can't," I tell him, straightforward and unemotional, though I'm not one hundred percent sure if I even believe it myself.

Then he starts crying. Grant, he cries a lot. I tried to be okay with it at first, but in actuality, it's too awkward for me. I don't wear my heart on my sleeve. Some people say that it's almost as though I don't even have a heart. Grant, on the other hand, everyone knows his heart inside and out. Mostly out. Always out.

"I'm going to go. I'll come later for my stuff. I have some work to do tonight, so I don't have time to pack it up."

"I can pack it for you." His voice is choked, sobbing. "I bought you new things for the bathroom. I honestly...dammit, Wendy. I honestly didn't expect this. I thought we were good."

"We're never good. You know that."

Laurent

"It's me, Etienne."

"Etienne?" I ask, hopeful.

"Your neighbor."

"Yes, I know. I know your voice. Where are we?"

"The hospital."

Hospital. What hospital?

"I can't see."

"*Oui*, the nurse told me."

"How did you find me?"

"They came to my house."

"Who did?"

95

I hear the fabric of his jacket lift as he shrugs.

"Someone from the hospital. I don't know. You have no next of kin. So they came to the address, I guess on your license, I don't know. And then they came to my house. And now I'm here."

"No next of kin?" I ask.

"Yeah. Unless you have family in the country? You never told me. All I know is that you live in that flat all by yourself."

"I have a family," I tell him.

I don't understand why I can't see. I've got to find out what's going on. I bring my hands up to my eyes and feel gauze patches over each socket, a loose bandage wrapped a few times around my head.

"They said you shouldn't touch."

"What happened? What happened to my eyes? Am I blind?"

"I don't know. They just said to not touch them."

"What happened to me, Etienne?"

"I honestly don't know. Nobody does. They told me that someone found you, a stranger. You were passed out on a bus."

"On a what?"

"On a bus. Some city bus. Were you in the city? What's the last thing that you remember?"

"I never take the bus."

"They said you were on a bus."

"But I don't take the bus."

"Well, then what's the last thing you *do* remember?"

"I don't remember the last thing that I remember."

I run the edge of my fingers over the gauze, and Etienne slowly clasps his warm hand around mine.

"They said you shouldn't touch."

Piper

I'm panting so hard, and I want to hide it, but I can't. Every thrust pushes the air right out of my lungs. Jesus, it's been a minute. This is *so* good. I forgot how good it was.

"Turn over?"

I shake my head.

"I'm almost there."

He pushes his face down into the pillow and keeps thrusting, not harder or faster, just continuously. Gasps of air keep puffing out my mouth, and I give up on trying to hide it. I'm close.

"Sam!" I blurt out into the darkness.

"Yeah?"

"Sam!"

The dark ceiling of the room lights up with stars. My legs are tingling. Everything is warm. I feel my eyes rolling around in my skull even though I'm squeezing my eyelids shut. He keeps pumping even after I'm done. I tap him on the back to let him know it's okay, he can stop.

"Turn over?" he asks again.

I open my eyes, and he's staring at me, expressionless, but seemingly full of hope. Or horniness.

"Okay."

He loves it from behind. I don't know why. I'm pretty. Doesn't he want to look at me in the face?

"I've missed you," he says as he slides back in.

"Don't talk."

The fronts of his legs slap softly against my ass. His arms are like ape arms on either side of my ribcage, his knuckled fists pressed deep into the mattress, elbows locked, shoulders hunched. When he finishes, he flops down onto the bed, and his penis stays hard for a few more minutes.

"Where are you going?" he asks.

"Dude, I have to clean up. You came all over my back."

"I wiped it off."

"Sam."

He shrugs.

In the bathroom, I close the door before I flip on the light switch. The brightness of the fluorescent light shocks me, though I don't know what else I was expecting. My eyes look dark, sunken in, bloodshot. My hair is a mess. I look as drunk as I feel. My heart floods with guilt.

Etienne

"The doctor says you can leave in a few days."

He frowns.

"With these patches on?"

"I suppose. I don't know."

"How the hell am I supposed to do anything if I can't see?"

"I'll be there to help you."

"Ettie, that's a full-time job. You don't have the patience for it. I won't let you."

"I'm not doing anything else. It'll be fine. And Simone can help."

"Don't drag Simone into this!"

She looks over at me from the chair and shrugs. He doesn't even know she's here.

"It'll be fine," I reassure him.

"But what about my family?"

Jesus, the poor guy. I don't know how many times I can keep telling him the same thing.

"Laurent, you don't have a family."

"But I do!" he shouts.

"Where are they? How do I get a hold of them? I'm happy to make some calls, find them. But you've got to give me some way to get a hold of them."

"They live with me, dammit!"

"No. You live alone."

"*Merde!*"

A nurse on the other side of the room pulls her body upright and sighs. I look back at Simone, and she shrugs again.

"Just a few more days, okay? Who knows? Maybe you can see after all and you just need some more time to heal?"

"Doubtful," he moans.

"We'll come back tomorrow, all right?"

"We?"

"Hi, Laurent," Simone says, smiling shyly.

Guy

"And he said, 'Two hundred thousand.' Just like that!"

"He just walked in? You'd not spoken to him before that moment?"

"That's right."

"But you don't even own the shop. How could it be worth that much?"

"Marion, it's the *business*. I own the business. The shop could be anywhere. It's the clientele, the pieces—you know, the inventory—and it's the reputation. The gallery is worth at least that much!"

"If it's worth at least that much, then you should get more for it."

"Why do you make me have to eat my own words?"

"You eat everything," she replies. "Words too."

"Two hundred thousand would be enough to pay off the house. I could retire. We could spend time in the countryside."

"That sounds so romantic, Guy. Really."

"But what?"

Marion shrugs.

"Two hundred thousand," I continue. "I mean, we don't have to pay off the house. I could take another job though. Maybe one closer to home. One that doesn't take up so much of my time. One that's less stressful, less hectic. This could be great for us!"

"Stress?" Marion laughs. "You sit in that gallery for ten hours a day, listening to your jazz records and eating croissants from the patisserie down the block. How could you possibly be stressed?"

"Marion," I chide. "I don't eat croissants from *that* patisserie. They're overpriced!"

"I see."

"Why are you so against this? I thought you would be happy. It's a blessing, no? Like a gift from God that just fell into my lap without me having to do anything! What could be better?"

She's stirring a pot on the stove. She's always stirring something. The poor woman, always cooking. Maybe she's just tired, worn out. Maybe we should get away for a few days and leave the kids with my brother.

"Whatever you think is best, dear," she murmurs, setting the spoon against the spoon rest.

"You always tell me to spend more time at home with you and the kids. I thought you'd be happy about this."

"Guy!" she shrieks, sharply turning her face up from the towel she's running over her hands. "I *would* be happy. I *would*."

"Then what is it?"

She sighs and goes back to drying her hands.

"Will you?"

Grant

Wendy's passed out on the hotel bed, her underwear loosely wrapped around her bony hips. She's wiped out, but I can't blame her. She just came ten times. Ten. I didn't know that was even possible. My tongue is already sore. Breakfast tomorrow will be interesting.

"Happy birthday," I whisper.

The hotel in Iguazú is the nicest hotel I've ever stayed at, though I only stay at nice hotels with Wendy. Shrouded in the middle of a legitimate rainforest. Infinity pools. Hanging bridge walkways. A five-star steakhouse in the land of Argentinian beef. And all for a hundred and seventy dollars a night. Yes. I could get used to this. I don't know if I'll ever go home.

My mind drifts back to last night. Lying on thatched chaise lounges by the pool. The sun is setting, and the sky has exploded into colors I've never seen back home. "Like a Star" starts to play on my phone. I'm staring at our knees, silhouetted against the palm trees and the streaks of purple, orange, and colors that might not even have names yet. I have everything I ever wanted in life, and I want everything I have right now. In this moment, I have it all. *We do it all the time, blowing out my mind...*

We could live here, Wendy and I, and start a life in this forest. Away from the office and L.A. and everything that our life revolves around now. I've got enough saved that we could live for at least a year, maybe more if we stick to a budget. We're always so good when we're on vacation. It's when we get back home that it all falls apart. Here, we could stay in a state of permanent bliss. Nothing would ever go wrong. We'd never fight. We'd have the world's most beautiful *cataratas* in our backyard, a symphony of falling water to lull us to sleep each night.

I look over at her, and her eyes are rolling around under her half-closed eyelids. She's not beautiful when she sleeps, but luckily, it's usually dark. Nobody's perfect, anyway. I'm not either. In Iguazú, though, it all doesn't matter. Everything's perfect here.

On the rollercoaster that is our relationship, we're two cars that have unintentionally disconnected and are now traveling on an endless loop. She comes around, and I'm all the way over here. I finally come back around, and she's over there. I used to think that eventually, one of us would change our velocity and we'd crash into each other and it would all change. But that hasn't happened yet, and I don't know if it ever will.

I flip open my laptop and go through my inbox. It's a slow week, and I'm finished before I realize I started. I'm bored. It's only ten o'clock. I think about waking her up, but I know that it'll just make her mad, so I start browsing the web at random. I close my laptop and lie down on the bed, then pull out my phone. I open Google Maps and type in *HOTEL MADELEINE PARIS*. A bunch of results pop up that aren't where we stayed. What was it called? Haussmann. I try *HOTEL MADELEINE HAUSSMANN*.

"There you are," I say softly to my phone before looking over to make sure I didn't wake Wendy.

I push into street view. I travel down the street a couple of blocks. I come to the corner. It takes me a few taps, but I eventually get it to turn the corner. I'm facing the gallery. I zoom in, but the paintings are different than when I was there. I don't know why this surprises me at first. Google Maps is great, but it's not as though they drive around Paris and take pictures every week.

I set the phone down on my bare chest and stare up at the ceiling fan above the bed. I should have bought it when I had the chance. I should have had Sophie call and arrange for them to ship it to me. It's surely gone now; it must be. Someone out there in the world has it. Someone that's not me. And I'll never know who it is. Seven billion people, and it's not me.

Laurent

"What do they say?"

He doesn't say anything for a little while. The papers rustling around remind me of being a schoolboy waiting in detention, listening to my teacher grading papers as I stared out the window. They say that scent is the sense most tied to your memory, but when your eyes aren't working, sound also becomes quite important.

"Nothing yet."

"Ettie, please. I'm telling you. There's got to be something in there. I have a wife. I have two kids. They're good kids."

I think. I actually don't know if they're good these days. I don't spend that much time with them anymore. Jacques, with his hair. He might not be a good kid. I just don't know.

"Laurent, I'm sorry, but I've known you for more than ten years now. You've never had a wife. You've never had kids."

"Do you think I am someone that I'm not?"

"No. I know who you are. I came here. I found you. Remember? I'm not the one who can't see."

"Did they tell you that? I'm blind?"

He sighs.

"I don't know. They didn't tell me anything. I'm just saying...you can't see, at least right now. And I can. So it's pretty unlikely that *I'm* mistaking *you* for someone else. Yes?"

"Are you sure you got the right box?"

The papers stop rustling. I feel him staring at me.

"You said the closet in the office. On the floor. Right side."

"Right side?"

"It was the only box in the entire closet, Laurent. I looked it over at least three times."

"Keep digging. There's got to be the marriage license in there somewhere. Maddy's birth certificate. Something."

The papers start rustling again.

"Whatever happened to you, it must have involved some sort of head trauma. I mean, obviously...with your eyes and all. But you must have hit your head. Lost your memory. Got confused. Something. I don't know. This isn't normal, Laurent."

"You're telling me? I've been holed up in this hospital for over a week now. I can't see! I can't go home! You're telling me that my wife and kids have run out on me!"

"I didn't say that."

"Did Margot find out? Is that what this is about? You'd tell me, wouldn't you, Ettie? You'd tell me if this was all a setup?"

"Hmm?"

"About my affairs. Did she find out? Did she strike me? Pay someone to hurt me? Take the kids and run away?"

"What on earth are you talking about?"

"You know Margot, for Christ's sake! Remember that Christmas dinner? She nearly killed me!"

"Laurent, honestly," he whispers. "You need to calm down. The people here are starting to get worried. You *do* want them to discharge you, don't you?"

"*Merde*! What's the difference?"

"Home is more comfortable, that's one. You can yell as much as you want about a Margot or Maddy or whoever else, that's another. And you can save all the money that you'll inevitably be charged for staying here this long."

"Ha! Not a chance! I have private insurance."

"Oh, I doubt that."

"What's that supposed to mean?"

"You're barely able to make payments on the flat. You've told me this much. I can only imagine it's even worse than what you've let on."

"Ettie! This is madness! I am not some poverty-stricken singleton that can barely pay my own mortgage! I am quite well off! I have been for a while, and you know this! The hotel may not be the Ritz, but it brings in fantastic revenue!"

"Monsieur," a nurse coos in my direction. "We're all aristocrats here. But you're still going to have to keep your voice down."

Guy

After I hang up the phone, I realize that I don't even know his last name. He's only gone by Jean this entire time. What a strange fellow.

"Marion," I call from the recliner. "Is dinner almost on the table?"

I cringe as I wait for her to respond. She says nothing and walks into the living room. Her apron is wrapped tightly around her hips. She takes a deep breath and holds it, her bust elevating and pushing up toward the lower part of her neck.

"Who was that?"

"Marion. Dinner?"

"Was that the buyer?"

I nod.

"He offered two hundred fifty."

"That's a lot of meat pies, isn't it now?"

"*Oui.* That's a lot of meat pies."

"Are you going to take it?" she asks, sitting on the arm of the sofa, her bust settling back to its regular position.

"I don't know. Should I?"

"You sounded like you wanted to. The other day, you were very intent on it. Even this morning, you sounded like it was a sure thing."

"Oh, Marion. Nothing's ever a sure thing with me, is it?"

"Your appetite is," she reminds me, and I laugh.

"What do you think? Two hundred fifty? Cash?"

"Cash?"

"Well, I mean, not in payments. I'm sure it'll be a bank check or a wire transfer or something secure. All in one lump sum is what I meant. Two hundred fifty, all at once."

She smiles.

"That is a lot of money."

"It is."

"We could do a lot with it."

"We could." I pause. "Think of all the meat pies."

"Would you be happy?"

"Would you?" I counter.

"Guy, I have the life that I always wanted. Two wonderful children. A faithful husband. A wonderful house in a safe neighborhood. I *am* happy. The question is, are you?"

"I think I am."

"Will you be if you sell the gallery?"

"I don't even know his last name," I murmur, wondering if that's strange or merely coincidental.

"*Balle*," she jokes. "Does it matter?"

We both sit in silence for a little while. A pot on the stove is quietly bubbling. Marion looks over her shoulder and shifts her weight back toward the doorway to the kitchen.

"So you think I should sell it?" I ask again as she stands up and begins to walk away.

"I support whatever it is that you want to do, my love. If you think this is the right move..."

Her voice trails off, and I hear the spoon clank against the sides of the pot. She never finishes her sentence. I sit in silence for a few moments, stroking the phone against my sweater.

"*Putain...*" I whisper to no one in particular, though maybe it's to the phone.

A few more minutes pass by. Outside, the wind is picking up, and it howls down through the chimney, scattering ash behind the screen.

"Dinner's almost ready!" Marion yells out. "Call the kids, love?"

I push myself up from the chair and walk over to the edge of the stairs. I rap on the wall.

"*Enfants!* Time for Papa's retirement dinner!"

Wendy

"This time I mean it," I tell him.

His eyes are full of tears, but they're not falling out. It's making me uncomfortable.

"You always say that. And then...you know what? What if I just say no? Hmm?"

"What do you mean?"

"What if I don't let you break up with me this time? What if I refuse?"

"What are you talking about? You can't *refuse*. We're breaking up. I've decided."

"You don't get to decide."

He's not usually this defiant. I take a step back, turn around, and look over my shoulder. My phone is on the couch. I'm hoping for a distraction, but it's not lighting up or making any noise.

"Yes, I do," I tell him.

Right? Don't I?

"No, you don't. *We* decide if we break up. And I am a part of *we*."

"Grant, look. I like you. Okay? We have a lot of fun. But you just...you just aren't what I'm looking for. Okay?"

"What are you looking for?"

"NOT THIS!" I yell.

"Then I'll change."

"What?"

"I'll change. To what you're looking for. I'll change."

"How will you change?"

He shrugs.

"You tell me. You obviously have something in mind. So, you tell me. And then I'll change."

"People can't change," I remind him.

"People change all the time. *All the time*."

"No. I don't think so. No."

He sits down on the couch and looks at my phone.

"Is there..."

"No."

"No what?"

"No, I'm not with someone else."

"Then what is it!?" he shouts. "You tell me you like me. You tell me you want something else. I tell you that I'll be that. But you won't tell me what that thing is. Just tell me! And I'll be that! And you'll—we'll—be happy!"

The tears still aren't dropping from his eyes, and I'm starting to worry that they never will, that he'll just have these watery, crystal blue orbs stuck to his face for the rest of his life.

"Grant, it's just not what I want."

He shakes his head.

"You can't get rid of me this easily. *I love you*, Wendy."

"Don't say that."

"But I do."

"You've got to go. Okay? You just...you've got to go."

"You love me too. I know it."

"You sound so creepy."

"You know it too. Don't you?"

"Grant. You've got to go."

He shrugs and then pushes himself further into the couch.

"Make me."

Guy

The wire transfer came in the day before yesterday. It's still hard for me to accept that in just a couple of weeks, I went from being the proud owner of my own gallery to the proud owner of a giant sum of money. On the brisk walk down Rue Pasquier, I stop and look at the patisserie with fondness.

"I'll miss you," I whisper delicately.

There's slush lining the gutters, and the street feels smaller than usual. My boots are squishing liquid between the grooves of my soles, and it reminds me of my childhood. I used to spend the entire walk home from school squishing out slush and trying to break my own personal distance record.

A police siren wails in the distance. I look up at the sky. It's clear and blue today, but brisk. The shade from the buildings all around the small street make it very cold and uninviting. I never did like the location of the gallery. But the lease was a good price, and the landlord was a fair man.

As I approach the gallery, I see large sheets of brown construction paper lining the windows on the west side of the building.

"What the...?"

On the glass of the front door, there's paper as well. The window to the left of the door is unblocked. I peek in and reel back in surprise. Then I knock on the door and wait for a few moments. A car drives by and splashes my pant leg.

"*Merde!*"

The door quickly opens, and a young man peers out.

"Gallery's closed," he announces.

"Yes. I know. I'm Guy."

"*Pardonne?*"

"I'm Guy. I'm the...I was the owner of this gallery."

"Oh! You're the guy here for the box, right?"

"Box?"

"Your things. We put them in a box."

"Oh, you didn't have to do that. I could get them myself."

"No worries. I have them back here. Just a moment..."

He leaves, and the door shuts behind him. I stand facing the closed door for a few awkward moments before he returns.

"Here you go," he says as he shoves the box into my arms.

"That's it?"

"That's it."

"You sure are moving fast. What's going on in there? Renovation?"

I try to peek around him, but he advances toward me and smiles.

"Sorry. Construction code doesn't allow civilians inside."

"You're already under construction? We just completed the transfer but two days ago!"

"The owner moves fast," he says with a smile.

"I'll say!"

We stand here for a while, not saying anything. Then he shrugs and wishes me a good day. The door closes behind him, and I hear the lock click.

"Goodbye, old friend," I murmur to the papered door.

Grant

I nudge Sam.

"I think it's the same one."

He looks over his shoulder at me and frowns.

"Same what?"

He turns back around and continues walking down the aisle.

"Flight crew. Same as the last time I came *back* from London."

"You memorize flight crews now? What else do you have in that big head of yours?"

I nudge him, and he turns around again.

"That one," I whisper.

In front of us, leaning over the footrest of 12G is a beautifully round ass in a red skirt, a freshly pressed white buttoned shirt tucked delicately inside the waistband, for sure the luckiest shirttails on the plane.

"You remember asses now?" Sam asks.

The flight attendant bends upright at the hips and turns around to face us. I shake my head. Fucking Sam.

"Good evening, gentlemen," she says as she smiles in our direction. What a professional. She didn't even bat an eye.

"Good evening," Sam responds, then turns around to wink at me.

"Hey. My seat is right here," I tell him. "You have fun back there in economy."

"Free alcohol back there too, right?"

"Yes," I reply, and he smiles.

"Then I'll have fun."

I slide my laptop bag into the overhead compartment and toss my jacket on top of it. Then I take the plastic bag from I Love L.A. with my

Smart Water and my Junior Mints and my Starbursts and my two unnecessarily expensive magazines, and I toss it onto the seat in front of me. The water makes a soft thud against the loose leather. I fidget with the air nozzles before shifting the bag to the side and sitting down.

A male flight attendant walks by after a few minutes. I've already gotten to the "What's Inside" section of *Wired*.

"Champagne?"

"No, thanks."

"Newspaper?"

I hold up my magazine.

"All good, thanks."

"Will you be dining with us this evening?"

I nod.

"Wonderful. I hope you enjoy the flight. I'm Davy."

"Thanks, Davy."

What kind of name is Davy? I don't remember him from the last flight. Maybe he was in Economy and just got promoted to Upper. I'd have remembered a Davy. No adult man should go by a nickname that ends in Y. It's just a mistake.

I get drunk, and I read through both magazines, regretting that I chose *Muscle & Health* to read second. Bloated from the steak, the gin and tonics, and the wine, the last thing I want to see is a magazine full of bodies that I just steered myself further away from having. I flex my right triceps and rub it with my left hand. I do the same with my left and then again to my right.

I watch a movie, then I take a nap. When I wake up, I ask for a drink, gulp it down quickly, and then I take another nap. When I wake up the next time, I check the flight tracker, and it says we have four hours and fifty-five minutes to go. I've spent an eternity in the sky for this job. My bladder urges me to walk to the bathroom, but when I try the door, it's locked. I stand here for a little while. A little while turns into a long while.

I no longer want to go in the bathroom. I know what's going on in there. I don't want to walk into the aftermath.

I push back the curtain and walk slowly through Premium Economy. Most of the people are asleep, mouths gaping open, eye masks plastered against their faces. I don't use the seats as my own personal guidance bars like some of the other passengers. I just walk down the center of the aisle, politely unobtrusive. I push back the next curtain and look up at the sea of people in Economy. I hold back a shudder. *That used to be me.*

Sam is five or six rows back from the front of the cabin. He's watching a movie and doesn't see me approaching. Whatever he's watching is very blue, his face illuminated and shining back at me. I stare at him for a little while, wondering if I can guess what's on the screen, but I can't. I looked through the whole in-flight magazine and scanned all the film selections, but I don't remember any that would have an abundance of ocean or sky.

Eventually he looks up at me, smiles, then taps the screen a couple of times.

"What's up, borth?"

I shrug.

"Bored."

"I tried to send you an in-seat message. Did you get it?"

"Oh. I didn't look. What'd you say?"

He laughs.

"You'll see."

"Okay. How's it been so far? Not too bad?"

I look around. Less people are sleeping, but everyone's still.

"Yeah, not bad at all. I watched a couple of movies. The dinner was actually pretty good. And they just keep pouring me refills of my drink. I even got a nightcap. Did you get one?"

"A what?"

"Some cream thing. Bailey's or something."

"I'm sure we got it. I just...I don't know. I slept a little."

He shifts around in his seat, looks around.

"How much time is left?" he asks.

"Like five hours."

He smiles.

"Good!"

"Huh?"

"There's a couple more movies I want to watch!"

I laugh. Oh, to be new to certain pleasures. Everything seems great when you've never experienced it before. I wish I still had his exuberance. I sneer at practically everything now. It's never enough. It's a problem, I know it, but I don't know what I can do about it. Success does this to you sometimes, without you even realizing it.

"You more excited about that, or spending the week in London?"

"Hmm...that's a tough one."

"Yeah? Is it?"

"You know what?" he says. "Ask me again after I watch the movies."

Piper

If we just didn't have such great physical chemistry, I could get over him. I could get past it and move on. Lord knows that I want to, that I need to. I don't love him. I don't even like him, not like that, not anymore. He was fun. We had a good thing for a while. But I grew up, and he didn't. He can't, I don't think. He may be permanently stuck in this state of maturity. I wish there was something else that I could do, but there isn't. I grew up, and he didn't.

But the sex? Dammit. The sex is still good. We've only hooked up a few times since we broke up, and each time I was more drunk than the last. And each time I've left his place, or my place, or the car, or the porta-potty, or wherever it was that we did what we did, I left it feeling cheap, tawdry, a whore, a tease, an idiot. And he's left feeling dopey, happy, optimistic. And I've had to bring him down to earth the next time I saw him.

Again and again. I think the only way I can get the cycle to end is if I leave, like if I move away, or I stop seeing him as friends, or we stop hanging out, or I otherwise just stop being around him. Or, maybe I should stop drinking. I don't know. Something has to stop. Or all of this won't stop. And we'll just stay on this cycle, again and again and again and again...

Sam

I'm trying to explain to Grant that England didn't seem like such a bad place to live, but he's not hearing it.

"I mean, why did we leave in the first place? Everything is nice. The city is very classy feeling. There's a lot going on. Why would you get on a boat and cross the entire ocean to get away from all that?"

"Religious freedom."

"So?" I retort.

He shrugs.

The plane we're on feels like it's the same size as a Southwest plane, but it looks very different with the Air France colors draped all over it. It feels somewhat British, actually, like I'd imagine that this is what flying on British Airways feels like. All in all, Virgin was much better.

"So is that what you normally do in London, when you come out here?"

"Yeah, pretty much. I land on Monday afternoon, around four. Get to the hotel by around six. I shower. But first, I usually jerk off if I didn't on the plane..."

"You jerk off on the plane?"

"Yeah. Sometimes."

"Where do you go?"

He hovers his hand over an imaginary hard-on.

"Toilet paper."

"Why don't you just wait until you land?"

"Well, sometimes I do. You cut me off."

"Someone had to," I quip, hoping to stop his momentum again, but he either doesn't get it or he just decided to continue regardless.

"So then I shower and change my clothes. Maybe I'll check email for a little bit. Then I go to Waitrose—you remember that store we went to—I go there to pick up my snacks and stuff for the week. Then I go out to get something to eat. And then when *that's* done, I head back to the hotel, get on my computer for a little while, then I go to sleep. If I didn't sleep on the flight over, I usually sleep for a good nine or ten hours. Then I wake up..."

He keeps going. I don't know why. I was there with him the whole week. I saw him do literally all the things he's just talking about. He did all of them. But there's nothing else to do on this flight, so I sit here, and I pretend to listen. Most people tell me that I'm a good listener. I know that I'm just a really good pretender.

"You excited for Paris?" I interrupt. "When were you here before?"

"Couple months back. November."

"So, you can't be that excited then, can you?"

"No. I'm definitely excited. It'll be totally different going with you. I mean, it already is."

"How so?"

"It's just different."

The pilot comes on over the speaker and starts speaking in French. I don't have to pretend to listen to him. For one, he can't see me. And two, he's not speaking in my language. There's only so far you must go to pretend to be a good listener. No one expects you to listen in this situation. When he switches to English, I don't notice right away; and when I do, it's too late, and he's already almost done telling us whatever it was he was telling us. But it's okay. He still can't see me.

"Do we land soon?" I ask Grant.

He slides the window shade up and peers outside. The black night air is dotted with little yellow twinkles.

"We're about to start our descent. We'll probably land in about fifteen or twenty minutes."

"Is there still time to go to the bathroom?"

He points up at the seatbelt sign. I sigh.

"Don't you want to save it so you can have your first *Parisian* pee?"

Grant

He takes for-fucking-ever to get ready, but I knew this, so I'm not stressed. Still. What takes someone so long to shower and get dressed? Thank God I had to work all week, or I would have been miserable with all the time wasted waiting on him. I look over at the chest under the TV and at the empty bottle of Brouilly. I laugh.

Last night, I thought the wine that I bought from Nicolas was too warm, so I stuck it outside on the balcony to cool it down a bit. I waited a little too long. And I forgot that below freezing temperatures are colder than a regular refrigerator. When I brought the wine in, it was more like a popsicle in the shape of a Burgundy bottle than a fine French wine.

The bathroom door creaks open, and a billow of steam puffs out into the room.

"The showers get *really* hot here."

"Enjoy it while you've got it. I just checked the weather. It's twenty-eight out right now."

"Celsius?" he asks.

"No, you idiot. That's like eighty degrees. It's twenty-eight Fahrenheit."

"That's not that cold."

I scoff.

"All right, tough guy. It's cold to me."

He finishes getting dressed as I work through some late emails that came in overnight. Everyone in L.A. is sleeping now. Nothing new is coming in. But while we were out at the rum bar last night, my phone kept buzzing. It's the end of the week, and people are just trying to check things off their lists. It always is that way. I was too drunk to care, so I just ignored it and kept my phone in my pocket, telling myself I had restless leg syndrome or some other malady that caused me to feel phantom vibrations in my pants.

In the elevator, I give Sam a shove.

"Where's your jacket?"

He pinches the corners of his sweater and raises it for me to see.

"I dunno. I've got this. That'll be enough."

"You say so. Remember: twenty-eight."

"Celsius?" he laughs.

Outside it's not snowing, but there are little crystals floating around in the air in front of us, like it's snow for miniature people. I stick my tongue out to try to catch some of them, and the cold air chills my open mouth. We walk down the block for a couple of minutes, me looking down at my phone for directions and Sam just, well, being Sam. I stop and look over at him. He's rubbing his elbows. I stop walking.

"Dude. We're gonna be walking all day. You *sure* you don't want a jacket?"

He smiles.

"Yeah, I mean...maybe I should, huh?"

"Twenty-eight," I repeat.

He doubles back and runs down the sidewalk toward the hotel.

"You have your room key?" I shout at his bobbing back.

He slows down to a walk. I jog over to him.

"I'm doing great today, aren't I?" he asks.

He holds out his hand, and I slap the key—it's a real metal key—into his bare hand.

"Get gloves if you have any," I tell him.

"I don't."

"Yeah. Me either. Maybe we can buy some."

"Grant, it's not *that* cold."

Sam

On my third latte, I'm starting to feel a little tingly in my extremities, and maybe a little dizzy.

"I can't believe we haven't found one store that sells gloves so far!" Grant yells.

The girl behind the counter looks up and smiles. The French are so nice. I don't know what the stereotypes are all about. They seem like wonderful people to me.

"We haven't really been looking," I tell him.

"At this rate, we're going to die of caffeine overdoses if we keep buying these things to keep our hands warm."

"I've had way more coffee than this before."

"I haven't."

Grant pays with some leftover euros from breakfast, and we head back out into the cold. The wind wastes no time in maneuvering right through the fabric of my scarf and onto my otherwise bare neck. I grip the paper cup a little tighter, but not too tight. I don't want it to crumple and spill everywhere.

"Maybe we can go to Champs-Élysées," Grant offers. "There's all kinds of stores there. I'm sure we'll find gloves."

"Is it far away?"

"No, not really."

"What are we near right now?"

"The big thing that everyone comes here to see."

I smile, but Grant just looks like his usual stoic self.

Grant

Eiffel Tower, check. Seine River, check. Arc de Triomphe, check. Gloves from a sporting goods store on Champs-Élysées, check. Those are all the famous French landmarks on this side of the city.

I'm hungry, and Sam goes along with it, so we stop into a café for a late lunch. Sam eyes the menu, but as usual, waits for me to suggest ordering for the both of us.

"Anything in particular that you want?" I ask him.

"These chocolate crêpes sound good. Have you had them?"

"I haven't. You can order them though."

The waiter comes over, and I pick up my menu so I can point to the items when I inevitably botch the pronunciation.

"Could we get the steak tartare?" I point, and he says *oui*. "The foie gras? The escargots?"

"*Escargots à la Bourguignonne?*"

"Sure. That's...is that the normal way?"

He nods.

"Okay. Then that. And a bottle of the Fleurie? And two waters, tap?"

He turns to look at Sam. He slides his finger down the menu and rests it near the bottom of the page.

"Oh, um. Could I get the chocolate crêpes?"

"Chocolate crêpes?"

"Yes. I mean, *oui*."

The waiter huffs.

"You cannot have the chocolate crêpes with the escargots, monsieur."

He says the word "chocolate" like the Johnny Depp movie. His French accept is *dripping* all over his words, and his husky voice is adding to the effect.

"No? Why not?"

"You cannot."

Sam looks at me, and I shrug.

"Why not?" he asks again.

"Monsieur? Escargots? Chocolate? No. No, no, no. You cannot."

The waiter walks back toward the kitchen, stops partway, looks over his shoulder at Sam with a scowl, and then turns back and walks through the kitchen door.

"What the hell was that about? Why can't I have crêpes with whatever I want to have them with?"

"*Oooooh*, you're in *trouble*," I coo. "He's probably gonna spit in all our food now."

A moment later, the waiter emerges from the kitchen and walks back over to Sam. His face is curious and determined to get some clarity.

"Chocolate? With escargots?"

Sam laughs.

"Yeah. Is that, like, not okay here? They just sounded good to me."

"I will do it. But it is not good. You should not do this."

"Okay. Thank you."

The wine comes first, and I let Sam be the one to taste it. At this point I'm just hoping for some more entertainment between the two of them, but Sam pulls it off just fine, and the whole thing goes by uneventfully.

"Smells...French," he says after the waiter is out of earshot.

"I know what you mean."

The rest of the food comes out relatively quickly, and we plow through it without hesitation. All that walking built up quite an appetite. When we're finished, I leave a wad of cash on the table, and I wave to the waiter on my way out.

"Thank you. My brother...he's a little...*à la con*."

The waiter smiles and waves back. When we're outside, Sam stretches and rubs his belly through his jacket.

"Not cold anymore!"

"No kidding. That did the trick. Not a bad lunch, huh?"

"Not at all."

"I could eat escargots all day."

I pull out my phone to look for the next place to go.

"Yeah, they were good...hey, what did you say to him when we were leaving?"

"Hmm?" I mumble, fixated on my phone screen.

"You said something in French to him. What was it?"

I laugh.

"I said you were hungry."

Sam

Grant takes us to a church high up on a hill. He stops to take pictures of graffiti, and I look out over the city as the sun lazily sinks behind the tops of the buildings in the distance. Someone's drawn a large picture of a praying mantis with the word *URBANUS* underneath. Grant's tapping on his phone, trying to get the perfect shot(?). I don't get him sometimes.

"Nice view, huh?" he asks me as he turns around.

"You been up here before?"

He nods.

"Your girl took me up here. *Had* to see it."

"Stop calling her 'my girl.' She's not my girl anymore."

"She's nobody else's," he retorts.

We walk up the stairs, occasionally turning around to see how the view has changed as we ascend toward the large wooden doors of the basilica.

"We going in?"

"Up to you," he says. "I've seen it. You've practically seen it too. It's no different than Notre Dame. It's just a church."

"Then I'm good," I tell him.

He sits down on the stairs, crosses his arms, rests them on his knees. There's no breeze. The air is eerily still, considering how exposed we are on top of the hill, on top of the whole city.

"You're good," he repeats.

I take my phone out of my back pocket and sit down next to him. We sit in silence for a while. I'm not thinking about anything, really. I don't know what he's thinking about, but he looks deep in thought. I'm hoping for a gust of wind to make some noise, but all I hear are the soft murmurs of the other people on the stairs along with us. Surprisingly, everyone is fairly quiet.

"You like Wendy, right?" he finally asks me after probably ten minutes of solitude.

"Yeah. I like her."

"Do you think, like, she's...do you like her as a girlfriend?"

"For you?"

He laughs.

"Yeah, for me. Who else is asking?"

"Well, I don't know. Did you guys break up or something?"

"No," he starts, then pauses. "I don't know. I don't think so. It's complicated."

"I like her if you like her," I tell him, because it's true.

She's a nice girl, and I think she's a lot of fun. I have no problem with her being his girlfriend if they actually stay together. They seem volatile to me, and I think I don't even know a fraction of it. Grant's always looking tired, exasperated, beat down. I don't remember him looking like this before Wendy.

But then again, for all the ways that she might be a drag, he can't stop talking about her. He seems so *proud* of her. I think he really likes her. I don't tell him any of this. I stay quiet and out of it. I don't want to be on the wrong side of history. It's better to be thought dumb and remain silent...

"I like her," he declares.

"Well, all right."

He smiles and looks satisfied, like we *really* accomplished something here in this little talk of ours. His hands brush quickly against his pants, and I can't tell if he's trying to warm up his knees or his fingers.

"You want to get out of here, go get drunk?"

I nod and stand up, straightening out my jacket. I look back at the church, and I pause for a moment. I feel a sense of regret, like I should just go in there since we came all the way up to this place. Something doesn't feel right. But then I turn around, and Grant's already at the bottom of the stairs, looking up at me and waiting for me to follow.

"You can order another girly Hemingway!"

Grant

"What do you mean it's gone?"

He shrugs, then he shoves his hands into his front pants pockets.

"I can't find it."

"How? Where could you have left it? We've been walking around all day. And you had it in your front pocket?"

"Front and back, it depends. I usually switch it around."

"Dude! Don't walk around a major city like this with anything in your back pocket. There's thieves everywhere!"

That little French thief creeps into the periphery of my memory, but I shake her back beyond my comprehension.

"No one pickpocketed me. I'd have felt it."

"Really? Have you ever been pickpocketed before?"

"No."

"Then how would you know?"

"I just know. That didn't happen. I think..."

He pauses and looks embarrassed.

"Was it at the restaurant?"

He shakes his head.

"The Starbucks bathroom?"

"No."

"Then what?"

He shakes his head.

"I think I put it next to me while we were sitting on the stairs at Sacre-Coeur."

I laugh. I can't help it.

"You put it on the stairs? Why?"

"Because it was in my back pocket. I didn't want to sit on it on those stairs. They're cement, or stone, or something. I've broken phones by sitting on them before in situations just like that."

"So you'd rather just leave it behind instead of breaking it? At least a broken phone screen can be fixed! What are you going to do now?"

"You think I wanted to lose it? I didn't mean to! Shit!"

Sam doesn't usually get upset, and if he does, it's still very subdued. This is about as animated as I've seen him in a long time. I pat him on the back to try to calm him down, but he flinches with my first touch.

"It's all right, man. You can get a new one when we go home."

"Do you think it's still there?" he asks.

"I highly doubt it."

He looks at me like he wants to go back, but I shake my head.

"Really?"

"Dude. It's gone. But look...drinks are on me tonight, all right?"

He laughs.

"Drinks have been on you the whole trip," he reminds me.

"Top shelf then."

"Okay."

The streetlights have all switched on, the crescendo of their hums rising and falling as we walk under each one. We're heading away from Sacre-Coeur and down toward the hotel, near the river. We pass by brasseries packed full of people, both inside and on the sidewalk, with rectangular, glowing red boxes heating the patrons that ended up outside. Women in coats with faux fur collar liners sit in little, uncomfortable chairs and sip red wine from slightly frosted glasses, a stark reminder of exactly how cold it is out here. I reach into my pants and adjust my dick.

Even the pubs are filling with people. Everybody is out in the city tonight. It's full of life and laughter and cigarette smoke so thick that it almost makes me want to light one up. But I don't smoke, never have, maybe never will. I never understood people that did until I came here. Now I get why it's supposedly cool. Because, well, it *looks cool* to blow smoke out of your mouth no matter what it's doing to your body.

"Are we close to the hotel?" Sam asks me.

"Not really. Not our hotel. But...we are pretty close to the last hotel I stayed at..."

I knew this moment would come. I didn't want to tell Sam about the painting because I knew that going to see if it is still there would be the first thing he'd suggest we do. But I don't want to know. I'd almost rather not know now. It'll be too painful to realize what I let slip away, even though I don't understand why I care so much. I can barely remember why I am so obsessed with it, but it's somehow lodged inside my heart like an emotional stent.

Sam picks up on my apprehension.

"What?"

"Nothing," I say quickly, trying to think of something to change the subject.

"Is it..."

"It's nothing," I repeat.

Fuck. We were having a good day. Well, I was. Sam lost his phone. But that doesn't count. He left the fucking thing somewhere. That's on him.

"Is it the painting that got away?" he chuckles.

I snap my head toward him.

"She told you?!"

"Oh yeah. I heard you were *real* bent out of shape about it. I've been wondering why you hadn't brought it up yet. Is it nearby? Is that why now you're suddenly all morose?"

"I'm sure it's gone now."

"How do you know? You don't know, do you?"

"I know."

"How?" he asks.

"Just...I know. Okay?"

"Is this like you and the Powerball tickets?"

"No. What?"

"You know, like...you don't check the numbers until you've got another ticket. That way you always have something to look forward to. Is it like that?"

"How could it be like that?"

"Because," he continues. "You don't want to *know* that it's gone, but most of you thinks that it might be. So if you never check it, there's still a chance that it's available. And that gives you hope."

"That's the stupidest thing I've ever heard," I tell him.

He laughs and shoves me.

"It's *your* theory about lottery tickets, not mine! I didn't make this shit up! I look mine up minutes after the drawing. Sometimes I even watch the drawing."

"Oh? You buy Powerball tickets?"

"You know what I mean. Anyway, what's so great about this painting? Can I see it?"

I sigh as I pull my phone out from my coat pocket. I've added it to its own album now to make it easier for me to pull it up whenever I want. I hold my phone out for Sam to examine. He wags his head from side to side.

"Hmm," he says.

"Hmm? That's it?"

"I mean…can you imagine waiting for a bus in the rain? Holding an umbrella, probably a bag or two, like that lady there? It sounds like…so much effort."

"You *would* see this painting and think about how much work it would be," I laugh. "But you know it's more than just a bunch of people waiting for a bus."

"What more is there? That's all I see. Just a bunch of people using up a bunch of their time and energy, getting wet in the process."

I shake my head. A scooter rips by, and as I follow its taillight down the narrow street, I recognize the bank up on the right as the same one that I took cash out the first night Piper and I were here. We *are* close.

"Fine," I blurt. "Let's go there. Let's go to that gallery and see if it's still there. Okay? Let's ruin my night!"

"You're so dramatic. C'mon. Maybe it's still there."

I pretend like I'm doing the best I can to navigate us back toward the hotel, but if I'm being honest with myself—which I'm trying not to be—I know this area like the back of my hand. I've been navigating up and down all these streets on Google Maps ever since I left. Up ahead on the corner, I see the gallery.

"There it is," I tell him.

Sam runs ahead as though he'll be able to spot anything before I do.

"Uh oh," I hear him say.

"What?"

I jog up behind him as he turns around and shrugs. The door is boarded shut with a heavy-duty padlock clasped to some equally heavy-duty chains. There's paper lining the windows.

"Renovation?"

I point at the sign over the door.

FERMÉ EN PERMANANCE

"That doesn't look good," Sam remarks.

"No. It doesn't."

He shrugs.

"Well, you tried. Right?"

I breathe out heavily through my nose.

"Let's go get fucking hammered."

Wendy

I want to start the message with *Dear Grant*, but it feels too formal. Should it be an email? A letter? A conversation? In my negotiation seminar, they said that only ten percent of what you communicate is delivered in the actual words you choose, and it's hanging over my head like a big body language guillotine. Should I just wait until he's back? But then what if we hook up first? I can never tell how a conversation between us is going to go. I may as well flip a coin. I may as well not look to see which side it lands on. It doesn't even matter.

Dear Grant, I type out, then delete. What if he thinks this is me trying to break up with him again? What if we're already broken up in his mind, and I don't even know it? He left for London with us on such uncertain terms. I don't know where we stand. All I know is that I miss him, and I want him here in bed with me. His hands combing down my spine. His forearms pressed up against my ribs in his embrace.

Hi Grant, I begin, and then I add an ellipsis. Too dramatic? *Hey hun,* I tap out, then delete.

"Shoot," I whisper.

My apartment is silent, save for the aromatherapy humidifier quietly humming on my kitchen counter. It's one of the only personal items of mine in the entire apartment. Everything else came with the place. The couch, the TV, the chair, the rugs, the bed. Fully furnished. Umma insisted on it. I just went along with it. I don't mind, anyway. The place is so sterile, but that's exactly how I like it. Besides, I'm barely here when Grant's not traveling. I may as well just get a hotel when he's out of town. Net-net, it'll probably cost me less.

Baby, I type, and then pause. Do I ever call him "baby"? Is it just babe? Bae? Babes? I don't even pay attention to my nicknames for him. What kind of girlfriend am I? I scroll back through our messages, looking at the blue bubbles on the right for any telltale names that I could latch onto. There aren't any. Just a bunch of angry, curt messages with hard punctuation marks at the end of each one: the text equivalent of folding my arms while talking. Why am I such a jerk to him?

But he deserves it, usually. Most times...practically all times. It's not my fault he keeps making mistakes. He should stop making me mad!

Grant, I miss you. There. I like that. Short, sweet, and to the point. Like me! My finger hovers over SEND, but I don't tap it. I switch to emojis, adding some purple hearts to show him some personality and emotion. I squint and re-read what I've written. No...that's way too many hearts. I can't look too lovey dovey.

Grant, I miss you. I can't wait to see you when yr home. There. No punctuation at the end. It feels softer, nicer. I like it! I should do this more often. I put my phone down and rest it across my belly as I kick the sheets around to better position my legs under the covers. I close my eyes and try to find my center and focus.

I can't. I open my eyes and look at my phone. The message is the same, but the elapsed time has made it feel different now. I delete the whole thing. I look back at the emoji keyboard, and I search for something even more poignant and meaningful. Then I swipe over to the ones that I use the most, all the way at the left. I frown.

There are all kinds of angry faces, a bomb, a gun, an explosion, and a bunch of hearts and animals. I sigh.

I exit the emojis and press my eyes shut. Think, Wendy, think. I open my eyes. The message is blank, and I stare at it until my eyes begin to cross, and I don't stop staring until they uncross. I wait a few seconds, and then I type the first thing that comes to mind.

ilu

Then I tap SEND, and I put my phone on the nightstand. It also came with the apartment, and it matches the bed frame perfectly.

Piper

"Do you *miss him* miss him?" Kana asks me.

I don't know how to answer that. I know what she means, but I don't know the answer. I stare ahead at the Starbucks sign and wait for the oncoming car to pass before stepping into the street. Kana follows alongside me.

"It's not like that," I finally tell her, though now I don't even know what I mean by it. It sounded so much better in my head before I said it.

"Not like what?"

"Never mind."

We walk into Starbucks, and I order a skinny vanilla latte.

"Sweetened?" the girl asks.

"No," I reply, then I look over at Kana and just stare.

She orders, I pay, and then we both walk over to the other side of the counter.

"Why would I order it *skinny* and then have them put sweetener in it?" I complain, barely under my breath, because I kind of want the barista to hear me, but not really.

Kana laughs.

"So, come on. What's going on with you and Sam? You said *it's complicated*. What does that mean? Are you thinking of getting back together?"

"I don't know. No. I don't think so."

"Did you hook up?"

"When?"

"Cynthia!" the girl behind the counter yells out.

"I still laugh every time I hear your Starbucks name."

Kana shakes her head.

"*Nobody* gets it right. *Connie? Karma? Caroline?*"

"There's no way anyone thinks *Kana* sounds like *Caroline*. That's not even close, not by a mile."

"I got it once. I swear."

"Piper!"

I look at her and smile.

"White people," Kana mumbles.

I take a sip, and it tastes like there's sweetener in it. WTF.

"So," she continues. "*When*? As in, you've hooked up with him, but you're asking me to confirm which occasion you guys hooked up?"

"No."

"Then why would you say *when*?"

"Okay, fine!" I blurt. "So what? You never hooked up with Daniel after you guys broke up?"

"We never *broke up*. We were never together, remember? But either way, no. We didn't."

"Never?"

"Not once. I was too mad."

"Well, I can see that. It was pretty fucked up. And Sam didn't do anything like that to me. I was the one who broke up with him."

"So you guys can screw whenever you want then, right?" she laughs.

"It's only been a few times."

"Poor Sam," Kana moans. "You know he thinks that each time, you're getting back together too."

"Stop it," I tell her, feeling guilty. Why does she have to make me feel guilty about this? I didn't ask her to get coffee so that I could feel worse about what I already feel bad enough about.

"You know he does," she presses.

"It is what it is."

"Do you want to be with him? Maybe he's grown up. Maybe he'd be better now."

I force an extra loud laugh to let her know how crazy her statement was. A guy in line to order looks over at me and winces. Fuck off, dude. It's a free country, last I checked.

"Grant had to handhold his passport application just to get him to come on the trip with him. He filled it out and everything. There was even some last-minute verification that involved a notary and some newspaper clippings from his childhood that they had to send in."

"Wait, what?"

"And Grant did it all. Grant and his *mother*."

Kana sighs.

"Okay. So what? He may not have figured out how to get shit done on time. But you clearly still have feelings for him. Right? Or else why would you even be considering it?"

"Who said I was considering anything?"

"Then why are we here? You said you needed to talk something through. What are we talking through?"

"Warner avails audit," I say without emotion.

Kana shakes her head and sits down at a table. I follow her and sit on the other side.

"Tell him how you feel."

"But I don't *know* how I feel," I tell her. "Really. I…I mean, I obviously still have feelings for him. But I don't want to be with him, not now. No. I don't think so, no."

"Then what is it?"

"I just don't know," I relent. "I'm torn."

A motorcycle revs its engine as it chugs down the road. The windows rattle in their frames.

"How about this," Kana begins. "How about you send him a message. An open-ended message. And you see how he responds. And you go from there."

"What kind of message?"

"Something that will give you clarity. Clarity on your feelings and on where you stand with him."

"But like what?"

"Piper, I don't know. It's your relationship. Or non-relationship. Or whatever. But if it was me, I'd say something that required him to respond in a way that I could evaluate him."

"I'm not following."

"Okay. So you think he's immature, right? He's lazy, he's not proactive. He's *Sam*. Right?"

"Yeah. We all think that."

"So, ask him something that requires him to demonstrate his maturity. Or his ambition. Ask him something, and see how long it takes him to reply, to commit to a decision, to...whatever it is that you think he doesn't do right. And if he does it right, then maybe he's changing, and maybe you can give him a second chance. And if he does it wrong, then you can take it as a sign that it wasn't meant to be."

"It's kind of like a choose-your-own-adventure story, in a way."

"Sure."

"I set the framework. I give him options. Not like A, B, C, but like, the way he responds will tell me what I need to know about whether or not he's grown since we broke up."

"There you go. Exactly."

I sip my stupid sweetened skinny vanilla latte and try to think of something to ask him.

"But I *know* he hasn't changed," I remind her. "I just hung out with him, like, I don't know, a week ago."

"Just do yourself a favor and send him the message. Assume he'll disappoint you, and then you can move on. But if he surprises you, maybe an old dog can learn new tricks. You know?"

"Wise beyond your years," I joke.

"Hey. No age jokes!"

I take out my phone.

"Now?" I ask her.

"Yeah, why not?"

"What time is it there?"

"He'll be up. When is Sam not awake?"

"That's fair. What should I say?"

"Jesus, Pipe. I don't know. What does he do that disappoints you the most? What was the straw that broke your back?"

"Please don't compare me to a camel."

"What was it?" she repeats.

I think for a bit. He had a lot of flaws. A lot of positives, of course, but the flaws stand out to me even more, especially now. He was always late. Slow to respond. Noncommittal. Never serious. He had no backbone, but he was unusually defensive and stubborn about being wrong. He baffled me with his trivia-like mind that somehow couldn't get itself out of its own way. But above all else, he was unreliable. I haven't been able to get past the fact that I can't count on him, not in the way that I think a girl should be able to count on a guy. Not for big things and not even for little things.

"Something simple?" I ask her.

"Whatever will get you clarity."

I start typing, and Kana peers over the table and tries to read my phone upside-down. She gives up and walks around to my side of the table, her hands grasping the back of my chair.

Can you help me pick up my furniture from Gary's house when you get back?

"What? Do you even have furniture at Gary's?"

"I don't know! What? What should I ask him?"

"It doesn't need to be that difficult. I think you're overthinking it."

"Kana, just help me. Write something."

I hand her the phone, and she holds it alongside me. Her thumbs hesitate for a moment before she begins tapping.

There's a cockroach problem at my apartment. Can I stay at your place until they fumigate?

"Cockroach? You make me sound like a *slob*!"

"Relax. I didn't say you turned into a cockroach. I just said you're having a cockroach problem. It's not like you own the place. It's not your fault. Relax."

"So, what's this going to do?"

She folds her arms and looks down at me. I feel awkward sitting here while she's standing, but I'm not ready to stand up yet, so I ride it out.

"You know he'll say *yes*. You're just waiting to see how long it takes for him to respond."

Etienne

"Okay. We're here."

"We're here?" he asks, bewildered. I don't know why he's bewildered. He asked me to drive him here.

"We're here."

"That was fast. Are you sure it's the right court?"

"Dammit, Laurent, yes. It's the right court."

"Well, okay."

"Let's go."

I tap him on the arm, and he reaches over to the door and pulls the handle.

"Wait until I get over there," I tell him as I step out and around the door, the gravity from the angle of the car shutting it closed without me intervening.

"I don't need your help, friend."

He's standing in the gutter, both feet directly in the runoff from a shopkeeper watering his plants a few stores down.

"If you say so," I mumble.

He looks like some kind of face-only mummy, with bandages wrapped around the top of his head and over his eyes, but nowhere else. Even though he tells me not to help him, I wrap my arm around his shoulder, and we walk up the stairs and to the front desk. The clerk looks at me, alarmed.

"Head injury," I tell her, but it does little to allay her inappropriate fear. What harm could a bandaged man inflict on a woman behind a counter?

"How may I help you?"

I look at Laurent, and he turns toward me. Okay.

"My friend here..."

"Name?" she blurts, staring down at a handful of papers strewn across her desk.

"Laurent Dubois."

"Yours or his?"

"His," I sigh.

"How may I help you, Mr. Dubois?"

He keeps looking at me.

"My friend—he's looking for a copy of his marriage certificate."

"To you?"

"No. To his...wife."

"Not you," she confirms.

"That's correct. I am not his wife. I am his friend, as I've mentioned..."

"Where is the wife?"

"Look!" Laurent suddenly shouts. "Is this the right place to look up marriage records? Or do we have to go somewhere else?"

"Sir, there's no need to..."

"Yes or no?"

She sighs as she widens her eyes with exasperation.

"Yes, sir."

"Okay then."

"Where is your wife?" she asks, calmer and more subdued.

"Out of town," he whispers. "Her name is Margot. Margot Dubois."

The clerk asks Laurent more questions, and he answers them all very convincingly. I can't imagine what's going on behind those bandages, but he's certainly delusional.

"I'll be right back."

The clerk pushes her stool behind her with her legs and then walks back to a door that takes her out of sight.

"You'll see," he says as he smiles.

"It's not that I don't believe you, friend. I just..."

"You just don't believe me."

"Laurent. You don't have a wife. I've known you for a decade. You've always been single."

He laughs.

"That unhelpful woman will show you exactly how wrong you are. Just wait."

I shrug. Poor guy. A few minutes pass, and then the woman comes back. There's a folder in her hands. I sit upright, confused. Laurent notices this and sits upright as well.

"Is she coming back?" he whispers.

"She's here," she says with a smile.

"Well? Tell him! Tell him I am a married man!"

"Mr. Dubois," she says as she flips open the cover of the folder. A single paper is contained inside.

"That's me. Yes. Yes?"

She looks up at me, then back at the folder. Then back at me.

"I'm sorry. There's no record here of a marriage."

"That's impossible! We got married in *this* courthouse!"

"We do not have any record of that, sir."

"That's...no! That can't be! You lost it!"

"Unlikely."

"Something. Something! Didn't you have a fire a few years back?"

"No records were lost. Just some furniture."

"How can you be so sure?!"

His hands are trembling. I'm glad I can't see his eyes, but it makes me wonder for a moment if a man can cry with gauze wrapped around his face.

"Excuse me," I interrupt. "But what is that paper in the folder you have there?" I turn to Laurent. "She's holding a folder," I tell him.

He turns his head toward her.

"Hmm?"

She looks down and then looks back up at us.

"I'm sorry. This is not your file."

"Then why are you carrying it?!" he shouts. People to our left and right both turn to watch the scene that's unfolding. A guard at the door stands up and steps away from his stool.

"Sir. I'm going to have to ask you to calm down, *oui*?"

"I'm...I'm just trying to understand why you don't have my marriage certificate. Margot Dubois. My wife. Of many years. Why isn't it here?"

"Laurent," I say softly. "Maybe we should go?"

"Go where? This is the court where we got married. This is the right court, isn't it? You didn't..."

"I didn't go to the wrong place, Laurent. It's just not here."

I look back at the clerk, and I pull my hands up in an apologetic gesture. Poor woman. Poor Laurent. Poor me.

Guy

"Two charcuterie boards are not *overkill*, Marion."

She gives me an *I beg to differ* face but says nothing. The waiter comes by and pulls out a small pad from his back pocket.

"Two charcuterie boards, *s'il vous plaît*."

Marion rolls her eyes. I stare back at her.

"These things never have enough cheese," I sneer. "That's why we need two."

"Anything else?" the waiter asks, looking impatient.

"Of course. But let us look at the menu and see. Two minutes? We'll take the charcuterie now though."

He walks away without saying anything.

"He's in a rush, isn't he?" I ask.

The kids are staring down at their phones. Marion is gazing off toward the bar. I took them all out so I could talk to myself, so this has turned out perfectly. I look at the menu and pick the biggest looking entrée. The kids had better have picked their meals out already. I'm not waiting when the guy comes back.

I lose myself staring over at the bar, at a blonde woman sitting next to a blonde man, her arm dangling around his back and over his shoulder like an ill-fitting human scarf. They're laughing and touching hands, and their drinks are sitting idly on the bar. They look happy. Intentionally happy.

"Here we go," the waiter announces as he lays one, and then another, charcuterie board on the table. The kids look up, examine the boards, then look back down. Marion stares emptily at the table.

"Everyone?" I announce, hoping to snap the daze that seems to have overtaken my family.

Minutes later, all the cheese is gone, and some shitty-looking Iberian ham and an equally shitty coarse mustard smear is all that remains. We order our entrées, and when they arrive, I eat mine too fast and get heartburn. I rush for the bill, and when we bustle out to the sidewalk, I'm wishing I had just stayed in. Or taken my time. Or not sold the gallery. Oh, the gallery.

Piper

Five hours. Nothing. I look over at Kana's desk and stare at her until she notices. I nod at her screen and then open a message window.

Me: *It's been like six hours*

Kana: *Eww*

Me: *Is it a sign?*

Me: *You said, see how long it takes*

Me: *This is long. Isn't it? This is long*

Kana: *Yea, it's pretty long*

Kana: *But maybe something's wrong*

Me: *Yeah. Like me texting him in the first place.*

Kana: *Ha*

Me: *What a waste of time!!*

Kana: *Do you have closure?*

Me: *I'm closuring this message and forgetting this ever happened*

Sam

Grant gets me an Upper Class seat on the flight back. I don't know how he does it, whether he uses miles, or he pays, or he expenses it, or something else altogether. When he was talking to the guy at the counter, I was watching a plane diorama as it slowly rotated in the atrium of the terminal lobby. At some point, he taps me on the arm and hands me my ticket. Seat 12K.

"Money," I say, referring to how cool it is, not asking how much it cost.

"Miles," he responds.

But then he reaches for his wallet, and it makes me think that he actually just paid for it. I pretend I don't see it.

We're waiting for the French version of TSA to do their thing to us. I've got a chunk of euros in my pocket that I fiddle with as the line inches forward. I don't want to forget to take them out before I pass through the metal detector.

"Any regrets?" I ask Grant. He's staring at a woman that's bending down to pick up her carry-on, the collar of her shirt swooping open and revealing some admittedly stare-worthy cleavage.

"Huh?" he mumbles, not shifting his gaze.

"Regrets. Things we should have done in Paris? You know, besides find that painting."

"Shut up."

"Other regrets," I clarify.

He doesn't look away, but I can tell he's thinking of an answer. He has the face of a guy that's simultaneously thinking and getting a slight boner.

"I kinda wish we got pictures of the café bathroom."

"Oh, with my dick?!"

"Not with your dick. Just...the bathroom. I told you, you could play Hemingway, *or* you could play Fitzgerald. It was up to you."

"You're so generous, you pervert."

"No other regrets," he decides.

The woman with the boobs passes through the metal detector, and it beeps. Now a very stern-looking French woman in a uniform is aggressively rubbing a wand across her limbs. The woman stares up at the ceiling.

"This shit is weird," I mumble, and Grant laughs.

Upper Class is a dream. Better than a dream, in fact. It's a wet dream. It starts with a separate entrance that I didn't even know existed when I was in Economy. The plane has an extra door just for rich people? Amazing! Then you get inside, and you realize the door was just the beginning. A full, lie-flat bed with free alcohol and quality food and attractive women hovering over you at any given moment...what more could anyone ask for? Free newspapers? Don't mind if I do! An eye mask? Sure! Complimentary noise-cancelling headphones that I have to return at the end of the flight and that might have been worn by a dozen other rich people? No, thanks, I'll pass. I brought my own headphones anyway.

The flight's choppy, but I don't notice because I get drunk off a few Gentleman Jack and ginger ales. Only the finest Jack for me in Upper Class. Only gentlemen here.

I sleep. I dream of Jeannie.

Grant

The week after Paris is long and sleepless. By Thursday, I desperately need to unwind. No one wants to go out, so I force Sam to meet me for a drink. He makes some excuse about having to get up early the next day, but eventually he relents.

"I used to love this bar," I tell him.

"Why are we here then?"

"It was cool back when it was called 3110, which was a terrible name, now that I think of it, since it was just the number of the street address. I don't even know what it's called now."

"Sounds like grounds for dislike, if you ask me."

I don't know what I'm trying to say. Since it's the same location and basically the same place but with a different person or group that owns it, it shouldn't make a difference. But it does. It's louder, maybe, and the people are younger. Or maybe I'm just getting older.

"I'm thinking of breaking it off with Wendy."

Sam's initial reaction is a sharp eyebrow raise, but then he immediately settles into the realization that this is probably the fifteenth time that I've had this conversation with him.

"What now?"

I shrug.

"Just don't think it's meant to be."

"Then I guess you should end it," he says matter-of-factly.

"Jeez. What, do you hate her?"

"Me? I like her. You're the one with the problem. Didn't we just have this conversation, like, last week?"

"It's a very fluid situation, Sam."

"I bet."

"It is."

"Like, bodily fluids?"

"I'm trying to have an adult conversation with you. This is *important*. Can't you see that?"

"Feels like a high school conversation to me. Just break up with her or marry her. I'm sick of it."

"You're sick of it? Think about me!"

"We're all sick of it, Grant."

"We? Who's *we*?"

"Me. And the rest of the group."

"Who? Kana?"

"Sure."

"Piper? Did she say something?"

"I haven't heard from her since we were in Paris. But I know she's sick of it too. You guys fight all the time. You ask us for advice all the time. Like I said, break up with her or marry her. It's getting ridiculous."

"You don't understand," I tell him, but I know that I don't understand it either, and I'm just being defensive.

"What's there to understand?"

Some girls come near our couch and sit on the edge, facing away. One has a drink, and the other is holding an unlit cigarette. I turn and tap the non-drinker.

"Can't smoke that in here." I flash a grin. She looks away. In turn, I stare down at my shoes.

"Fuck it," I mumble, then turn to face Sam. "Let's go home."

Laurent

It's cold in this house at night, but I don't know where the thermostat is because they moved it. Someone moved it. It wasn't me. I wouldn't move it. I wouldn't even know how.

"What did I do to deserve this?" I ask the empty night. "Is this my fate? To be a stranger, lost, in my own house?"

I think it's my own house, but I can't tell. When Etienne first removed the bandages, I honestly thought that I'd see just fine and I'd be able to get on with my life and with figuring out what the hell is going on. Sure, there would be some initial blurriness. But it would subside, and I'd resume my normal life.

I still can't see clearly. It's been weeks. Shapes are becoming a little more obvious in the brightness of daylight, but anything outside of that just blends into anything else outside of that. The thermostat is somewhere in a dark hallway. I've walked down a few of them, running my hands across the walls, hoping I'll bump into it. I can't bring myself to ask Ettie to turn the heat up. I've got to be able to do this by myself.

By myself. *Merde.* When did this become my life? This isn't my life, no. I have a wife—a beautiful, loving wife. I have children. Yes, I had a mistress. And many before her. But that is over, I swear. I mean, if I can get my life back, it is over. This feels like a ghost of Christmas past teaching moment, but somehow injected into my own real life.

"What did I do?" I ask the house again.

Grant

"For real. This time, it's over. I've...I've just had enough, all right?"

"Enough what? I've had enough of *you*!"

When I get mad, the veins in my forehead bulge ever so slightly. If you weren't really paying attention, you might not even know it. When she gets mad, the whole world quivers in fear.

"Okay. Then that's settled."

"You know what, Grant? Just get out. Go."

I look at the door behind me, at my shoes neatly slid against the adjacent wall. At the door handle. At the peephole.

"I think I'm going to move to Europe," I tell her, just to piss her off, though it's true. I'm thinking of doing it, maybe.

"Go away!"

"See you around," I say and then turn my back to her and bend down to retrieve my shoes. I'm half-expecting her to unsheathe a knife from the butcher block on the counter and ram it through my deltoid, pinning me to the ground, chipping the cool, grey tile beneath my chest, trapping me face-down in the foyer.

"I hope I never see you again," she snarls.

I don't turn around to look at her. I think she's still standing there, but I don't want to know. It's better this way. I slide my shoes on, and I open the door, still waiting for the smooth, metal plunge into my back, but it doesn't come. In the elevator, it smells like a fart. I shake my head, then hold my breath and hope it doesn't stop on another floor until I reach the lobby.

In the parking lot, tandem behind Wendy's car, I sit behind my steering wheel and cry. Not because I'm sad, but because I've been trained to feel these feelings any time we break up. How do I feel? I think I'm indifferent. Actually, I'm mad. Borderline livid. But it comes out as tears anyway. Wendy always makes fun of me for crying. She'll never know the alternative, and that's good for everyone. Some women just don't realize how they behave, how they drag their men through hell and expect them to stay calm about it. It must be easy to be a selfish bitch when you live in a bubble.

Wendy

"Eff you, Grant!"

Delete.

"Eff you, Brazil!"

Delete.

"Eff you, Iguazú!"

Delete. Delete. Delete.

"Eff you, Piper and Grant smiling!"

Delete.

Why did I even have that picture? Freaking Grant.

Delete. Delete. Delete. Delete. Delete. Delete. Delete. Delete. Delete. Select All. Delete.

"Move to freaking Europe, you greedy, conceited jerk! You'll fit right in."

Piper

"When?"

I feel like it's a joke. I'm always the last to know the important things in my life. I know that most people feel like they're the last to know, but I truly am. I must be. I heard about it from *Warren*. Why the fuck does Warren know anything?

Kana looks at me, puzzled.

"You guys haven't talked about it?"

"Do I look like we've talked about it? This is the first I'm hearing about it."

"I thought you said Warren..."

"Whatever. This...that doesn't count, right? This counts. This is the first. Fuck that weirdo."

"Well, to answer your question, I don't know when. He said as soon as he could talk to Aaron, and if Aaron was on board with it, he'd make plans."

"You think Aaron will be okay with it?"

"Grant said he'll do it on his own dime. He just wants to get away. He'll still work and manage the team and all that. Just from the London office."

"Aaron will go for that?"

"He said he's going to position it as an opportunity to bring the London team closer to the day-to-day."

"Okay. But why? Why now?"

Kana shrugs.

"That dude has issues. I don't know. He's hurt from the breakup. He's floundering. He's coming on thirty, and he doesn't know what he wants to do with his life. You know, typical white guy shit."

"The breakup? What, they're not back together again already?"

Seriously. They've broken up more times than Van Halen, though I may need to run a fact check there because I don't know if Van Halen ever actually broke up or if they just constantly replaced people. Whatever. Same thing.

"Not that I know of."

"Why am I the last to know about these things?"

"You're not the last," she says, but she's looking around the office like she's trying to think of someone who doesn't already know. Her eyes turn up empty.

"We're supposed to be best friends, and he doesn't even fucking tell me that he's leaving the country for, what, for how long?"

"Indefinite."

"You've got to be fucking kidding me."

"You know Grant. This might be a two-week trip. I wouldn't put much stock in it."

"Does Sam know?"

Kana shrugs. That's all she's good for, most days. An informed shrug. I guess I can't blame her. This is too dramatic, even for me.

"Maybe I'll just move back to Ohio then."

"What would that prove?"

"I don't know. Just don't tell Grant. Let him be the last one to find out."

Sam

"Are you having another? Because if you are, then I will too. But if you aren't..."

I trail off intentionally, hoping she'll pick up on it fast enough so that this waiter doesn't just hover over us, anticipating the drink order that never gets placed.

"Sure."

"I'll have the same," I tell him. Piper nods as she flicks her index finger up in the air. The waiter interprets that as her having the same drink that she had previously, or at least I think he does, because that's how I interpreted it.

"I can't believe he didn't tell me himself."

Jesus, Piper, with the melodramatic concern over Grant's stupid little European moving fantasy.

"I don't think he's *moving* moving. I think it's just a long trip."

"How do you know?"

"Who cares? He's a big boy. And I should know, you know. He's always been like a big brother to me."

"Funny."

I thought it was.

"So what else is new? Seeing anyone?"

Why did I ask that? I don't want to know the answer, and I equally don't want her to think that I'm cool with it if the answer is *yes*.

"Seeing you right now," she says, smiling, her first smile of the night, maybe.

"Same."

That doesn't make sense.

"So all your photos from Paris are gone?"

"You had to remind me. Yes. *Yes*. They are. Every photo I've taken in the last two years is gone. They were all on that phone, and I've had it since, well, yeah...two years ago."

"You don't back them up?"

I can tell her a long, drawn out story about how I started to back them up using iCloud, but then I ran out of storage, and how it keeps asking me to pay for more storage, and how I try to delete things that are currently on there, and every time that I think I do it right, I don't, and I can never back up anything more than the first 5GB that I backed up. But I don't want to tell her this. And I *know* she doesn't want to hear it.

"I live my life on the edge, Piper."

"Well, then that settles it. No one needs memories on *the edge*."

She laughs, and I do too. I miss this.

"So what's after this? Want to watch something?"

Her eyes get serious.

"We're not hooking up."

"I said *watch something*. Like a movie or TV."

"Right."

"Why can't I..."

"Do you want to hook up again?"

The guy sitting next to me blurts out a laugh, then covers his mouth and apologizes under his breath. Man. Communal tables really ruin the intimacy of a meal.

"I want to watch something," I clarify, though that's what I've already said a couple of times now. "I'm not tired, and I don't have to be in to work until noon tomorrow."

"I have to work at nine."

"I still want to watch something. I was just seeing if you wanted to watch it with me."

"I don't want to hook up," she repeats.

"Got it."

I look over at the guy, and I shake my head. He smiles, and there's kale in between his teeth. I'd tell him, but he's dining alone, so who cares if he ever finds out.

Grant

Wendy and I are over, and Los Angeles and I are going to take a little break too. It's not you, city, it's me. Actually, it's Wendy. I can't stand to see her right now. My emotions are too raw, too delicate. I need to be somewhere else.

Ideally Paris. But it's going to be London. I contacted a guy with a long-term Airbnb on Greek Street and another in Islington. Greek Street would be a quick walk to the office, and I'd be stumbling distance from all the bars and restaurants, including that wack Mexican restaurant that most people in London probably don't realize is wack (and that I still sometimes go to anyway).

Islington is, well, much farther. I'd have to take the tube, but it's just four stops on the Victoria line. I've never tried that stretch during the commute hour. It may be impossible to get on, like that time I tried taking the Northern line out of Clapham at 8:30 a.m. Fuck that.

After very little consideration, Greek Street rises to the top of the short list of two. Maybe I can finally try to get a Soho House membership. Alison could give me one reference, maybe. I'm sure I could find another person too. Skye, maybe, though I doubt if he even remembers me. I wonder how long it takes to get approved?

It's been a couple of months since I backed up my laptop, so that's how I'm spending my evening. I rarely wait over a month. There's too much stuff on here to let it be open to chance. A hard drive head crash, a theft, an egregiously spilled coffee—these are all possibilities that I don't want to even have to consider.

Scrolling through Excel docs and Word docs and PowerPoint decks, scrolling past macros and scripts and avails, scrolling past photos and sub folders of more photos.

Paris

Double-click. My trip with Piper. I wonder how she'll take the news when I tell her I'm moving. There's us at that snooty restaurant, not the one where she stole the napkins, but another snooty restaurant. There's me pretending to orally satisfy the Eiffel Tower (that was a request from Matt).

There's the river. A lot of the river, in fact. Okay. We get it. The river is cool. Sometimes what I think will turn out to be a great set of photos just falls flat the next time I look at them.

Our hotel room, so tiny.

The bathroom, amazingly, somehow tinier.

A blurry shot of the front desk.

Delete.

The two beds pushed together.

The sidewalk, blurry.

Delete.

The painting.

My mouth tries to curl into a smile, but it immediately dissolves into a frown.

"So beautiful," I moan softly. "But where are you?"

I stare at it for a few moments, and it's still as captivating as the first time I saw it. I don't know what it is about it. The style: smudged, smart, intentional. In the bottom right corner, there's something I hadn't noticed before: a smear of suspect paint, in sharp contrast to the palette used in the scene. I mean, *maybe* it's supposed to be there. What else would explain it? It just looks so...odd.

There's a glare on the window in the picture, and I try to find my reflection in it, staring like it's one of those magic eye puzzles, and if I look hard enough, it'll appear. But it doesn't, and I feel stupid because the payoff would just be seeing myself, which I can do anytime. With my eyes back in focus, I shift my attention to the top left corner. There's a white square of paper, cropped by the edge of the photo, but visible enough to display a few lines of text.

Palmieri

Encadrée: 950€

Frantic, I pop open a browser and translate *encadrée*.

"Framed."

Even though I think it's an Italian word, and seemingly a name, I try to translate *Palmieri*. It returns: Palmieri.

"Damn."

Okay, Google. "Palmieri painter palette knife bus Paris" returns a bunch of palette knife paintings of Paris. Most of them by a guy named Afremov. Pretty, but not what I'm looking for. "Palmieri painter Paris" does the same. "Palmieri painter" gets me a little closer. There's a Frank, a Marco, and an Antonio. One painting of a boat in a wild sea catches my attention. Stylistically, it's very similar. Could this be from the same artist?

"Who made you?"

A little more searching, and I think I've narrowed it down to Antonio. There's a Russian website with a number of his paintings, but it has conflicting information. It says he was born in 1946, but then another part of the site says he died in 1891. Unless he is Benjamin Button, this does not seem to add up. My phone buzzes on the corner of the counter, and I glance up for a moment to see who it is. Wendy.

I'm not going to answer.

"Move over, girl," I whisper. "I'm working on a new love now."

Etienne

It's hard to see him this way, but he was always the loner type, so it doesn't feel too different. Still, with whatever he's struggling with after his injury, it's sad. I assumed that by now he would come to his senses and realize that he never had a family, but he's still stuck on it and asks me about it every day.

I was given approval from the city board of health to act as his primary caretaker. Since I live so close and I am one of his only friends, the city agreed that this was a preferable option. The alternative is that he would be committed somewhere, and I just couldn't stand to see that. I requested a small stipend to pay for my services, and the clerk laughed in my face.

"What would you like for lunch?" I ask Laurent. "And don't say, 'My old life back.'"

"What else is there to say?" he says, smiling slightly. It's the first smile of his that I've seen in a long, long time. He never was much of a smiler anyway.

"Salade Niçoise, you could say that. Is that what you want?"

"You're going to make me a Salade Niçoise?" he laughs.

"Not now, you asshole. Instead you get some couscous. Hmm?"

Laurent shrugs.

"I don't think I've had couscous since I was in Morocco," he mutters.

"Like hell you have. You've never left France!"

"You're mad," he tells me, stirring in his seat but clearly not intending to arise. "I've been all over. For work and for pleasure."

"Laurent, my friend. I'm sorry to say, but you don't travel. Period. You never have. I'm really sorry, I am. But your injury is affecting your memory again."

"Morocco. I've been! The food was excellent—even the couscous, Ettie—well, except for this one night. I overindulged on tabbouleh, tahini, and hummus...I didn't have enough filler to keep it all together. I got diarrhea. It was not good. I remember there was this cute girl at the hotel that I couldn't stop making eyes with. But I had the runs, and I didn't want to risk it."

The poor guy. I don't know what movie he saw that somehow lodged this idea into his brain, but this was not a memory of his actual life.

"You?" I play along, now just feeling a bit sad and trying to entertain him. "I cannot believe that you let a little diarrhea stop you from a *conquest*."

156

"Ha. Well, my friend, you are right. I just didn't want to sound like the buffoon that I was. But yes. We made love in the empty freight elevator. She came so loudly, one of the servicemen thought there was a person trapped in the elevator car and called the technician. It was a whole thing. Meanwhile, I'm clenching my buttocks, holding back some gas that had the potential to be much worse."

"Impressive."

"Margot was in the room the whole time. She had no idea," he laughs, and now I feel sad, but for a different reason.

"You dirty dog, Laurent."

He shrugs, clearly proud of his nonsense story and his impression that I believed it. He raps his fingers on the table as he stares straight ahead.

"Now, how about that couscous?"

Grant

"You can't handle my *Trois Mec!*"

Sam stumbles back as I lay it in off the glass.

"No, I cannot," he pants, his hands on knees in the traditional tired-sports-player stance. "What's that mean?"

"I dunno. It's a restaurant. You never heard of it?"

"Traw Mech?"

"Jesus, Sam. How did you turn it into *that?*"

"Try Mech?"

"Just stop. *Trois. Mec.* I don't even know what it means. Three good looking dudes, I think."

"Sounds like your kind of restaurant," he says as he shoves me.

"Your ball."

I pass it back to Sam, and he dribbles for a moment before staring me straight in the eyes and driving directly at me.

"You can't handle my *Troy Match!*"

I step aside. Fucking idiot.

"*Merde*," I mutter.

Sam looks over at me and shrugs.

"That?"

"It means *shit*. Like, *oh fuck*."

"Which one is it? Shit? Or fuck?"

"Shit. I think."

"Well, *merrydee*, you're going to have a hell of a time over there if you don't know your shits from your fucks."

"Last I checked, they speak English in London. I'll be fine."

"Wait, you're not moving to Paris?"

"Why the fuck would I move to Paris? I'm just going to London so I can be closer to the team. And I'm not *moving*. I'm just...taking a little break from L.A."

"*Merrydee*," he whispers, passing the ball back to me.

"The Airbnb I'm staying at looks dope."

"Wait...why are you practicing French if you're just going to London? You just want to try to learn a new language, or what?"

"I'm trying to learn enough so I can find my way back to that painting."

Sam laughs as he shakes his head.

"Are you for real?"

"Yes, I'm *for real*. Fuck off. I want that painting. And I can afford it, so, fuck it, I'm going to get it."

"Determination."

"You know me, man. If I want something, like *really really* want it, I'm going to get it. I just have to. I'll keep trying until it happens. I'll never give up."

"Never give up. Never surrender."

"Uh, what?"

"Nothing. Just the tagline on some guy's LinkedIn I saw the other day. Can you believe that?"

"I can't believe you were on LinkedIn. Why?"

Sam shrugs.

"Bored. Just like I am with this conversation. Are you going to play or what?"

"Pass it to me," I tell him.

"Why? It's my ball."

"C'mon. Just pass it."

He does, and I place it on the ground.

"I've got to get back and pack. Let's finish this another time?"

"Finish a pickup game of basketball? Why not just start a new one?"

Piper

If Grant wants to go to fucking London, then fine, go to fucking London, *dude*. Don't fucking tell me, don't even bother to tell me at all. But he knows I know. I know he knows I know. But he's not acknowledging it, so now it's awkward. Fuck this. Maybe I'll move too. Show him.

I'm sitting at my kitchen counter, my leg tucked under my other leg and squashed up against the stool. My laptop is open right in front of my face, and the brightness is way too aggressive considering how dim the lights are in here.

"What good is auto-dimming if you don't actually dim?" I mutter.

All the apartment websites that I'd normally use here are turning up nothing for Cleveland. Maybe there's been some new apartment website that's come up since I moved away. I text my mom, and she texts me back promptly, which is odd since it's almost ten here, which makes it tomorrow where she is. She gives me the name of a website to try, so I try it.

"There we go!" I exclaim, then start scrolling, my eyes opening wide. "So *cheap*..."

I'm staring at the living room of a one-bedroom apartment/industrial downtown loft that's only $850 a month.

I scroll for what seems like hours. There are so many options, I don't even know how I would choose. I guess first I'd need to find a job. Maybe until then I'd live with my parents. Or I bet I could stay with Megan. She has all those extra bedrooms, and they still haven't had the baby. I'm sure they'd let me stay for a few weeks until I found a job.

Or I could start looking for work now and then move only when I have something lined up. But...the interview process would probably have to come out of my own pocket. And more than one or two flights out there would make it not even worth the cost. No. I'd have to just outright move and figure it out; that's the only way it'd work.

I sigh and close my laptop. Out my window, a bird is chirping a sad little melody. Or maybe it's happy, but I'm just melancholy at the thought of leaving a place where I can keep the windows open even during the winter and not have a drift of snow piled up on the floor alongside my curtains. The air that heaved from my chest is still floating around in front of me, the faint odor of my rosé lingering softly as though someone was pouring a brand new, fragrant bottle in the other room with a high-powered fan a few feet away.

"Cleveland..." I begin, and then trail off.

Who knows? Maybe I'll stay in L.A. forever. Or maybe I'll leave and come back. Or maybe I'll never come back. I could sure use a change of scenery, even if it is the shittiest time of year to move back home. Snow might be nice. I still have all these cute scarves and gloves that I never get to wear here. It'd be nice to get to trot them out, and not just for the handful of days where it drops below sixty here.

One thing I know for certain. Whether I move, or I don't, or I don't, but I eventually do...I am not giving Grant a single fucking indication of what I'm thinking. He'll have to find out from someone else.

Laurent

Merde. This life, what the hell is happening to me? Each morning, I wake up and say to myself, *Laurent, let's try to do something on our own. Today, let's make eggs. You can do this.* Can I do this? No. I get eggs all over the stove. I don't even realize it, not right away. It took until the smell of rotting eggs filled my nostrils as I stood in the kitchen. So then the next day, I say to myself, *Laurent, how about toast?* I get out of bed, I walk to the kitchen, and I take out the toaster. *How could this go wrong?* I think. I put the bread in the side of the toaster that doesn't heat up. I didn't even know there was a side of the toaster that doesn't heat up. Either way, I end up with regular bread.

Sure, I could toast it again. But then I'd have to wait, the time that slips away a reminder of the insult that is my condition.

Is this punishment for all of the women? I know plenty of other men who do the same thing, and none of them have had their lives taken away. Sure, some die here and there, natural causes and other expected maladies, but this? This is worse than death. This is hopeless. None of them are left to wonder if their entire existence was a facade, decades of memories of raising children and maintaining a house and avoiding the destruction of a marriage transformed into what others are calling a complete fabrication created in the recesses of my mind. What has become of me? And why *me*?

Desperate to steer the ship in the other direction, I spend countless hours sifting through my memories. There must be a clue somewhere, something tangible in this real world that I can remember and, well, *use*. All I've had thus far are memories. And when you've been diagnosed with memory loss after sustaining a head injury, your memories may as well be the currency of a banana republic.

But I sift regardless. There must be something, I think, but I never come across anything. He's a good-natured man, but Etienne is wrong here. I did not conjure a life that never existed. I did not simply conceive of a rather mundane and ordinary life that I didn't actually live. These were real things that happened! The world knows it. My only ally, the silent world around me. Though sometimes I wonder if even the world itself doesn't know what I'm talking about, as though everything I thought I lived through happened in some other dimension, and this world knows nothing of it.

Merde. Just fucking *merde.* It's all gone to shit, all of it. I might end it, I don't know. It'd be a different story entirely if I were able to truly start over. But I'm old now, and apparently poor. No women to call my own, or even women to consider trying to contact. Worst of all, I'm impaired. Relegated to a house, I'm learning what comfort there was in having a spouse. Someone to care for me, to look after me. Someone who knew me and actually cared for me. But it's too late now. It's always too late—the gratitude, it's never on time. That's just how it is, I suppose.

Sam

"*Un, deux, trois, quatre, cinq,*" he breathes in deeply, then exhales as he continues. "Six, se-e-e-e-pt," he sputters, taking another deep breath. "HUIT!"

The bar slams against the rack, and he flexes his wrists in circles like he just came in second in a masturbation contest.

"Did you help me at all?" Grant asks.

"Nah. That was all you."

"Still can't get back to what I used to bench."

"When?"

Here we go. Some story about the heyday of Grant's strength. Who fucking cares.

"College. I maxed out at two forty-five once."

"That's cool."

"I can't get anywhere near that now."

"Do you need to? What good is two forty-five? Are you afraid that one day you'll be stuck underneath a two-hundred-forty-five-pound object and you won't be able to get out?"

"It's the principle," he moans, ducking his head around the bar as he sits up.

"Eight reps of two hundred seems pretty solid to me."

Grant smiles.

"I'm actually pretty happy with it, if I'm being honest."

"Yeah, be honest. Or, actually, just don't even talk about it. Maybe just keep counting in French. That's much more pleasant for me."

"Fuck off."

Two girls walk by and step up onto side-by-side stair machines. Grant follows them with his eyes.

"*Les babes?*" I laugh.

"I can't wait to get to London."

In a low voice, I try to say *babes* with a British accent, but it doesn't work at all. It just sounds like I said *babes*, but I had a TBI playing football in high school and this is how I talk now.

"I thought the girls were decent everywhere in Europe."

"They are. I mean, girls are decent everywhere, you know? You just have to always be looking."

"Or, you know...not. You can just be okay being solo too."

Grant huffs and shakes his head.

"You gonna do your set, or are you pussying out already?"

"I'll do my set," I mumble, sitting down and feeling the heat his back left behind on the nylon bench cover.

"How much do you want me to take off?"

"Just leave the forty-fives."

"One thirty-five? Come on. You did one fifty before; you can't go *down* on your next set."

"Says who?"

"Says strong people. You just can't do that. I'm going to leave tens on each side as well."

There's no arguing with him, and besides, he's my spotter anyway, so he'll just have to do more work if I can't finish the set. I start, and it feels fine. I'm pretty sure I can do at least eight reps, maybe even more. Is this lighter than the last time? It seems easier.

Then it starts to get heavier. What the fuck is happening? My fourth rep feels like my eighth. Grant is just hovering over me, his crotch less than a foot from my forehead. I can't believe in all the years that people have been lifting weights, that we can't come up with a better way for someone to spot you when you're bench pressing.

I shake my way to the top of the fifth rep. I don't know if I can do six, let alone eight. I give it a try.

"Fu-u-u-u-uuuuuu-c-k-k-k," I blurt, a strange staccato rhythm overtaking my words.

"Come on!" he yells, but it doesn't help.

The bar isn't moving up or down, and my arms are quivering like a leaf about to fall from a tree on the last day of October, somewhere cold and windy, like New Hampshire.

I stare straight ahead at the ceiling tiles and wait for him to realize he has to help me. Eventually, the bar somehow makes its way to the rack and crashes down with a lot less emphasis than it felt like it would have, at least from my perspective.

"Good job!" he yells.

A guy looks over while doing some weak-looking, bent-over curls, his ass barely perched on the edge of his bench, his eyes bulging from his face. He's holding a fifteen-pound weight. Unless his ocular muscles are the ones doing the lifting, I don't understand the juxtaposition of his face and that dumbbell.

"I got five good ones," I tell him, but he already knows, and we both ignore my worthless words.

"*De rien.*"

"Hmm?"

"No problem," he translates.

"I still don't get why you're learning French. Can't you just have Siri translate whatever you need to tell the painting guy?"

"Don't start, okay? I'm learning French. It's not like I'm learning to suck dicks. Why does everyone give a shit what I do with my free time? Why is this such a goddamned controversy with everyone that finds out?"

One of the girls on the stair machine looks over at us, but mostly she's looking at Grant. Maybe she was intrigued by the idea of him learning to suck dicks. He smiles, and she looks away.

"Was I too loud?" he asks, a slight hint of shame in his voice.

"You're always too loud," I remind him.

Piper

We're riding the elevator up together. It's a long twelve floors, and I don't have anything to say to him right now, so I stare ahead at the screen and wait for the news headlines to update.

"Salad?" Grant asks.

I nod.

"I forgot to make my lunch this week," I explain.

He shrugs.

"We have our one-on-one in a little bit, right? Want to just do it while we eat?"

No, you asshole, I want to say. *You didn't even fucking tell me that you're moving! I don't want to have lunch with you.* I don't even want to be in this elevator. I swear, if it stops on another floor before we get up to twelve, I'll jump out and just start working wherever the hell the doors open.

"I guess so," I say quietly.

The door beeps, and we arrive on the twelfth floor after what felt like *minutes*.

"See you in a few," he says over his shoulder as he heads in through the opposite door to our area.

I don't question where he's going, even though I'm curious. I wait at my desk for a few minutes, contemplating what he'd think if I just leave my lunch at my desk to avoid giving him the pleasure of my lunch company. What's he thinking, co-opting our one-on-one with something social anyway? We're not friends now; maybe we never were. He's just my boss, and I'm just his employee.

Grant comes by my desk after a few minutes and nods his head toward his office. I reluctantly pick up my salad, not having the courage to leave it behind and see his reaction, and I follow him inside. He nods to the door, and I close it behind me. He sits down behind his desk and opens the plastic carton in front of him, grabbing one half of his sandwich and taking a large bite. He looks up and me and smiles with his lips pressed together as he chews.

"Did you have that call with Tokyo yesterday?" he asks.

Who fucking cares, I want to scream at the top of my lungs. Are we friends, or are we not? What is this non-confrontational bullshit?

"It got rescheduled."

"Ah," he replies, and then he takes another bite of his sandwich.

"Tomorrow," I add.

The room is quiet for a little while, and I try to see if he feels as uncomfortable as I do, but he's steadily munching away and staring over at the whiteboard. He leans back in his chair and places his hands behind his head.

"So, what's new?" he asks.

I let out a deep sigh.

"Same old," I reply.

He laughs.

"Not much to say, I take it."

"No," I lie. "Not really."

"Okay. Do you want some updates from big room planning?"

I want you to tell me you're moving, I'm dying to shout in his face. I want some updates from my FRIEND. I want to have a real discussion like we used to have. I want things back the way they used to be. I don't even know why they changed or what happened that caused this to get so awkward between us. Though, admittedly, he doesn't seem fazed by it. I want to know why he's okay with all of this too.

I must have been quiet for a while, because he's staring at me with a WTF expression. I feel my skin flush as I look down at my salad, still unopened in its container.

"Sure. Tell me about big room planning."

Grant

Every five minutes, the motion sensor on my office light thinks I'm not in here, and it flicks the lights off without notice. So, every five minutes, I then wave my hands around above my head until I hear it click and the light turns back on. It's a little game we play, the light and I, when no one else is around.

It's nearly 11 p.m. Sometimes I like being the last person in the office. There's a certain solitude that you can't get anywhere other than an empty office late at night. Even the cleaning crew has left the floor. Everyone who worked in this office today is at home now, except me. I look down at the words on the paper in front of me, and I breathe out all of the air in my lungs. My hand taps nervously on the black screen of my phone.

I wrote it all out, but I know that once the person on the other end starts to talk, it's all going to fall to shit. That's why I'm going to start by saying that I barely speak French and that I'd really appreciate it if the conversation were slow and, if necessary, sentences are repeated upon request.

I've locked and unlocked my phone about a dozen times. I don't know why I'm so nervous. It's just a phone call.

But it's not. I know it's not. It's a big deal. It's me actually pursuing this thing that I can't get out of my head. It's me putting myself out there. Shit, I'm moving halfway around the world, at least in some way trying to get closer to it, and this is me, calling to see where the hell the thing is. Of course it's nerve-wracking. Of course I keep locking and unlocking my phone. This is huge...for me.

Finally, I unlock my phone and start the call. After a few seconds, it begins to ring. I stare down at my notes, scrawled in terrible handwriting and what I can only hope is perfect French syntax. I repeat the lines under my breath as the phone continues to ring.

Then, someone picks up.

"*Allo?*"

Okay. Game time. I breathe in deeply, but the voice cuts me off.

"Is this an American number?" the voice asks.

"Uhh," is all I can say. The words on the paper in front of me are worthless now. We're already off-script.

"*Allo?*"

"Uhh, yes, this is an American number."

There's a long pause, followed by another long pause. If you weren't paying attention, you might think it was one very long pause, but it wasn't. They were definitely two different pauses.

"You...speak English?" I ask.

"Yes. How can I help you?"

I shake my head.

"Are you the owner of the gallery?"

"The gallery?"

"Yes. Is this the number of the gallery on the corner of—"

"No," the voice barks.

"What?"

"No," he repeats.

"It's not? I didn't even finish—"

"Gallery's been sold. It's not a gallery anymore."

My heart drops. "But you still have the number? Are you the owner?"

"What are you looking for?" the voice asks, finally offering something that resembles a helpful tone.

"I'm looking for a painting that was hung in the window of the gallery a few months ago. I was hoping to talk to the owner of the gallery."

"There is no more gallery, I'm afraid."

"That's it?" I ask.

"That's it."

This time there's one long pause. Definitely not two.

"You don't have a forwarding address, or a phone number, or...anything?"

"Hang on."

He slams the phone down. If my ear could wince, now would be the time. A few moments pass as I hear faint rustling in the background. Then the voice comes back to the phone.

"Got a pen?"

"Sure."

Then he gives me a phone number and an address.

"The person's name is Guy. This is his home phone number and his home address."

"Wow, really?"

"Don't tell anyone I gave it to you."

Weird.

"Okay."

"Anything else?" he asks, impatient again, whatever sense of hospitality I sensed earlier completely evaporating into the hypothetical air our conversation floats within.

"No, that'll be it. Thank you."

"*De rien.*"

"Say, what's your name, if I may ask?"

"Have a nice day."

He hangs up.

Wendy

"He can move to freaking Abu Dhabi, I don't care."

"Why would he move there?"

Kana, come on. Not now with the practical retort.

"It was an example. Just...I'm just over him."

"He probably needs a change of scenery. You guys, I mean...you guys have been on-and-off for what feels like the entire year now. Dude probably just needs a break."

"Why are you defending him?"

"I'm not! You need a break too. I'm just saying, that's probably the only reason he's going. Because he's hurt."

"You think so?"

She shrugs.

"You need a break too."

"Okay. I mean, whatever. I'm still *so* busy with all these deals. Did I tell you about how many amendments Rohit and I are working through right now? Stupid DMA, triggering MFNs..."

"Wendy, come on. You need a break too."

"Why do you keep saying that? Maybe I'm fine."

She shakes her head.

"Let's go somewhere."

"Where? I have a meeting at two."

"Not right now. Like, let's take a trip. Let's go somewhere for a weekend. If Grant gets to get away, why can't you?"

I consider it for a moment. It's not the worst idea I've ever heard. But I am super busy right now.

"Where? Like Vegas?"

"You want to go to Vegas?"

"Hmm. I mean...kinda, yeah. Would you go?"

"Sure. I love Vegas!"

"Even though you don't drink?"

"You don't have to drink in Vegas to have a good time. We can go to a club. I love to dance, you know that."

I didn't know that. I feel like I don't actually know that much about Kana, but she thinks I do.

"Yeah, good point. I forgot."

"Let's do Vegas," she announces, then unlocks her phone.

"What, like, you're booking it right now?"

She raises her eyebrows.

"Leave it to me."

"All right."

"What DJs do you like?"

Shoot. I don't know. Grant always picks out any of the music we listen to. I've never been able to stay on top of current music.

"You know..." I trail off, searching my brain for at least one DJ I can reference so I don't sound like I'm completely out of touch.

"I know," she smiles. "Don't worry. I'll get it all sorted."

I'm worried, but I don't say anything. As long as I don't have to think of a DJ, she can plan the entire thing.

Guy

Merde. That boy, he can't be more than twenty, he has such nerve! Calling me at this late hour, telling *me* that someone was asking for me, for the gallery, for a painting. What kind of peon does he think I am, that he can call me at all hours of the night with such inane ramblings, possibly not even from a real person? Or at the very least, not an important person. Who cares what the person who phones the defunct gallery wants to say?

Marion left the window open in the bathroom, and as I'm standing here, my boxer shorts around my knees, I feel the lingering touch of a slight breeze. The breeze gives way, and all I can think about is the audacity of that boy and how his parents probably never taught him any manners. To call past midnight...about *someone else* inquiring about a painting?

A larger, chilly gust blows in through the window. Why Marion would leave the window open at this time of year is beyond me. Certainly, a mistake, perhaps after she had a particularly fragrant encounter with the toilet. I rush to think of something else to scrub such an uncouth idea from my mind. My sweet Marion would never...

The breeze continues to blow in, unencumbered. My stream is tapering, but I still have some time until I can pull my shorts back up, wash my hands, and reach over to securely close the window and shut out this awful breeze. The hairs on the back of my buttocks stand up. It's a terrible feeling.

There. Done. I wash hastily, and before I even lay the towel in my palms to dry them, I'm reaching toward the window to slam it shut. The sound is loud enough that the dog jolts to a start, all the way from under the bed back in the bedroom, his collar jingling a few times before he settles back down.

"Sorry," I mutter, drying my hands with the towel as I clutch the edge of the window frame for no meaningful reason.

The boy, he said the caller was an American, asking about a painting that was hanging in the window back in November.

I cannot remember what was hanging in the window in November, nor would I remember an unnamed American. Certainly, lots of Americans come through and look at paintings. Most never buy. Rarely does one call after the fact. This sounds like a most serious collector, perhaps a lucrative art dealer, or an artist himself, or a celebrity, or a billionaire. So who was this mystery man, and what painting did he want?

I'm standing in the bathroom, hands on the window for far too long, staring out at the leafless branches of the maple tree in the backyard. I could call the boy back; his number was the last to ring me. Or I could let it go.

I walk back to the room and stare at the hollow impression I left in the bed, unperturbed since I left. As though the bed believes, as it is warranted to do, that I have not moved; and in fact, I am still there, laid in place, pressing the sheets into the familiar shape of my body. Staring at this outline of myself gives me an out-of-body experience. I rub my shoulders with my opposing hands and take stock of the room.

No, there's nothing I really want from here right now. Not even sleep, back in the imprint of myself. No, I can wait. That can wait until later.

I walk out to the living room with my phone in my hand. In the recent calls list, I see the unfamiliar number that I know to be from the boy who just rang me less than ten minutes prior. I sit down on the recliner and, without hesitation, dial him back.

"*Allo?*"

"You called me earlier," I declare.

"Who's this?"

"Guy."

"A guy? So what? Who's this?"

"Guy. My name is Guy. You called me not less than ten minutes ago. I am the man with the gallery."

He chuckles.

"Yes, the gallery man. How's it going? Did you need something?"

"What's so funny?" I ask.

"Nothing."

"You laughed."

"I laugh often. Don't mind that."

"Hmmph."

"How can I help you? Do you need something? You know, it's late."

"Yes, *I know*. You woke *me* up. I know exactly how late it is."

"So then, what do you want?" he asks, indignant and almost seething.

"Who called for me?"

"Didn't catch his name," he mumbles.

"You didn't ask?"

"Didn't think it mattered. Gallery's closed."

"Sure. But this was a call for me. You didn't think to take down any information to help me contact this person in return?"

"Is that something you want to do?"

I pause.

"What do you think I am calling you about?" I finally breathe into the receiver.

"Maybe you're lonely," he jokes, but I can tell that he immediately regrets it. Or maybe I just wish he'd regret it.

"I'm calling to get a hold of whomever just called me."

"Well, I don't have his name. But he was an American."

"You said as much."

"Okay," he says. "So?"

"So?"

"So, what now?"

"Now you give me his information, you ingrate!"

"Let me see if I can get his number from when he called," he says quietly, then slams the phone onto some sort of hard surface. I can only imagine it to be the desk, the very desk where I wrote countless accounting statements by hand, where I wrote hundreds of bills of sale, dozens of transfer of ownership decrees, scores of artist recommendations. The wood was becoming so soft, even a heavy lean with a hard object would create a slight crease in the surface. I could only imagine what damage the receiver would have inflicted when it met the wood.

He returns faster than I was prepared.

"You have a pen?" he asks.

"Sure."

"It's an American number," he reminds me.

"Okay."

"You ready?"

"Jesus Christ, yes, I am fucking ready. What is taking you so goddamned long?"

He laughs softly.

"I don't do anything twice. So I just wanted to make sure."

Laurent

I've only been talking to Etienne about it, but it feels like the whole world is denying me my former existence. As though I didn't have the life that I had. What is this universe I have woken up into?

I'm holding the newspaper in my hand, hand in lap, trying to focus long enough to read the front-page headline. I think I can see two words start to materialize, but then the pain creeps back into the base of my skull, so I stop. Looking around has seemingly been fine, at least with the pain, but when the task requires me to focus my eyes, I struggle. I simply cannot do it. The pain is too much.

And so my vision goes, back to muddied, back to the blur. It has not progressed significantly, and I've now been back out of the coma, or whatever it was, whenever that accident happened, for weeks now. Possibly a month, maybe even two. I've lost track of time. I never was much of one to maintain a calendar, but it would be useless now anyway.

The doctors said that by all accounts—all medical accounts, that is— my vision is restored. They could see nothing wrong with my pupils, my irises, the rods and cones and nerves and corneas and whatever other parts of the eyes they can assess. They saw nothing wrong with any of those things. Told me I was fine. Told me they couldn't explain it. Told me it was okay to go home.

Now the world in front of me is a garbled mess. Colors run into each other without regard for boundaries. Boundaries melt away with barely a fight. One moment I think I'm focused on Etienne's mouth, my eyes beginning to calibrate and home in on the rest of his face, but then the next moment I realize it was never his mouth. It wasn't even Etienne; it's just a bowl of apples on the table. No wonder he was so quiet.

Who brought the apples anyway? Whoever it was should have told me so that I knew I had some apples to eat. They look like a bowl of Etienne's mouths to me.

It gets lonely when you can't even see your reflection in the mirror anymore. I am the crowning epitome of solitude.

Guy

"Guy, my love! The meat pies are out of the oven!" she calls from downstairs.

Marion—what an angel. I stare down at the phone in my hand, then up at the ceiling, trying to decide if calling the American is worth my time. I am not very busy these days, but I do like to maintain the illusion that I am. It makes it easier to justify anything unsmart that I may choose to do, at any time. A busy person makes mistakes, and everyone accepts this. Idle men that make mistakes may as well be publicly shot.

I look down at the phone and then again at the piece of paper with the number scribbled down, matching each number on the screen to the number on the paper. *Oui.* It's the right one.

"*Merde*," I mutter and press the call button.

It rings that funny American ring that you only hear in the American movies. So many rings. I start to salivate thinking of the meat pies. And then...

"Hello?"

"*Allo?*" I respond.

"Who's calling?"

"You called looking for me," I say factually.

"What now?" the American voice barks. "You just called me. Who is this?"

"Who I am is not important. But, alas, you must know who I am anyway, as you called for me. Did you not?"

There's a pause. Then:

"Is that a French accent?" the American asks.

"*Oui.*"

"Oh my...um. Are you...are you the owner of the gallery? I mean, the former owner. Is that...is this you?"

"My name is Guy. Yes. This is he."

I lean back into the chair, hoping it will give more than it does. For being such an old chair, it still puts up quite the fight.

"Wow, wow. Thank you for calling me..."

The line goes silent.

"*Allo?*"

The voice finally returns.

"Hang on. How did you get my number?"

"Ha! I presume that boy also gave you mine, no?" I counter with a guess. "What's the difference?"

"That's right. Well, thank you, nevertheless."

"So, American...what can I help you with? There was a painting you were interested in, is that right?"

"Yes. I have...I have a picture of it. Is this your mobile? I could text it to you. Or, uh, Whatsapp. Do you use Whatsapp? I can send it that way too."

"Boy, slow down. Perhaps you can describe it. What was it a painting of?"

"A bus."

"Just a bus?"

"No, no. A bus in the middle of a rainy intersection. With ladies walking by under umbrellas, and the paint is all—"

"*Palmieri!*" I shout, aware at once which beauty he's referring to.

"Yes, yes. That's right! You remember it?"

"Of course. That Palmieri. What a genius."

We both say nothing for a little while. A little while turns into a long while.

"*Allo?*"

"Yes, sorry. I'm just...I just can't believe I am finally talking to someone who knows about this painting."

"I know it well."

"You sold it, yes?"

"Indeed."

"Would you be able to tell me to whom?"

I glance out the window, then down at my lap.

"I'm afraid I cannot. That is a violation of the customer's privacy."

"It's really important," the American breathes heavily.

"What is it? What for?"

He certainly seems emotional for an American. Not the John Wayne type at all.

"I just...are you sure you can't simply give me a name? Or an email address or something?"

"Fool!" I shout. "You must tell me what business it is of yours who has this painting. I do not know you from the hole in my floorboard! Why should I compromise *my* customer for you?"

"I thought you sold the business," he murmurs.

He has a point. This is not my customer anymore. This is just a man who transacted with a business I no longer own.

"Sold it, so what," I retort, not giving him the satisfaction yet of knowing that I'm considering his question more seriously than he believes I am.

"Sir," he starts, even more wistful and sad than he sounded earlier, and that was pretty sad already. "I don't know what it is about this painting, but I've got to have it. I just must have it. If you'd just let me talk to the owner, if you'd..." he trails off, and when his voice returns, it is much more direct and to the point. "Do you even know who it is? The person with the painting, that is. Do you even keep records like this? Am I asking a question you literally cannot answer?"

"I know who it is," I tell him, instantly feeling a little suckered into answering so quickly.

"But you will not tell me," he says.

"Listen. I could be persuaded. But the fact is, I don't have the records anymore. They went with the business."

"So that last guy knows? I can ask him?"

I recall that boy, that insolent boy. No way will I involve *him*!

"I will find this name for you. Okay? No need to worry."

"Ohhhhhhhh," the American breathes heavily. "Thank you so much. Just...thank you."

The relief surges through the phone and into my ear. He must have been telling the truth. This painting seems to really matter to him.

"It's nothing."

"How long will it take?"

"A few days. I am a busy man."

"Sure, of course. I just...so, I live in Los Angeles, but I am moving to London next month. Right? I was thinking of coming out later this week to search for places anyway. I could come down for a day to meet you, if that would be all right. Would that be all right?"

"You're really serious about this painting, are you?" I ask him.

"You can't see me, Guy, but I'm smiling."

A whiff of the meat pies hits my nose, and I pause, remembering Marion's sweet face.

"Yeah, yeah. We're all smiling, friend."

Grant

The window is open in the kitchen, and across on the other side of the room, the other window is open too. A cool current of salty sea air is slowly, lugubriously blowing by me. My dinner, once a heap of steaming eggs and rice mixed with sausage and cilantro, is now nothing but the cool, eggsmattered remnants of said cilantro, the quantity of which I severely underestimated.

"Holy. Mother. Fucking. Shit."

And then again, just inside my head. *Holy shit! Holy holy holy holy holy holy shit!*

Okay. It's probably not that incredible, but I'm beside myself here. I don't even know how long it has been, but I'm finally within reach of the thing. Oh, the angst of not having it...soon it'll be gone. I deserve the damn thing, definitely more than whoever this person who bought it does.

They'll have to say yes. I won't accept anything less than a sale. Whatever it takes. Whatever it costs.

Leaning over the edge of the dish—which, upon second consideration, really should have been cleaned off and put away by now—I tap the trackpad with my index finger to confirm the purchase of my ticket. One way to Charles de Gaulle, in two days. Fucking expensive, but irrelevant...and somehow, in this feverish, inexplicable tornado of desire, worth it.

I can't wait, can't *fucking* wait, to get back. This place, I'm just sick of it. Sick of the cool salty air, sick of the palm trees as they sway gently from side to side like they do in all the cliché whatevers that they appear in. No, I want some grime. Some real diversity, not fake L.A. diversity where all I see are affluent young people that don't really look all that diverse. Paris is *diverse*. London is *diverse*. L.A. can suck it.

The doorbell chimes from down below.

"The fuck?" I mouth, cognizant of the open window and the short distance down to the landing in front of my door.

The doorbell chimes again as I'm halfway down the stairs. It's probably just Rick, now that I think of it. He said he needed to talk to me about the sewer main, some digging they had to do under the driveway. I open the door, and it's not Rick.

"Can we talk?" she asks.

"Wendy..." I start, but she's already walking in.

"I just...I need to say some things."

"Okay."

Maybe it's the look on my face, or maybe it's how I said it, but either way, she's already looking mad.

"Is that *okay*?" she asks, a little bite at the end of her sentence.

"Yeah, sure. It's fine."

"Jeez, I thought you'd be happy to see me."

I laugh, but just enough to not be too disrespectful.

"Happy to see you? This is going to be hard, I already know it. *Happy* is not the word I'd use."

We're standing in the foyer, her shoes still on, almost as though she's poised to just turn around and walk out if the next few exchanges don't go to her liking.

"Look, Grant. Do you actually want to be with me?"

"Wendy," I say softly, unsure what else to say, really.

"Have you ever even stopped to think about it? Like, *why* do you want to be with me? It doesn't seem like I add a lot of positive value to your life. We're always fighting, you're always sad. It's a vicious cycle. Right?"

"It is a cycle, but I don't think that means I haven't thought about why I want what I want."

Her hands are on her hips.

"Then what do you want? Hmm?"

There are so many ways to answer this, most of which are not going to go over very well.

"I'm leaving on Thursday," I casually announce, almost sneeringly.

"No, you're not," she says indignantly.

"No, I am. I literally just booked it, like, minutes ago."

"You're really doing it? You're just running away?"

"Flying," I joke, but again, bad timing.

"So you don't care about this relationship?"

"Hang on," I reset. "What relationship? *This*? This is not a relationship. This *was* a relationship. Now this is just, I don't know, the aftermath."

"I can't believe this," she mutters.

"I'm going to get that painting," I tell her, as though that will make her happier.

"Who the freak cares, Grant?"

"Look, what'd you want, Wendy? To come back over here and make up? Or just fuck and then break up for real right after? What was your plan? I've got to imagine it's a great plan, something that *really* takes my feelings into consideration."

"What's your problem?"

"My problem, Wen, is that you are constantly fucking with me! I'm sick of it. I am crazy about you, but you're...you're just crazy. Like, I literally think there is something wrong with you. You are fucking crazy."

"Eff you!" she screams, with more hurt in her voice than I expected.

She spins around and bolts toward the door, completing my earlier prediction almost precisely.

"I hope I never freaking see you again!" she yells from the driveway.

Sam

There's nothing I hate more than driving Grant to LAX. The stress of it just ruins my day, and usually the evening before as well. That is, if I remember that he asked me to drive him until he messages me, usually on the day of his trip.

I don't get why he doesn't just Lyft there like everyone else does. He asks for a ride. The guy can afford twenty dollars if he's spending who-knows-what to fly to Paris for a stupid painting. But whatever. That's Grant. He's peculiar.

I can envision the ride there. He's backseat driving the entire time, sitting shotgun, defying the very label of his behavior by being in the front along with me. *Switch lanes. Watch out for that truck. Exit here and take Sepulveda the rest of the way.* Checking his watch incessantly. *Can you go faster? My flight is in a little more than an hour.*

"How about you drive yourself," I want to say. But I just bite my tongue and drive him there. It's the least I can do, I think. He drove me to school every day for two years. I can drive him to LAX once or twice a month. But goddamn if it isn't the bane of my current existence.

I roll up to the curb alongside his place and honk my horn twice. Then I text him, because honking a car horn in L.A. doesn't mean jack shit. Everyone honks. If you come to a complete stop at a stop sign, someone will honk at you.

I'd walk up, but I'm comfortable in my seat, and the A/C feels good, and, well, Grant can just come down if he's in such a hurry. He takes longer than usual, and for once I'm thinking that maybe he'll be a little more casual about things. When he finally emerges through the doorway at the end of the carport, he's towing a large suitcase behind him, wheels a few inches off the ground. *Shit.* I unbuckle my seat belt and step out of the car.

"Hang on," I tell him before he gets too close to the hatchback. "I have to move some things around."

He sighs, and I take back my optimism about him being casual. Maybe the best I can hope for is that he's at least cheery.

"It's fine," he moans, and leans over the suitcase as he presses both hands into the handle on the top.

The 405 looks gnarly, he tells me, so we take Centinela. I can see him eyeing the crosswalk countdown as we approach the intersection at Colorado. He's thinking, *speed up so we can make the light.* I'm thinking, *what's the rush?* Or, more accurately, I'm using my temporary position of power to make decisions counter to what he'd decide on his own, were he to be the one driving. Because he's not. That's the whole point.

"So, you have a ceiling on how much you'll pay for this thing?" I ask, trying to shift his attention from staring down the subsequent crosswalk countdown.

"No ceiling," he mutters.

"That can't be true."

"No ceiling, in concept. I can't pay the dude a million dollars, but he's not going to ask for a mil. So, no ceiling, not really."

"Then what?"

He smiles.

"Nice job making it through that intersection."

Goddammit. In my effort to distract him from his objective, he distracted me from mine.

"You're not the only one who can risk lives to get to the airport a few seconds earlier," I reassure him.

Wendy

"Like that one," I say, loud enough that if we were anywhere other than a plane flying at thirty thousand feet, the target of my focus would have heard me.

"Probably," Kana replies. "They probably all do."

"I don't know. What about that one?" I say, nodding my head toward the front of the plane. There's a heavier flight attendant completing the first pass of her tray service.

"Probably," Kana repeats.

I didn't realize I was leaning forward, with my back arched and the muscles that gather around my shoulder blades taut and tense. I sink back into the seat, and the worn leather presses against the back of my neck. The seat is not comfortable, but it's Southwest. I wasn't expecting comfort. Besides, it's a forty-minute flight.

The pilot comes on over the intercom and starts to talk, but like most times the pilot comes on, I can't hear anything he's actually saying.

"This is why we need more female pilots," I preach. "A woman would *enunciate*. We'd all know what she was saying. We'd know that we're beginning the descent, that the co-pilot was celebrating his birthday, that the airline thanks us for our business. We'd know everything, because she'd say it all *clearly*."

Kana squints and scans the ceiling for the nearest speaker.

"I think it is a woman."

I turn my face up in disgust.

"Poor woman."

We land. The throngs of people in the aisle of the plane give me anxiety. I stare ahead at the seatback in front of me. There's no screen, and that's perfectly fine with me. After a few minutes, Kana stands up and signals for me to do the same. We're exiting the plane when suddenly I panic and fling my purse around to the front of my body to make sure I didn't leave my phone behind.

"Oh no!"

I'm rifling through my bag as we step out of the plane and into the tarmac.

"Hang on," I tell Kana, and the flight attendant at the door looks over at me. "I think I left my phone back there!"

People are brushing past me, and Kana's looking like a lost puppy. I shake my head and keep digging. And then I feel it; the rubbery case is unmistakable.

"Never mind," I mumble, and shuffle the contents of my purse back to some sort of new unorganized order.

We walk out into the terminal. The air is stale, and the inescapable sadness of Vegas hits me as I see the travelers on the slot machines, unable to stop throwing their money away, even as they're moments away from leaving this sinkhole of a city. All the cigarette smoke and ashtrays are equally as sad. It reminds me of Appa, when he used to smoke in the house and make me empty his ashtray while he sat on the couch and watched people playing Go on the Korean channel.

The cab line is extraordinarily long, and it looks just like it does during CES. Last year, Grant and I waited in the line for almost an hour. That was before we were dating...but after we started hooking up. When I think back to those times, I can't get wistful or nostalgic. I just get mad.

"What are we doing tonight?" I ask Kana through my gritted teeth. I'm trying to look like I'm smiling.

"What do you want to do?"

"Kana. I need you to be decisive. Please? Just this once."

She nods. Kana gets it.

"Martin Garrix is at Omnia tonight."

"Is he good?"

"He's like the rest. He's hot though."

"Yeah, but he's busy."

"Hmm?"

I wave my hands around in front of me like an invisible set of turntables are floating just in front of my hips.

"He'll be DJing," I explain.

"So?"

"Will there be hot guys that I can *talk to* as well?"

Kana laughs.

"Sure. There are always hot guys. Is that what you want?"

I look through the tinted window of the terminal and into the baggage claim area. I can still see the rows and rows of slot machines in the distance. They're still pissing me off.

"I want to be reckless tonight," I tell her. "I mean, you know...within reason."

"We can do reckless," Kana confirms.

She's smiling as though she's secretly been waiting for me to come out of my shell and be some other type of person that I haven't been able to be since I've been with Grant.

Since I was with Grant.

Shoot.

"I'm making out with at least one hot guy tonight," I declare.

A sad-looking fat man sits down at one of the slot machines. Maybe he's not sad, but his entire existence is sad to me. We inch forward in the line, and Kana is flipping her phone back and forth between her hands.

"Could just call an Uber," she reminds me.

"Takes just as long. Are you going to make out with someone tonight too?"

"I'm sure Bertrand would love that."

"Well, he's not here."

She raises her eyebrows.

"No, he's not. But..."

"But he's friends with Grant, right? So doesn't he deserve to feel like crap too? Guilt by association. Right?"

"Okay. We'll see," she shrugs.

"Will we?"

I know her. She's loyal, almost to a fault.

"No. Come on. I'm here to make you happy, Wen. But I'm not about to ruin my relationship to make you *slightly* more happy. Would you even want that?"

I think about it for a moment.

"All I know is that I want to make out with a hot guy tonight."

Grant

The Air France lounge at Tom Bradley is non-existent, so I'm sitting in the Korean Air lounge instead. Somehow these companies have an agreement between them. I'm not inclined to look up their ownership, but I assume there's some sort of overlap or *alliance*, as they call it. Either way, the spread is modest, and the seats were all taken when I first walked in. I had to wait a good ten minutes, eating rolled deli meat and crackers while holding my plate in front of my stomach. I paid a shit ton for this flight; I'd think the least I could get is a chair when I walk in the damned lounge.

A nice-sounding, slightly Korean-accented voice emerges through the soft music playing on the speakers overhead.

"Attention, passengers. Air France flight number 65 is now open for boarding. Air France, flight number 65, now open for boarding."

I glance over at the deli meat array and consider grabbing a few for the journey, but then I let the idea slip away as I rub my hands across my belly. I've already had enough, especially if this is just a snack. We'll be having dinner within the next two hours.

My seat isn't as plush and spacious as what I'm used to on Virgin, but it's fine. I'm too excited about what's about to happen, this adventure of mine that really has no logical beginning, middle, or denouement. But it will have a logical end, with me, the sole owner of that painting, at long last.

"Newspaper, Monsieur?"

This one isn't a looker, but her voice is borderline sublime.

"No, thank you," I tell her. "But I will take another flute of champagne."

"Very well," she smiles.

I sleep through dinner and wake up to the majority of my cabin sound asleep. *Merde*, I say in my head, practicing without even realizing it. There are no snacks in the galley, and I can't find any of the attendants. It's like they're all off duty and forgot that there was still a cabin full of potentially awakened fliers who are depending on them for sustenance.

I reluctantly shuffle back to my seat and open the overhead compartment to access my backpack. The Junior Mints I had bought at the I Love L.A. store are in there, but I don't want them, not yet. I want fucking dinner. I sit down, dejected. I don't even put my goddamned seat belt on, because, fuck it. If the plane hits a patch of rough air, I want to fly the hell out of my seat and call attention to the fact that yes, I am still awake here, and I want my first-class meal that I paid for with my own dollars.

Finally, an attendant comes by and asks me if I want anything. I'm too irritated to be irritable, if that makes sense. I utter something soft and forgettable, and she returns with a plate of sliced apples wrapped in cellophane. After she leaves, I eye each slice suspiciously before eating it.

"What did I do to deserve this?"

Piper

There's no way around it. I have to get this dress. The flares on the sides are doing something amazing, and they're hiding my extra whatever that I don't want to show. The pattern is killing me with its pure beauty, a veritable tapestry, of sorts. The length, ahh...it's perfect. Yeah. I have to get this dress.

Never mind that it's thirty-four degrees back home and there wouldn't be one single girl even considering wearing something like this for at least two more months. Maybe three. That doesn't matter. This dress will still be extremely cute once spring finally hits. And besides, if I'm back home, I can't go out and buy something like this. Cleveland doesn't have stores that sell things like this. Cleveland has stores that sell Lebron jersey dresses. I'm not about that.

I pull the sleeves, and the dress slides over my head. I try my best to not bunch it up too much, but I know there was another size four on the rack, and I'm just going to bring that one up to the register anyway. With the dress gripped in my right hand, I'm staring at my body. This bra needs to go. I think I've had it since the surgery.

There are faintly appealing curved lines where my abs should be, and this is good, considering the time of the year and how infrequently I've been exercising. My legs look trim. My butt—I turn around to get as straight-on of a view as I can—it's basically the same as it always is. A little flat; flatter than I'd prefer, at least, but nonetheless cute.

"Who wouldn't?" I say, trying to hype myself up a little bit.

"Sorry?" a voice calls over the fitting room wall. "Did you say something to me?"

I shake my head and don't say anything.

"Excuse me?" the voice asks.

Time to go. I shimmy my jeans on and pull my shirt over my head, grabbing the dress again, and then I open the door and head out. I'm not about to have a conversation with a random who-the-hell-knows-who-you-are over a fitting room wall. Especially not over a conceited comment that I immediately felt awkward about uttering. My illusion of privacy was promptly dismissed.

At the checkout line, an insecure girl is standing in front of me, holding her boyfriend's hand. She looks back at me and does the elevator eyes before looking back at his face. They're almost a foot different in height, and she's basically beaming up at him to get a sliver of attention. He's staring off at some mannequin, or at least that's how it appears to me. The girl looks back at me again as the line contracts and we inch forward.

Relax. I'm not going to steal your man. Though I am cuter than you. And this dress is *definitely* cuter than whatever crumpled up shit you have in your hand that you just picked out.

Grant

Landing in Paris is exhilarating, but it's nothing compared to the taxi ride into the city. Which is nothing compared to waking up in the city. Which is nothing compared to walking around the city.

Fuck. Paris. Why am I even bothering with London? This is where I ought to be. The home of this wonderful painting, nonetheless. Or, at least, the home of the gallery in which I saw the painting hung. For all I know, Palmieri, with his clearly Italian-sounding name, was a resident at a Venetian studio hundreds of miles away.

Regardless, it's morning, and I'm embarking on a walk out into the Parisian landscape. The air is still, and there are remarkably few cars on the streets, the novelty cobblestone segments experiencing roughly the same volume of traffic they initially experienced in their first years.

I walk down into the Metro and scan the map to gain my bearings, even though I had already mapped out the route a dozen times in my room an hour earlier. A few stops on the purple line and then a few more on the green one. That seems to be it.

On the train, a cross-dresser that clearly had a rough night is slumped against a railing, his neck extended backwards as far as needed for his head to rest against the window behind him. It's a grotesque contortion, and one that I simply cannot stare at for more than a few moments. I also can't look away. I walk to the end of the train car and consider exiting at the next stop to enter the subsequent train car. Other than the cross-dresser, there's an old man and a teenage boy. *Where the fuck is everyone else?*

Eventually I get to the stop where I change lines, and thankfully I make my way to a much more populated train car. That last one was freaking me out. A few more stops and I'm again aboveground, the air almost chillier than before, but mostly because of the comparative staleness of being underground.

My phone takes a long time to regain service. In the meantime, I'm standing idly just to the side of the exit to the Metro stairs, waiting to see the network appear in the corner. Finally, it comes through, and I type in the address Guy gave to me. It's not his house, that much seems evident. What I cannot tell is if it is a Starbucks or just something with the same general address as a Starbucks, like an office above it.

When I arrive, I realize that I have no way of knowing how to identify him. Yelling out "Guy" is probably not going to be entirely effective. I pull my phone out from my pocket, aware of how cold the morning air is against my bare hands, and I text him. It's our first text. I'm not even sure he texts. He sounded older. This all might be a moonshot.

I look up at the sky and examine the layer of clouds that are slowly floating overhead. It's a delicate mist, with intricate strands connecting from mass to mass as though it's one giant, connected organism. But it's not. It's just water vapor.

My phone vibrates.

I'm at a table in the corner. Latté

Starbucks it is. It's okay. Playing it safe is fine by me. Besides, Sam and I frequented no less than a half-dozen Starbucks during our brief trip here. I walk in and immediately spot him. A heavyset man with thick glasses and a virile mustache, he's less French and more Spanish, at least through my (American) eyes.

"Guy?" I ask, even though I'm ninety-nine percent sure it's him. It's got to be him.

"American?"

Does he not know my name? Shit. Did I not give him my name, ever?

"*Oui*," I say, now extremely self-conscious about the fact that he may not even know my name.

"Come. Sit."

"I'm Grant," I say as I approach.

"Yes," he replies.

I sit down.

"Will you get something to drink?"

"I'm okay."

He frowns.

"I chose a Starbucks because you Americans love your Starbucks. Yes?"

"I'm just not thirsty," I lie.

The truth is, another coffee will make me too jittery, and my nerves are already pulsing so hard through my veins, I feel like I can see them beating just underneath the surface of my skin.

"Just business," he replies, seeming slightly dissatisfied but overall indifferent. "Fine."

"Sure. And, I mean, thank you," I stammer. "I...I can't tell you how much this means to me."

"No problem," he reassures me, reaching down to the side of the table to pull a folder out from what I can only assume is a bag or a briefcase of sorts. He sets the folder down on the table in front of us and looks up at me.

"You understand that this is a violation of my code of ethics, yes?"

I nod, even though I'm not sure exactly what code he's referring to. One man's ethics are not formal enough to warrant an entire code, but I play along because, well, obviously.

"Here," he says, sliding the folder over to me.

Inside is a single post-it note with a single word written on it.

"Laurent?" I ask, befuddled at the lack of a full name.

"Yes. You've not heard this name before in America? It is a common name. A great name."

"No, I...I've heard the name Laurent. I worked with a guy named Laurent. I just thought you'd have his full name."

"What difference does that make?" he nearly shouts.

I take a breath and look around. The crowd in this Starbucks feels shifty. I don't want to be here too long.

"How am I supposed to find this painting if all you've given me is a first name?"

"Fool!" he shouts, this time not nearly, but fully.

I shrug.

"There are two pieces of paper!"

I look down and realize that he's correct. The second post-it has a last name.

"Ah," I say sheepishly. "Why did you write his name on two separate post-its?"

"*Merde*," he mumbles, and I laugh.

"I know that word. That one, I do know."

"Figures."

"Is he expecting me?" I ask, unsure of how much digging he's done and trying to ascertain exactly what kind of situation I'm walking into.

"Did you want me to do everything for you?" he scoffs, then looks around incredulously. "Why don't I just paint the painting for you, yes?"

"Okay. It's fine. I was just wondering if you had spoken to him."

"Spoken to him? No. No, I have not."

"Very well."

We sit in silence for a few moments.

"No address?"

"Boy!" he shouts.

"Okay, okay. I'll find him. This is helpful. Thank you."

It's silent again and getting awkward. Guy's fumbling around with the cardboard sleeve on his latté.

"Can I get you anything?" I ask, unsure how to break the stalemate.

"As in what?"

I don't know what I had in mind, so I improvise.

"Another coffee. A water. Lunch?"

"I'm a busy man," he begins.

"Sure, yes. Of course. I was just trying to..."

"But I could take a meat pie," he says with a smile. "There's a fantastic shop just around the corner. I know the owner. Great work he does. You should get one for yourself."

"All right," I say, feeling relieved. "A meat pie. Shall we?"

Guy

"This time, I will stick to it," I tell her, and she's shaking her head, almost laughing. "I swear!"

"How many times have I heard this, Guy? How many?"

I need to say something to prove to her how serious I am.

"I swear on our children."

"Don't do that..."

"No! I do! I swear."

She pauses and stares out the bay window at the back of the room. It looks like it might snow outside, but I don't remember seeing that in the forecast. Never mind. What's she looking at? What's she waiting for? I just swore on the kids' lives. Is there some answer outside that's telling her that I'm being honest this time?

She turns and looks back at me.

"You're really going to commit to this diet?"

"Yes."

"Why this one?"

"What do you mean?"

"Of all the times that you've attempted to lose weight, of all the times that you've told me that you'd change your habits, none, none of them have stuck. Why will this be any different?"

"You just have to trust me, Marion."

"I've trusted you before, and look where that's gotten me."

I'm getting frustrated. She's supposed to be *supporting* me, not questioning if I'm actually going to go through with it.

"Marion, look. I told you. Today, when I was out with the American, we went to Gabriel's. You know Gabriel's, with the meat pies?"

She stares straight at me, expressionless, imploring me to continue.

"The American bought me one. And I was eating it…and, I don't know how to explain it, but I just didn't want it anymore. I didn't want any of it. I didn't want the feeling of having overeaten. I didn't want the looks from people when I attempt to fit in a space that's a little too small for someone my size. The risk of early death. The wheezing at night. The tingling fingers when I awake. Any of it. I don't want any of it, Marion. It scares the hell out of me that the thing I've loved for all my life may be the thing that takes it all away from me."

"Eating?" she asks demurely.

"Yes. Eating. I've loved food as far back as I can remember, and it's dominated my life. More than the gallery, or the jazz collection, or anything. It's truly dominated me. No more!"

She sighs and walks over to me, stroking my back with her delicate, open hand. If I were to do the same thing, the rough skin on my palms would snag my sweater. Her hands are so soft, it's as though the sweater might snag her.

"We want you to live a long, long time."

I kiss her on the forehead.

"I swear, Marion. This time I mean it."

"What happened? Did the American say something that got you?"

I shrug.

"I don't know what it was. I just felt a flood of emotions, like I had received a sign from the Lord above and that sign was directing me away from my premature death. I don't want to die..."

I trail off. Nobody wants to die, not usually. But self-inflicted death comes in many forms. Some obvious and direct, like a gunshot to your temple or a razor down your wrist. Some less obvious, like alcohol-induced organ failure or an accidental overdose. Some even less obvious, like heedless dietary habits that ultimately consume your body's ability to maintain itself.

"What did the American say?" she asks me as I'm in mid-thought.

"Huh?"

"The American. What did he say when he bought you a meat pie and then didn't finish it?"

I smile and try on my best John Wayne accent.

"Guess it wasn't that good after all."

She laughs and pats me on the back.

"No, I guess not."

Grant

The internet returns thirty-two Laurent Dubois results in Paris, though many of them are related to a fromagerie chain that is apparently well-reviewed, if you consider 4.5 out of 5 internet stars well-reviewed. I wonder if the buyer of the painting, my guy, if he is the proprietor or if it is just a common name here. I don't eat dairy, or I'd consider starting at one of their locations. Instead, I make a list and plot out the most efficient path I think I can take. After culling some obvious ones to skip, I am left with fourteen. That's no small feat for a single day. And I'm certain the path I selected is not the most efficient, but it's as good as I'm going to get, so I go with it. Ideally, there would be an app for something like this, but there isn't. At least not that I'm aware of. So I just plotted them all on a map and tried to find the shortest line through all of them.

At the first house, the widow of Laurent answers the door, and we have a somber and extremely harrowing, albeit brief, conversation about his death. Falling beneath a street sweeper in a drunken stupor, they found his mangled body the following morning, crushed into a sewer grate, some of his mushier organs spilling down into the tubes below as they burst through his ruptured skin. It was in all the papers, she insisted.

I walk back out to the sidewalk and try to shake off that terrible image. And that poor woman! I can't believe she just rattled that off to a complete stranger. She must be severely fucking damaged emotionally. I don't know how you couldn't be.

The Laurent at the second house is a nice gentleman, willing to help, but not the right one. The sparseness of the walls behind him as he stands in the doorway tells me that he is not exactly the art collector type anyway.

No one is home at the third and fourth houses.

It's past noon, and my stomach is rumbling. I told myself it was going to be a low-carb day, but all the lunch options are profuse with bread. Oh well. I need energy if I'm going to make it to ten more houses before the sun sets.

I choose a delicatessen that looks promising, mostly due to the medium-sized line extending out the door. No line means it's not that great. A super long line means it's all hype. The line contracts slowly, and within a few minutes, I am barely inside and amidst the familiar smell of processed and cured meats. I inhale deeply. I wonder if they would just serve me a pile of meat?

Eventually I make my way up to the counter.

"*Oui?*"

"Hi," I start.

"Yes. What will it be?"

Damn. No time to even try the French. That's how it's been the whole trip. Every time I think I'm about to get some practice, my American aura gives it all away. I should have started with *bonjour*.

"Do you just do meat, no bread?"

"For lunch? Or to-go?"

"For lunch."

"No, monsieur. For lunch you must order a sandwich."

He points up and behind his head at a sign of sandwich options, not even bothering to look back to make sure it hadn't disappeared since the last time he turned around.

"Can I just order meat to go then?"

"I just said 'no,' monsieur. It must be a sandwich, from the menu. See?"

Now he turns around and points, then looks back at me.

"Right. But I just want meat to-go now. You guys surely serve just meat, right? You're a deli. Yes?"

"You said 'lunch.'"

His hands are on his hips. I can feel the people in line staring at me, like, *hurry the fuck up, American.*

"I changed my mind. I just want deli meat, to-go."

He smiles.

"You can order a sandwich. Go ahead. Pick one."

Jesus Christ. This is turning out to be a fucking annoying place to get my lunch. If I hadn't waited nearly ten minutes in the line already, I'd just walk out. I sigh and throw my hands up in the air as I study the menu.

"I don't know, man. Whatever has the most meat, okay?"

"Okay, monsieur. Anything to drink?"

I give him a *fuck off* look as I slide down toward the register. The woman smiles at me, and I watch as the obstinate guy to her left retrieves what I can only assume is the largest roll he could find amidst all the rolls in the bin. He's blatantly fucking my low-carb plan squarely in the ass.

"Real strict policies here, yeah?"

She looks up from whatever she was punching into the register and shakes her head condescendingly.

"You can't *always* get what you want," she hisses.

I smile.

"Thanks, Mick. We'll see about that."

Wendy

Spins. Freak. I hate the spins. What time is it?

I look over at the nightstand, at the wall, at the sliding door of the hotel room. At anything. There's no clock anywhere.

Where's my phone?

Where's Kana?

The ceiling fan above is spinning, though it's not on. It's just spinning in my mind's eye, my vision blurring and chafing against the edges of my optic nerve. If I had to estimate, this is the result of two too many Red Bull vodkas. It's definitely the result of at least one of them, no less. Possibly three. I can't tell.

Spins.

What time is it?

Where is Kana?

I turn my head to the right to see a mass of a body lying motionless, save for the slight rise in his back as he slowly inhales, pauses, and then exhales deeply.

What's his name?

Freak. *Where's Kana?*

I slide my hands down from their clasped position over my chest, and I feel around for the seams of the pockets of my jeans. All I feel are the strands of my underwear as they stretch across my hips.

Where are my pants?

I grope around amidst the sheets. *Where's my phone?*

The guy next to me, *what's his name*, he breathes out extra hard; and for a moment I lie still, hoping he doesn't awaken and try to, I don't know, do something with me. He rustles for a moment and then settles back into whatever contorted shape he's currently in.

Finally, as though an angel landed my hand in exactly the right position amidst the heaps of sheets and the obscenely heavy comforter, I find my phone. I drag it across the surface of the fitted sheet beneath me, beneath *us*, and I raise it in front of my face, instinctively tapping the messages app.

Where's Grant?

I don't see his name in any of the recent contacts, which makes sense, since we haven't spoken for days, maybe weeks. Actually, just days. It feels longer though.

I type in his number into a new message, too lazy to scroll and find him in the mix. I get a few numbers wrong, but only because my drunken brain isn't properly telling my fingers what to do. It pains me to know that even in this state, I still remember his number. I don't remember anyone's number. But his, it's like it's burned into my brain.

The ceiling fan refuses to cease spinning, and for a moment, I contemplate walking over to the light switch and actually turning it on, an act of defiance that I hope will counteract the irreverent spins. But that's a good twelve or so feet away, and I can't be bothered. The spinning isn't *that* bad.

I try to conjure up the right words to say.

You're in parts and im here, in vegas, missing yu

I study what I wrote. *Parts?* No. That's not right. I change it to Paris.
Yu? Come on, autocorrect. I thought we had an understanding.

I look it over once again. Then I delete it and start over.

How's Paris? I miss you

Nope. Delete.

Just slept with another dude, how does that make you feel

Yikes. Hard delete.

What's the weather

Nope.

Did you find it?

I sigh, and the mass next to me reciprocates. For a moment, I think
he's awake, reading my messages and judging me as harshly as I'm judging
myself. But then I realize it's just a coincidence, and he's passed the heck
out like he has been for the past hour.

I hope it's what you wanted

I pause and consider the message I just composed. I could be referring
to the painting he is bent on finding. Or I could be referencing the state of
our relationship. Or his life. Or anything. It's so ambiguous, it's almost...

The ceiling fan has stopped spinning, and it alerts me to the change in
my perception. Is the fan actually on now? Or am I sober?

Do sober people ever ask themselves if they're sober?

I close my eyes and search for answers. There are none, and I fall
asleep.

Laurent

Oh, how I miss the curves of Patrice's thighs. Wrapped tight around
my hips, her full breasts pressing against my chest, our bare skin gliding
together with ease. Her thighs were pure magic. I could come just touching
them. Or when I would rest my face against the inside of her leg before

devouring her. The supple skin against my cheek, reminding me exactly how long it had been since I had shaved.

"Can you pass the *haricot vert?*"

I look up, even though I still can't see much other than a vague blur where Etienne sits across from me at the table.

"Sorry?"

"The beans. Can you pass them?"

I look down at the table, searching for something green. There's something pinkish-peach. Something yellow. And then green, ensconced in white.

"This?" I ask, offering what I assume is the right plate to him after a few missed grabs at its rim.

"Thank you."

"Of course."

"Still not getting better, is it?" Etienne asks.

I shake my head.

"Just blurs. The doctors said it should be getting better by now, but every day feels just the same."

"They said," he pauses, clearing his throat. Coughing. Coughing. For a moment, I worry that he is choking. My legs tense. Coughing. "Sorry." My legs relax, but only slightly. "They said it *may* get better over time, but they really didn't know."

"What use are the doctors if they can't even tell me what's wrong with me? Why did we even go there? I should sue them!"

"It's not their fault. You are...a medical anomaly. They simply do not know what caused your vision loss."

"Head trauma, they said. They know what caused it."

"Sure. But why it hasn't come back?" He coughs again, as you do when you nearly choked on something and now you're trying to just get back to regular life. "They don't know. *We* don't know. You know? It's just...*c'est la vie*, right?"

"Forget that," I wave him off. "It's the twenty-first century. They should know why I can't see more than blobs of color."

Etienne doesn't say anything for a while. I grope around the table for my fork. I must have set it down somewhere elusive. I've gotten very good at not doing this, but alas, I've slipped up.

"Ettie?" I ask.

I see his blob shift, and at the same time, I hear the sliding of metal against wood.

"Thank you."

"Of course."

"Ettie, this is killing me."

"What is?"

"This. All of this! I can't make sense of it. Not only is my life not what I remember it to be, but I can't see a goddamned thing. It's awful! It's quite literally killing me."

"Literally, you say?"

"You know what I mean. I mean, yes. Yes! It might be killing me, in fact. I want to die. This much I know."

"No, you do not. Don't say that."

"Ettie, please help me."

He sighs. A siren wails outside, and I wonder if he's left a window open. It sounds too loud to be on the other side of the windows. I just had them replaced last spring. Double-insulated and exceptional at noise reduction.

"Help you how, Laurent? I mean, more than I already am. You realize that—"

"Yes," I acknowledge, hoping he won't finish his thought so that the words don't actually make it out into the universe.

"Well, then. Yes. Then how *else* can I help you?"

"I just want some clarity. Some understanding."

"Sure. But how?"

My fork is resting on the table, but my fingers keep probing it, making sure it is never too far out of reach that it gets to the point that I don't know where it is and have to ask him again.

"You have the police report, yes?"

"From your arrest?"

"I was arrested?! I thought I was just taken to the hospital."

"Procedure," he tells me. "They arrest anyone who is not conscious on public transportation."

"*Merde*," I mutter. "So that's the majority of the police report? Me being arrested under suspicion of drug or alcohol abuse?"

"Do you want me to read it to you? It's somewhere around here."

"Yes."

Etienne stands up, pushing the chair out behind him.

"All right. Give me a moment."

He scuffles around, and I hear papers shuffling against each other. I think back to Patrice's thighs. God, I wish I could be laying between them right now. My old life. It was so nice.

I slip into a daydream, a fragment of a memory of a life that I'm told is not even mine. Patrice and I are in my car, on the second floor of a subterranean parking garage. I'm parked right alongside a broad cement wall, with a large truck immediately beside me on the other side. Patrice is stroking my leg as we sit in near-silence. There are no passersby.

I give her a look that tells her everything I'm thinking. She starts to unbutton my jeans.

"Found it!" Etienne calls.

I wince, inhaling sharply.

"Great. Let's see it."

He walks back into the room, though I'm unsure where he actually went to find it.

"See it?" he asks.

"*See* it. A figure of speech. Let's *hear* it, *oui?*"

Etienne clears his throat. I can see a white blob in front of the now-more-obviously-less-than-white-blob that is him.

"Okay. It begins with a lot of procedural things. Date, time, cross streets, etc."

"Sure. Ettie, can you do me a favor?"

"What's that?"

"Just read the whole thing. All of it. I don't care how inconsequential it seems. I just want to hear it all."

He obliges and begins reading through some impressive minutiae that I clearly underestimated. Date, time, location, and not just location, but full address, cross streets, and coordinates, as though that is at all necessary. Weather, environment, and witnesses, replete with their names and addresses. He's rattling off all the details before we can even get to the description of what happened. It takes a few minutes. Then, the meat.

"A man, identified as Laurent Dubois, 52, was found unconscious on City Bus 21, at 3:42 p.m., as the bus was heading westbound. His identification proves to be consistent with his character."

Etienne pauses.

"Go on," I tell him.

"That's it."

"What? What do you mean?"

"That's all that's written."

"All that pretense for, what, two sentences?"

"I don't know what else to say, Laurent. That's all that's written."

Incredible. Everything seems like a waste of time these days. I don't even know why I bother. I should just walk into traffic. I sink my face into my hands and consider weeping, but I will not do that in front of Etienne. I will ask him to leave if it comes to that.

We sit for a while, in silence. I'm unsure what to do. And then, it hits me, or at least I hope it has.

"Ettie, what did you say the bus number was?"

Etienne

I let out a deep sigh, and Simone strokes my back knowingly. It's chilly tonight, but we're outside on the rear patio. Moments earlier I was staring up at the stars. Now I'm holding my face in my palms. I feel tears welling up, and I press my face deeper into my hands, trying to make them go away.

"You're doing what you can," she reminds me, but it doesn't change the momentum of these emotions.

"Am I?"

I don't expect her to answer, and she doesn't. After twenty-something years of marriage, I knew what to expect, and it was what I wanted. Sometimes you just have to ask a question to get it out there in the world.

"Simone," I start, but my voice quivers.

"Ettie, it's okay," she croons. "You're doing what you can."

I rub the heels of my palms into my eye sockets and try to stamp out whatever moisture is there, ideally smashing it into my skin so that it's entirely unnoticeable.

"He's in such a bad state, you know?"

"He's been in a bad state for a while. He's never had his life together."

"He thinks he did," I mumble, and she perks up.

"What's that?"

"He's delusional, Simone. He has it in his head that he is a well-off, philandering hotel owner—a hotel owner!—with no mortgage on his house and a loving wife in bed, whom he readily cheats on. He thinks, *he truly believes*, that this is how his life was before the accident. That it suddenly was taken away, that it's being hidden somewhere, and if he can prove that it existed, then he can have it back."

"We've lived next to him for almost ten years now. He's never had much money."

"I know. This I know."

"He's never so much as had a lady over for dinner, let alone a bevy of mistresses."

"Simone, I know. He's delusional."

"Why does this upset you?"

I think about it for a moment, though the answer feels so obvious, I have to rethink just to make sure I'm not simply being reactive with my answer.

"It's awful. It would upset anyone!"

"Sure. It upsets me too," she says. "But it's not making me tear up. Why's it having such a profound effect on you?"

Her hand migrates away from my back, where she had been steadily stroking my sweater to the point where I didn't even notice it any longer. She picks up her wine glass and takes a sniff before sipping.

"I simply feel terrible for him. No one deserves to suffer through a delusion. I wish he could just realize that none of what he believes his life was like is actually real. I wish he could know that, so he could go back to being just a regular, sad, partially blind version of the man who has been our neighbor for all this time. That's sad, but it's not pitiful."

"You're really torn up about this?" she asks.

I nod.

"I used to envy him, you know."

She looks startled.

"Him?"

A sizeable part of my brain knows that it is a bad idea to even bring this up, but for whatever reason, perhaps the sheer emotions I'm feeling, I do it anyway.

"Look, I mean, don't take this the wrong way. I love my life. *Our* life. I just...I would see his independence, his lack of concern for the things that consume my every day...yeah, I would be jealous at times."

"What is the *right* way to take that? You're saying you wish you were a single, lonely slob?"

Merde.

"I'm just saying that I used to envy him, in a way, in a very certain, isolated way. And now...now I just feel pity for him. It's sad, really." I turn my head up to see if I can see any stars, but a film of low clouds now hangs above us. "When did that happen?"

Behind me, the door creaks open, and I hear Simone's footsteps as they trail in through the kitchen.

Grant

Laurent Dubois #8 is a crotchety old man who, despite having the same name of the fromagerie, absolutely hates cheese, or at least that's what he's telling me right now as I stare at him in his tattered bathrobe, a shadow of a man leaning against the door frame.

"I'm sorry. I was just—"

"Any kind!" he shouts. "Swiss? Forget it. Muenster, how dare you? Cheese is the devil's music."

"The what?"

Shit. I should have known better than to engage with this nutcase.

"The devil's music. You've never heard the phrase?"

He pauses and then gives me a look that tells me it's time to leave. I can't tell if he's just going to roll into a never-ending rant or if he'll shut the door in my face. Either scenario achieves the same purpose for me. This guy isn't the purchaser of my painting, so he is simply wasting my time at this point.

I wave and turn to head down the walkway and back to the sidewalk.

"Americans," he mutters.

I shake my head and keep walking, though I'm cognizant of the fact that I am not doing our reputation any good by being a brash and annoying door-knocker, asking about, of all inane things, a painting of a bus. What's more self-absorbed and American than a good-looking guy inquiring about a painting? Perhaps the American calling himself good-looking. Otherwise, maybe not much else.

Laurent Dubois #9 is dead. That's two dead Laurents. Google is not my friend today. I consider visiting the cemetery to have better luck. Perhaps he was buried with the painting.

I stop still in my steps and think about what just crossed my mind. This painting, while important to me, may not even have been a blip on the radar of the life of the man who purchased it. He may have obtained it, only to rip it off his wall and throw it in the trash in the alley behind his house. He may have actively destroyed it, appalled and motivated by the very opposite sentiment that is drawing me toward the painting in the first place. Obviously this is not likely, but the possibility remains that this painting may not even exist anymore!

I can't walk. My feet are glued to the sidewalk, and as I turn my head slowly to look back at the house that I just left, I wonder what the fuck I am even doing here in the first place. Chasing after a painting that someone, not me, had purchased. Legally, honestly, and for whatever reason they purchased it. Who am I to come knocking on their door, asking for it? What right do I have?

My stomach rumbles, and I think about the relatively minimal amount of deli meat that was on my stupid sandwich earlier. It's like they were intentionally fucking with me, withholding the very thing that I wanted. I doubt the two hundred fifty or so calories I did consume will hold me over much longer. Five more Laurents to go. Maybe I should just quit.

A young girl rides past me in the street, her bicycle replete with streamers and a bell. She's wearing a pink helmet, the epitome of a sweet little girl on a bike. I feel like a creep just staring at her as she rides by, but for the first time in my life, I consider the idea that I might want to have children one day. To have a daughter of my own. To teach her how to ride a bike. To watch her proudly as she rides down the street. I turn and look over my shoulder, mostly expecting her father standing with his arms folded, satisfied.

There's no one. It's just me and a bunch of dead leaves and maybe the remnants of some snow, though it's brown and it may just be debris that has been swept up into a pile. When I turn around, the little girl is gone.

Laurent

The wall has a smattering of colors all over it, and as I stare straight ahead, I think of those magic eye puzzles that were all the rage twenty or so years ago. Whatever happened to that craze? Did people realize that seeing objects embedded in ugly stereograms was not actually entertaining or highbrow or interesting at all? Nevertheless, I wonder if I stare long enough at this blob of colors, if I'll see something start to emerge. That would be interesting, if only to me and only me.

My house, albeit seemingly the same layout as I remember it from before the accident, doesn't seem to have the same furnishings as I remember. We had a plush leather couch in the sitting room. I bought it from a bespoke furniture shop and paid quite a good deal of money for it. But when I was in the sitting room the other day, and I sat down on it, the fabric felt like mere cotton. Certainly not leather. Certainly not expensive.

This blob of colors, though, reminds me of that painting I purchased just before everything went to shit. The alignment of the colors seems to match with what I recall the subject to be: a bus gliding through a rainy intersection, with passersby holding umbrellas to shield their dainty heads from the precipitation. It was a dark, yet colorful piece with streaks of vibrancy interspersed with soft amalgamations of grey. I suppose it was a beautiful piece; maybe Patrice was right about that.

Now, as I stand here, I wonder if this is the same painting. Surely, it can't be. I brought the painting to the hotel...

The fine lines and details that I so badly desire to see are simply elusive. I can't focus my eyes on anything more than a smush of color. And even then, it erodes and dances out of my sight before I even know what's happening. Damn this condition. It's ruined my ability to perceive even the simplest of things.

I sit down on the floor and secure my knees with the insides of my elbows, propping my body on my tailbone and teetering from side to side. Where do I go from here?

I miss Margot. Despite the weakening of our passion, we still had the memories. All those years together. And now this. I don't even know what *this* is. Just some make-believe puzzle version of my life, but with all the pieces out of order and a few of them just plain missing. I search back through my memories, trying to find a corner piece to use as my foundation. Something concrete, unmistakable, and instantly recognizable.

"What's my corner?" I mutter, still teetering from side to side.

Then it hits me, and I spring up to my feet before I know what's come over me. I stumble around the house, and my newfound excitement for a moment has me thinking that my vision is improving. But it's just the sheer speed of my actions that's making me think this. When I slow down as I attempt to cram my shoes onto my feet, I realize that nothing has changed, at least not measurably.

Alas, it doesn't matter. I find my phone on the table, and I use the familiar pattern Etienne taught me so that I could reach him if I needed to. It's only a few taps, and I must have practiced it a few hundred times by now. His poor phone. Poor Simone. Hopefully she wasn't at home while we were doing this, over and over and over again.

"*Allo?*"

"Ettie, I need a favor."

"What is it?"

"Take me to a bus stop."

"What? Can it wait? We are just about to head to the market. How about after?"

"No, it must be now!" I shout, unsure why. I mean, I have nothing else going on. Waiting an hour or a day or a week would be no different than waiting a minute.

"Wait," he pauses. "A bus stop? What are you going to do there?"

"Board a bus," I state flatly.

"To where?"

"That's not the point, Ettie. I need to get on this bus. It's the 21 bus. Can you take me there?"

"Laurent, but why? It cannot wait? Surely it can wait. I can go with you to wherever you're going. Or I can just drive you, if you can wait long enough."

"Is the 21 on your route to the market?" I ask, ignoring his generous offer.

"*Merde.* I don't know. I don't take the bus."

"Neither do I."

"What's this about? Have you gone mad?"

"Ettie!" I shout. I can hear how frantic my voice is, but there is nothing I can do to control it. "The 21 bus! Can you take me? I swear, I won't ask for another thing all week. Please! On the way to the market. Simone can sit in the front. I'll just ride like a lump in the backseat."

"Of course she'd sit in the front," he starts, then backtracks. "Hang on. Let me...just give me a moment."

I can hear muffled sounds through what I assume is the earpiece of his phone as it presses against his shirt. It's not quite Charlie Brown adult voices, but it's reminiscent.

"Laurent?" he asks as he returns.

"Yes, I'm still here."

"I don't know what you're up to, but you're in luck. There's a stop for the 21 less than a mile away."

"I'll be waiting on my front steps," I declare, then hang up.

In maybe twenty-five or thirty minutes, I hear a horn honk a few times. While this could potentially be anyone, I assume it's Etienne's car, and I stand up and brush the back of my pants off as I walk gingerly down the walkway. Leaves crinkle beneath my shoes. I think one of my shoelaces is dragging, but I don't bother to reach down to check.

"Laurent," Etienne yells, his voice closer than I expected. He's come out of the car and is guiding me down to the back seat of his sedan.

"Hi, Laurent," Simone whispers from the front seat.

I can hear the sadness in her voice. I try to ignore it, but it gets inside my heart just for a moment.

"Hi, Simone. How have you been? Thank you so much for taking me along today. I know how—"

"There, there, Laurent. It's fine."

She has such a soothing voice. I've never noticed it. She was never the looker, but her voice, it's rhythmic. For the first time, I can imagine what Etienne sees in her. What he *has* seen in her for all these years.

Etienne's door closes, and the car lurches forward. He's driving more erratically than usual, but at the same time, it still feels patient and measured. He's a good guy, Ettie.

After a few minutes of sitting in silence, I open my mouth, feeling obliged to put forth some topics for small talk. But then the car suddenly slows to a stop, and I feel Etienne pat me on the knee.

"What on earth are you going to do now, Laurent?"

I smile.

"I'm getting on that bus."

The car is silent. The hum and rumble of the engine is the only thing I'm aware of at this moment. I sit still for a few seconds, absorbing all that's around me. Then I pull the door handle and kick the door out with my leg. It slams abruptly into...something. I wince.

"Sorry," I call out as I step into the gutter along the sidewalk.

"It's fine. Laurent?"

"Yes?"

"What in God's name are you doing?"

"Ettie, I just have to ride this bus. Okay? It's the bus where they found me."

"Yes, I knew that. So?"

"Trust me."

He sighs loudly.

"Call me when you need me. We'll be at the market for the next thirty minutes. Then I should be available."

"Don't worry," I tell him, but I have no idea what to expect or what I may or may not need in the way of assistance. It'll be a miracle if I can get on the correct bus.

I close the car door and slowly wander over to what I believe is the bus bench. Covered by a little awning, I sit down and hope that I am not uncomfortably close to another passenger waiting alongside me. No one says anything, so I settle back into the bench.

"Excuse me?" I announce rather loudly.

"*Oui?*"

"Is this the 21?"

"This is a stop for the 21, yes. Are you...are you impaired, sir?"

"I'm blind, yes. Somewhat."

"Do you not have a caretaker?"

"I do. He just dropped me off."

"Like that? Why?"

"I asked him to."

Why else would he drop me off?

"I am not taking the 21, sir."

"Okay."

"But I can tell you when it arrives."

"Thank you. That would be most kind of you."

Some time passes, and we do not exchange any more words.

"Are you still there?" I ask on more than one occasion, to which the voice replies *yes*.

Eventually the 21 arrives, and the voice lets me know that it's my time to get up and board the bus. The body attached to the voice guides me to the open door of the bus. I extend my right leg out and up in front of me, anticipating the first step. My shoe connects with the front edge, and I propel myself up.

"Thank you," I shout as I face forward, aware that if I turn around so that I could use a more rational voice, I might fall back down the stairs.

There's no one behind me, and the bus door lets out a hiss as it closes shut. I step up toward the driver and extend my hand. In it, a small number of coins.

"Not to worry," the driver murmurs. "This one is on me."

His voice sounds familiar, but that might be the case with everyone these days. Sound is all I have.

I nod and begin to travel down the aisle. I find what seems like an empty seat, and I sit down slowly, afraid that someone's possessions might be on the seat but of a similar color as the fabric. There's nothing.

The bus heaves forward, and I'm slammed against the back of my seat. As the momentum dissipates, I lean forward and place my face in my hands.

"God help me," I mumble, hopefully quiet enough that no one hears. I let out a deep sigh and try to gather my thoughts. The bus rumbles along and stops a number of times as I sit frozen in place. I don't know what's next. I don't even know why I'm here. For a moment, I fill with regret, and then sadness, and then anger. Then back to sadness. What has happened to me?

Eventually, a voice off to my right emerges through the steady hum of the bus engine.

"Sir, are you all right?"

I pull my face off my hands and look over in the direction of the voice. A college-aged boy is sitting against the window, a pile of books in his lap. My eyes open wide, and I marvel at the words on their spines. They're all garbage books, but it doesn't matter. There are words! And I can see them!

I look up, and his face has a rugged yet gentle quality, but it, too, is irrelevant. I can *see* his face!

"Sir?" he asks. "I was just checking to see if you're okay."

Bewildered and feeling as though I was just given a second chance at life, I smile as wide as my face could possibly permit.

"My boy, I'm fantastic."

Grant

Laurent #12 was a transgender that looked right at the precipice of becoming the other gender, though I was admittedly uncertain which direction he or she was heading. Laurent #13 refuses to open the door. He's just peering out through a crack in the curtain that obfuscates the room behind him. I see him, and he sees me see him. I knock again. He won't budge.

"Did you recently purchase a painting?" I shout, hoping he'll hear me through the door and decide to give me a listen after all. But he doesn't. He simply stares out at me with his beady, unblinking eyes.

I shrug.

"One left," I mumble, shoving my hands in my pockets and fishing in the corners with my index fingers for any lint remnants that need discarding.

I take a look at my map. Laurent Dubois #14, the last on the list. His place is not too far away. In retrospect, I did a pretty good job of lining these up in order. I tilt my head up to the sky to assess the waning slivers of daylight as they peek over the top of a nearby apartment building. A grey aura is beginning to permeate the sky. I suppose nightfall will descend rapidly, so I get to walking.

Humming along the way, I have a strange sense of dread and hope, intertwined and confusing as hell. On the one hand, I hope more than anything that this is the right Laurent. On the other, I will simply be glad that this ordeal is over, no matter how it ends. It's been a long-ass day.

When I arrive, Laurent #14 has a nicely kept house, with freshly trimmed hedges and a tidy lawn, despite the fact that they're still somewhat in the throes of winter here. It's not green, but it's tidy, and that impresses me. The brick walkway that leads up to his front door looks freshly swept, maybe even hosed down. I put aside the natural judgement I have for someone using a hose in a wintery place.

There's a charcoal grey, recently washed Mercedes in the driveway. From what I can see, there is no garage. The house, a two-level anomaly amidst a long row of single-story homes, sits majestically atop a slight hill that leads up from the sidewalk to the steps. I walk up the walkway, feeling like the man inside knows a thing or two about keeping something in good condition.

I slide my phone out of my pocket, checking for messages, but there are none. I'm procrastinating and I know it, but for a moment, I let it happen and watch myself lean down to tie my shoes as though I'm a spectator of my own life. *Why is he doing this? Well, he is you.*

I snap out of it and knock on the door with three quick raps. Then I wait. I let the customary ten or so seconds pass before I elicit another set of knocks. There's no answer. The car is in the driveway, and as I look back at it again to make sure it's still there, I realize that it doesn't necessarily mean anything. My car is somewhere in L.A., after all, but I, clearly, am not. Still, it feels like someone is in there. I don't know if that's just the optimism or if it's an actual feeling, but nevertheless, it's there. I knock one more time, a series of three.

Peering over to the window beside the door, by habit from the previous house, I'm now staring through the crack between the curtains. Why is it that curtains always seem to have a crack between them? Can't we solve this problem so that people like me can't take unsolicited glances at whatever's behind them? I mean, not right now. But after I've left this house. We need curtains that do their damn job.

No one appears in the crack to stare back at me. My eyes begin to focus on the room behind the curtains. I'm squinting and shifting around, trying to see all possible angles through the little sliver afforded to me.

The only thing that's apparent to me is a small framed photo of a family. I knock a few more times, and then slowly, a desperation washes over me that I haven't felt until this very moment. If this is it, and I've truly run out of Laurent Duboises to seek, I've got to do something to make all of this effort amount to more than just a list of crossed-off addresses. But what? Without much actual thought, I press down on the thumb latch, and miraculously it gives way. The bolt slides out of the jamb, and for a moment, I'm terrified. Then I push the door forward, half-expecting the shrill siren of an alarm to begin ringing out. But there's nothing, just the slight swoosh of the door as it slowly opens into the foyer.

"Hello?" I call out, now hoping more than anything that there's no one home, since this will be hard to explain.

I step in slowly and look at my surroundings. There are keys in a little bowl on an entryway table and a bucket on the floor with umbrellas poking out like the reeds in a diffuser. The framed photo I spied from the other side of the curtains has a happy-looking family with a wife, a daughter, a son, and, ostensibly, a Laurent Dubois. He looks familiar, but maybe that's just because he's ruggedly handsome and decisively French and my envy of his European looks impedes my ability to be objective. For a moment, I wish I'm him.

"Hello?" I call out again as I trace my finger across the top of the frame.

No one ever answers my calls into the empty house, and after a few minutes of holding the frame and staring off at a handsome leather couch outfitting the room in front of me, I place it back on the table and make my way back to the door. Outside, my eyes dart for any witnesses, but the street is as empty as when I arrived. It's a funny little neighborhood, quite outside the main parts of the city, with actual houses—not apartments—something I haven't seen in all my time here.

I let out a deep sigh and pull out my phone, searching for the fastest route to bring me back to my hotel. It's the same one I stayed at with Piper; the travel agency had a special rate, and I was too lazy to be creative and find some place new. There's a metro not too far off that I find with ease. When the train pulls up, I step in and flop down onto the hard, plastic seat. Another sigh escapes my mouth, this time with a forceful breath of hot air behind it.

All of this work, for what? I bury my face in my hands, searching for a plausible next step. I don't bring my face up until the conductor announces the next stop, though it's not mine, so I rest my face back down into my hands. I repeat this pattern until it's actually my stop.

As I approach the hotel, I glance to the end of the block where the gallery is. I'm tempted to walk down there again, just to see, just in case...but I know it's not the gallery anymore. I know the painting isn't there. I just don't know where it is.

The overwhelming sensation of despair is welling in my gut. I feel queasy, so I stop and crouch down, my elbows tucked inside my knees. The air is sticky and thick tonight, a quality I didn't notice until just this moment. It's hard to breathe, but maybe it's just my hunched-over position. I can feel tears forming in my eyes. I consider letting them fall freely, letting it all out...but instead, I force the emotion out of my mind and shove it deep down somewhere, the same place I keep the rest of the things that hurt me. I look up at the hotel and give in to this shitty feeling.

Inside, the lobby is desolate. I search my pockets for the key to my room, but I can't find it. Frazzled, I search my jacket pockets and then my pants pockets again, but they're all empty. I stand dumbly in front of the reception desk, unsure what to do next.

"Hello?" I call out, waiting a moment to hopefully see someone emerge from the hallway alongside the desk. No one comes out.

After thirty seconds or so, I take matters into my own hands. Damned if I'm going to stand here and rot in this lobby. Not after this day! I walk around behind the desk and toward the little doorway, presumably the manager's office, or at least some place where a real person might be. The first room is, in fact, what looks like the manager's office. A modest light hums on the desk, filling the room with a soft sound. At the rear of the office is another doorway. Curious, and clearly not being helped anyway, I walk around behind the manager's desk and peek into the next room. It's like the first room but larger, with a proud, mahogany desk occupying the center of the space. This room is equally as quiet and empty as the previous.

Something poking out from behind the desk catches my attention, and before I realize that I'm walking around the other side, I'm there. In front of me is a half-revealed painting, wrapped in torn brown paper with splashes of color peeking out to look at me.

"What the fu—"

It's the painting! THE PAINTING! I recognize it instantly. It's even more stunning than I remember it.

"What the fuck?" I finish.

A flurry of questions races around in my brain. How is this happening? Is this one big ruse? Is Guy just fucking with me? How could this be it? Here? *Here?!*

I reach down and peel the paper back further, running my hand along the rain-slicked road, tracing the path the bus tires have left in its wake. My heart starts to race. I'm overcome with a feeling of déjà vu. *What is it about this painting?* I know I haven't been here in this strange office with this painting. Not before. This is absolutely the first time.

My head spins a little as I continue to trace my finger along the road. My knees get weak, and my hand begins to tremble, though I can't feel it. The dark edges of my vision are creeping inward. Everything is becoming blurry. All of my feelings have escaped my body. I'm just a shell, not a human. Just a vessel. My eyes shut, I think, or everything otherwise just goes dark.

Wendy

The Vegas hangover still hasn't worn off. It's been two days. I know that as I've gotten older, my hangovers have sometimes lasted an entire day, but this is the first time that it's eclipsed the night and continued on the following morning. I wonder if I'll ever get back on track. I need to go to yoga.

Kana and I are both playing hooky from work today, though hers is a little more official than mine. I'm working from home, just not very productively. A strangely high number of people are out of the office this week anyway, with either meetings in Tokyo or San Diego or San Mateo. Everybody seems to need to be somewhere. So Kana and I decided we needed to be nowhere.

I'm bored, but I don't feel like opening my laptop. I'm trying to come to grips with the pangs of regret about the length of time that has passed since Grant and I last spoke, or even worse, since we last saw each other. I miss him.

For all the messed-up ways he's made me feel, I think I do truly love him. He has been good to me, in his own way. He's been good *for* me. This much I know. My family says as much, and they haven't even met him yet. I wish we were less volatile. I'd bring him down to visit. They'd love him. He'd be so novel. Just a white guy, out of his element.

I pick up my phone and scroll back to the last message Grant and I shared before he left. I see my previously unsent-yet-composed message and quickly delete it, as though there's the possibility that by me simply seeing it, it will automatically send itself. No, I can't let that happen. Sober now, or at least somewhere in that direction, I know that I can write a better sentence that explains how I feel. Or, at the very least, that he cares enough about when he reads it that he feels like he should respond. Then again, it doesn't need to be surgery here.

Hi. How's Europe?

At this point, I don't know if he's in Paris or London or Copenhagen, for that matter, but I know he's not here. Europe seems like an appropriate catch-all to summarize the situation.

* * *

A few days have passed now since the last time I texted him, but he hasn't replied. I decided to call him yesterday, but I couldn't get it to ring. It didn't even drop to voicemail; it just hung up. I tried again today and got the same result. I've been thinking about it ever since. Something doesn't feel right, so I call Sam.

"Hello?"

He sounds like he just woke up. What the freak time is it? How could he be sleeping *now*?

"Hey, Sam."

"Wendy?"

"Yes. Hi. Did I...are you awake?"

The sound of his face brushing against the microphone is unmistakable, if only for the fact that I can visualize his beard as it scrapes along his phone case and the resulting sound that it might make as it amplifies over cellular signals and into my ear.

"I'm awake. I'm...what's up?"

"Have you talked to Grant lately?"

He sighs.

"That guy has *not* been returning any of my messages. Same with you?"

"Yeah."

"Are you guys even talking though?"

"That's beside the point. If he's not talking to *you*, that's something, right?"

"I guess. I just figured he's busy. Maybe he found that painting. You know that's what he's doing out there, right? He's just chasing some stupid painting."

"Yes, I know. So...you haven't heard from him, not at all? When was the last time you did?"

"I dunno. Few days ago."

"A few days *when*?" I demand.

"Ummm..."

He's silent for a while, and I'm hoping he's reviewing his messages; but moments pass, and then I hear someone talking in the background.

"Sam!" I shout.

"Hey. It was, I don't know, maybe two days ago."

"Can you *check*?"

He's quiet for a moment, but now I have doubts that he's actually checking.

"Yep. Two days ago."

"Really?"

"Wendy, what do you want? The guy has gone off the grid. He moved to fucking Europe for the time being. I don't know what to tell you, okay?"

"Tell me you'll try to find him, you lazy jerk! Tell me that!"

Sam laughs.

"If you want me to do work for you, you can't be mean to me like this."

"Sam, buddy. Sam. Listen. I just want to know that he's okay. Don't you?"

"I'm sure he's fine. He's a big boy."

"Can you try to find out, for me?"

He's quiet for a while, and I'm half-expecting a voice to emerge in the background again, but it remains silent.

"But are you guys even talking?" he asks.

"Sam!"

Sam

I don't get what he sees in her. She's a total control freak. And he's a control freak. Don't they say that opposites attract? Then why the hell are they so drawn to each other if they're the same Type A personality?

"Hello?"

"Hey, Pipe. How's it going?"

"Fine. What's up?"

"I, uh...are you busy?"

"What's up?"

Yeah, she's busy. She's usually not *this* impatient so early into the conversation. I mean, I get it. I can take a while to get to a point. But we just got on the phone. She's hardly had enough time to already be exasperated. She must be busy.

"I can call back later. Sorry."

"No, Sam..." she starts. "I don't want to talk later. I'm busy."

"I knew it!"

"What is it? Why did you call?"

"I just wanted to see how you were doing?"

"Seriously?" she shouts.

All right. Cut to the chase, Sam.

"No. I mean, yes. I care how you are doing. But I am calling for a reason."

"And...? That reason is?"

"Have you talked to Grant recently?"

"You've got to be kidding me..." she mutters.

"What?"

"No, I haven't talked to Grant!"

"Okay. Wow. What's the matter?"

"That bastard didn't even tell me he was moving to Europe! I found out in our *team meeting*. In the fucking team meeting! Can you believe that? I found out after fucking *Warren* found out."

"So, you haven't spoken to him, like, since the meeting or whatever?"

"No."

"Hmm."

The pauses in our conversations have historically been so uncomfortable that for the past few months, I've been pretending my signal is bad and I hang up the phone, only to call back in hopes of resetting the mood. At this point, she's convinced that my apartment is a cell signal vortex and the only way I can talk steadily on the phone is to pace around in the street in front of my apartment.

"Hmm what?" she asks.

"Warren?"

"Fuck you, Sam!"

"All right. I dunno. No one can get a hold of him. Have you tried?"

"I haven't tried."

"Can you?"

"Can I what? Try calling him?"

"Yeah."

"To say what? Thanks for abandoning me without even telling me?"

"Uhh, if you want to say that. I don't really care what you talk about. I just want to know if you can get a hold of him. You can talk about whatever you want. That's up to you."

"Thank you for that generous allowance. Is there anything else I can do? I'd like to know what rules I'm operating under before I begin this journey."

Salty.

"That's not what I meant. Just...Piper, can you just try calling him to see if he's okay?"

She lets out a deep, intentional breath.

"I'm hanging up if I hear his voice."

Piper

Fucking Sam. Always doing his brother's bidding. I'm staring angrily at my phone, though the phone didn't do anything wrong, certainly not today. The very idea of placing a call to reach Grant has spun my gut into a thousand uncomfortable spirals. What if he answers? What do I say? What if he doesn't? What does it mean? What if I don't call? What if he's in trouble?

Stupid fucking phone. I mean, no offense, phone. I just...why the fuck did this asshole just abandon me, and abandon everything? He clearly did this to everyone, because no one in his life can seem to get a hold of him. But it has to be hurting me more than anyone else. We were best friends. *Best friends*. And now he's just Mr. M.I.A. in who-the-fuck-knows-where.

I hope he's okay. I do. But I also hope, actually, I hope even more, that he realizes what a mistake he's made. Wishful thinking, I suppose. Grant has never been one to realize any of his mistakes. Everything in his life, to him, is a series of outcomes that resulted from decisions he's made under his own free will. And when they go awry, he accepts that in some kind of perverse, unaffected way, where he believes that his decisions had no impact on the negative things that ultimately came to pass. Like it was always meant to be that way, and his decisions—which he fully believes are under his control—had nothing to do with it. It's a completely self-absorbed way to view the world, but such is Grant's life. And, if I'm being honest, it has served him very well.

The stupid fucking opaque blackness of the iPhone screen is just screaming at me: *Hey, call him, Piper!* Its blackness absorbs me, and for a moment, I'm suspended in air, staring at an oblong representation of the inside of my soul. Then I snap out of it and remember it is only glass and metal and circuit boards.

Fuck it.

I pick up the phone and go to my favorites, because goddamnit, Grant is the third one, right behind my mom and Megan. Whatever. I forgot to change it.

I stare at the little, red handset icon as the phone rings. I remember to tap it to speaker, even though it's virtually silent here and I could hear him if he answered without it. It rings a few times, then drops to voicemail.

Is he ignoring me? Or is something wrong?

Fucking fuck.

All I know is that my dread over whatever is happening in my life has not gotten better, and I'm simultaneously stuck between reminiscing of memories with a friend who ditched me and angrily scratching out any remnants of him from my memory in the first place. They counteract each other, and I know there's no point. I also know that I'm not as unforgiving as I wish I were sometimes. The guy might just be going through some real shit, and if he comes out on the other side and needs me, I might just be there for him.

Or I might not. Fucking asshole.

Grant

The first thing I notice is the familiar smell of a diesel-burning engine. Not like it's directly under my nose, but it's in the general vicinity, permeating the atmosphere around me. My eyes are shut tight, like I'm lying face-up on the beach, attempting to tan while avoiding any eye contact with the bright sun above. The more I notice how tightly shut my eyes are, the more I wonder if I am shutting them voluntarily or if something else is forcing them closed. I can't will them open, or at least I don't know how to at the moment.

I concentrate on the sounds around me as I begin to notice them. A low, dull roar. Muffled chatter, indistinguishable. Something like a window with a draft of wind coming through. Shifting gears of an engine. Where am I?

I scrape the insides of my skull, trying to remember what I was doing last. Was I at a bar? Did I black out and here I am, in an Uber, being shuffled back to...where am I? Is this L.A.? Am I...

A distorted voice interrupts my thoughts as it blares through a speaker overhead.

"Prochain arrêt, Saint-Honoré - Valois."

Well, scratch L.A. Remnants from my memory begin to seep in. Obviously, this is Paris. I was at that sandwich shop...I was walking around the city, door to door...I was looking for a man named—what was his name? Something French. Something very French.

It's all too hazy. My head starts to ache. Slowly, and without thought, I begin to open my eyes, dispelling my previous notion that there might be something binding them shut. Everything is blurry at first. As objects come into focus, I fixate on a seatback directly in front of me. The fabric that stretches between the unapologetically drab steel bars is colorful yet worn. It's tired. I'm tired. What time is it?

Around me, the sounds and smells begin to coalesce into an understanding of my environment that my eyes can now validate. A city bus. I'm on a city bus.

How did I get here? I look around. It's half full, a mix of young people and old, put-together professionals and students and possible transients. The smell of diesel becomes stronger, but that's probably just because I know where I am now.

Outside the window, I see the Seine as it winds through the city. It's a beautiful river, and this is an okay bus. But how did I get here? Did I really drink that much? It's daytime. I'm unclear what time exactly, but it looks like early afternoon. I rub my eyes.

"What the fuck..." I mumble, intending for it to be quiet, but based on the reaction from the person in front of me, who turns around abruptly, I suppose it wasn't so. "Sorry," I add.

The bus slows to a stop, and a few people disembark. I consider going off with them, but I don't really know where we are. I'm still a little too disoriented anyway. I don't even want to take out my phone to check my location yet; it might make me puke. I sit back and rest my head against the top of the seat. A few more stops come and go, and people come and go with them.

A man sitting near the front of the bus stands up from his seat while we're in motion, and he turns around to face the rest of the passengers. He has a strange look on his face, and for a moment, I think he's a crazy person and he's about to begin some nonsensical rant, maybe about Bostrom's Simulation Argument or the Occupy movement. Instead, he places his hands on his hips and smiles wide, beaming in my direction. *Shit.*

He slowly starts walking down the aisle, careful to not lurch forward or to the side with each jerky move from the bus as it chugs along down the street. I look down at my shoes, then back up again, hoping he's passed me by the time my eyes are level again. But he's right here, right in front of me, smiling. Suddenly, he looks familiar to me. He extends his right hand in front of his waist, tucking his other arm behind his back.

"I've been waiting here for God-knows-how-long," he rasps, a cool French accent dripping over his English.

"I'm sorry...waiting for what?"

He shrugs, but his expression is motionless.

"*Merde.* I think I've been waiting for *you.*"

Laurent

He's handsome enough, but certainly I would have hoped for better. Then again, it shouldn't matter. He has an almost effortless grace to him, an affability that doesn't strike you immediately and certainly isn't what you'd call describable. But it's there. It's surely there.

"Waiting for you," I repeat.

Like Morpheus from the only American movie I actually remember fondly, I've been searching for *the one*. It's been ages now, it seems. I don't even know how long I've ridden this bus, looped the 21 route, over and over and over and over...it's a never-ending monotony that I wouldn't ever have imagined could be a sizable part of my conscious life. I honestly don't know how long it has been since I've been here. It could be years, or merely hours. It feels interminable, this much I know. At times like this, accurate measures of time are nothing compared to gut feelings. This is a long time. It's in my bones. I *feel* it.

"Have we met?" he asks, looking as confused as one would expect he might look.

"Yes, we just might have, once upon a time." My extended hand is still hanging in the air; he has not shaken it nor even acknowledged that it is hanging there. "My name is Laurent."

"Dubois?" he asks, laying his terrible American accent over my beautiful surname.

"*Dubois*," I correct him, though he hardly seems to understand the nuance.

"You're *the* Laurent Dubois?" he asks.

"As far as I know, yes. I am he. Maybe I'm a little worn out these days, but I'm still me."

He looks confused again, his assuredness completely wiped off his face.

"Wait. Where are we?"

"The 21 bus."

"Sorry?"

"There's nothing to be sorry about. We're on the 21 bus. Paris. The city bus."

"How did I get here?"

"I don't know," I tell him earnestly. Then I ask, "How *did* you get here?"

He gives me a don't-fuck-with-me look and then basically says as much.

"Look," I cut him off. "I didn't choose this; you didn't choose this. But in some weird way, we both chose this. Okay? And here we are."

He shakes his head.

"Where is *here*?"

"I told you. The 21 bus."

Like an exasperated student at the onset of a final exam, his face is worrisome and exhausted. He's staring straight ahead, unsure what to do next. He buries his face in his hands, only for a moment, and then bursts upright and stares into my eyes. But he says nothing.

"My boy," I coo, hoping to soothe him, though clearly not yet succeeding. "Relax. It'll all make sense soon enough."

There's a long pause. Long enough for the bus to slow to a stop, let some passengers off, let some passengers on, and then resume its slow, laborious route.

"I mean, somewhat," I add.

Truth is, there is no "sense" to any of this. There is just what I've deduced in this interminable period I've been here. And it's not a whole hell of a lot.

"Who are you?" he asks me.

"My name is Laurent Dubois. But you know this," I tell him.

"You're not...hey, all right. I get what's happening. Did you...did you go in my pocket while I was asleep, read my list?"

"I've only just walked over to you now. I know of no list in your pocket."

He eyes me up and down.

"I don't know if I believe you. No. I don't think I do. What is happening? Like, what *exactly* is happening?"

"My boy, it's hard to explain. It's a good thing you're sitting down. Can you promise me you won't stand up anytime soon? It may knock you over, and then you'll have a head injury, and then who knows how it will all pan out. Believe me."

I stop and think about the hospital for a moment.

"I'll stay seated," he tells me.

"Well, then. Here we are."

I look around and try to think of how to best describe to him where we are.

"I believe that you and I are connected," I tell him finally.

"Okay," he says flatly. Then he smiles an awkward, not-actually-happy smile. "But what of it? And how? Just help me out, man. I'm so confused."

His voice is genuinely sad.

"The painting," I tell him.

"The painting?"

"That is, I presume this is why we are linked. After countless hours ruminating over my current condition, only to find myself bound to this damned bus, I've deduced that my condition has been laid upon me by virtue of the fact that the painting—the one I presume also conjured you here—it wanted me here. It *needed* me here. It's the only thing that seems to make sense. My life was normal until that damned thing showed up. Then, somehow, I ended up here. I don't know why. But here I am. And now...here are you."

"The painting," he says slowly, then stares off into nothing. I follow the line his eyes are tracing, but it leads nowhere.

"Yes," I assure him.

"How do you know? What does this have to do with me?"

"I don't know," I admit. "But I've been here a long time, and it's the only thing that makes sense. I knew it as soon as I saw you in this seat. You came out of nowhere. You didn't just walk onto the bus like any of the other passengers. It was just like, one moment, you're not here. The next? Poof."

I spread my hands wide in front of me. He rubs his chin and stares at me.

"Let me guess...was the last thing you saw was that painting?"

"Was it?" he asks, searching the air for answers to his foggy recollection.

"What was the painting of, tell me?"

He pauses, and then his eyes grow wide.

"This is the bus?!" he nearly shouts.

I shrug. "That's my best guess."

"How...I mean, what? What the hell is this?"

I'm tired of his American antics. This boy needs to get his head straight.

"Look," I tell him. "I didn't want this any more than you. I didn't even want the painting. I was just buying it for my...I didn't want to be sucked into the world *of* the painting, you know? It just kind of happened, at least I think that's what happened. I don't know why, or how, or if we're even alive...I don't know anything, except a few precious things that continue to reaffirm what I've just told you."

He eyes me over cautiously.

"What things?" he asks.

"Well," I start. "For one, I, too, awoke on a bus, unaware of what had happened or where I was. It was this very bus, the 21 line. Except I wasn't as fortunate as you. I didn't come to my senses on my own. Someone summoned the paramedics, and my first memory of this world was of me lying in a hospital bed with gauze wrapped around my eyes and head."

"Why?"

"Head injury, they said. I don't know why the eyes. But when they took the gauze off, I couldn't see. Not properly, at least. Everything was blurry, smudged. Like...well, like the painting. But I didn't realize that yet."

"Go on," he says, unamused but entirely enthralled.

"On this bus, my vision is normal. I can see the world as it normally appears. I look out the window, and I see the river, the buildings, the people going about their days. I see everything as clear as anyone would see it. But when I step off the bus, everything turns back to the smudged nightmare I lived in after I awoke in the damned hospital. But when I'm on the bus? I can see just fine."

"Really," he says flatly. Then he asks, realizing his tone did not match his intent. "Really?"

"I've tried it a number of times. Disembark the bus, and the vision goes to shit. Get back on, everything is fine."

"So here you are," he says, rather smugly. He has a kind of punchable face.

"And here you are," I remind him. "Likely in the same predicament as me, by the way."

He shakes his head.

"No, that can't be right," he tells me.

I laugh.

"None of this is *right*."

Grant

The guy is probably crazy. He has to be crazy. I don't know how he knows about the painting; that I can't explain. But he isn't normal. This conversation isn't normal. I'm not *in* a painting.

"So," he says as he sits down on the seat across from me, finally withdrawing his extended hand. I didn't notice, but I think it may have been in front of me the entire time we've been speaking. I'd feel bad, but there are more important things to feel right now. "What will you do?"

"What do you mean?" I ask. "Do about what?"

"Everything."

Everything. This guy is starting to make me lose my patience. I can handle a crazy person for a little while, but a vague crazy person is ultimately too much work to humor for any considerable length of time. At least be a specific crazy person. I shift around in my seat, trying to physically indicate through the slightest of movements that I'm considering standing up and getting off the bus.

"I don't know," I tell him. "It's been nice talking to you. It really has. But I think I need to go."

He smiles.

"And what will you do?" he repeats.

"I'll do whatever it is I normally do. Whatever I want to do. World is my oyster, right?"

Suddenly, a look much sadder than I was expecting washes over his face as he lowers his voice and says, "*This* world is nobody's oyster."

I look at him, puzzled, but I shake it off.

"Maybe not. But I'm going to just do whatever comes next. Probably get off the bus, go get something to eat, then head back to my hotel."

"You don't believe me, do you?" he asks.

I consider how to respond to him for long enough that he realizes it, and then that slows me down, and then *that* slows me down, and now it's been at least twenty seconds and I haven't said as much as a word in response.

"No, I don't think I believe you. No offense though. I'm sure you believe it. And I believe that you believe it. I just..."

What's the point? The guy is crazy. I don't need to rationalize why I don't want to do anything. He's just some guy on some bus.

"I suppose you're as hard-headed as me."

I shrug.

"Pleasure talking. I think I'll depart here."

He returns a shrug back to me. I stand up, looking around my seat for any of my belongings, and then I begin walking toward the front. The bus is steadily humming down the street, showing no signs of stopping. I'll just wait near the front until the next stop.

"Suppose I'll be seeing you sooner or later," he calls out.

I don't turn around. It's time to go. The bus begins to slow down, and the speaker overhead crackles as the microphone is turned on. I'm close enough to the driver that I can see his lips part as he prepares to speak.

"Glacière - Nordmann."

Yeah, sure. That'll do.

The doors hiss as they open, and I prepare to step down toward the sidewalk, but a horde of people already trying to come aboard send me reeling backwards, my back pressing up against the driver's shoulder. Even in Paris, a city supposedly *oozing* with refinement, people still don't understand the proper etiquette when it comes to getting on and off transportation. Let me off, then you come on. It's easy, but no one ever seems to do it right.

The driver rests his hand on my shoulder, and I turn around to face him. He's a middle-aged man, nothing special or remarkable in appearance. He's vaguely Italian-looking, but beyond that, he may as well have been a mannequin. "Maybe this is not your stop," he says to me, smiling.

"No, it's my stop," I reply. "Really." The stream of people ends, and I descend the steps down to the sidewalk.

As I step outside, I realize only now that the bus windows were heavily tinted. I squint as the sun overhead drowns out my vision. For a moment, I'm lightheaded; it's that feeling when your blood sugar is low, and you stand up too quickly. I take a few steps farther onto the sidewalk to get out of the way of the crowd, and I let my eyes adjust to the brightness. It's not warm out, but the sun is absolutely sharp at the moment. The air is sticky and sweet, laced with the aroma of roasted pistachios, undoubtedly emanating from a street vendor nearby. Slowly, my eyes adjust to the bright sky over my head.

Laurent

The bus *chug-chug-chugs* along, and I slump back against the seat. The driver, he never seems to leave his position at the wheel. Even when we stop at the end of the route, at the time when most bus drivers step out and take a leak, smoke a cigarette, text their mistress, whatever, he just sits there, hands clasped neatly and placed on his lap. After a few minutes with the engine off, he turns the key and it roars back to life, and then off we go.

This is no ordinary bus, this much I know. I presume the man driving this abnormal bus is also abnormal, like a spirit or a phantom or an otherworldly agent who seemingly does not have a need for food, sleep, or bodily relief. I've engaged in a few conversations with him, and he is always pleasant, but he speaks in generalities and never stops to look me in the eye for more than a passing glance. He may not even be real. I don't know if any of this is real. There is a nonzero possibility that I am already dead.

I rest my chin on my hand and stare out the window, watching the girls as they stroll up and down the sidewalk in their springtime skirts, little buttons lining the front—the latest fashion, I suppose. Oh, to be out there again. To be young. To be...anything but bound to this bus. I'd do anything, *anything*...if I only knew what to do. But I don't.

After we complete the entire route again and park in the bus lane at Gare Saint-Lazare, and after all the people shuffle off, and after all the new people shuffle on, I walk up and make small talk with the driver.

"Think that boy will be back?" I ask him.

"What boy?" he asks.

"The one I was talking to. The one that exited at *Glacière-Nordmann*."

"I'm afraid I didn't notice whom you were talking to," he says, but I can tell that he's lying.

"Is that so?"

"Doesn't matter now. They all come back."

"Oh?"

He nods, staring ahead as he turns the key in the ignition.

"They all come back. Now go on and take your seat. We're about to go."

Grant

I'm either drunk or tired or some other kind of impaired, but I can hardly make out clear shapes or figures. Everything feels a little blob-like. I think back to when I got LASIK; Wendy took me there, some well-reviewed doctor in K-town. In my consultation, he said he'd done over sixty thousand LASIK surgeries. That seems like enough to know what you're doing. I wasn't alarmed, not in the least, when he also tried to sell me on some indoor golf driving simulator that he had patented and invented. People I told about this later on joked that I was crazy to trust such a Renaissance man, but my feeling on this never changed. It was a good price, and I didn't want to spend that much to improve what was already a superficial vision deficiency anyway.

My appointment was on a Wednesday. I don't know why I chose a Wednesday, but it was nearing the time when my flex spend would run out, so I just took whatever I could. Wendy laughed as I struggled to keep my eyes open when the doctor's assistant attempted to lubricate them with some sort of eye drop solution in a long, cylindrical container. "You're going to have a hard time with the surgery if you can't keep your eyes open for something as simple as an eye drop," he said. I wanted to shove him. You're not even a doctor. Get the fuck out of my face.

Wendy was great through all of it. And when they took the clamps off my eyes, and my vision was absolutely blurred, and they put these ridiculously large sunglasses on me, she was right there. She held her hand on my shoulder the whole time we walked out, all the way to the car. She held my hand as she drove me home. She was so sweet to me back then.

I wasn't allowed to use my phone or look at any screens for the rest of the day. This was when I learned that Siri pronounces emojis if she's reading out your messages. My mom texted me something that came out as: *How did the surgery go purple heart purple heart purple heart.* It was a fun game afterwards to hear Siri read out the names of all the other emojis.

A hurried pedestrian, clearly en-route to somewhere that she thinks is important, slams the front of her shoulder into the back of mine. I lurch forward, not so much by the sheer force, but due to my lack of anticipation. No apology. No acknowledgement. I can't exactly tell, but I am fairly certain she didn't even turn around. She just kept marching along on her predetermined, highly important route. At the very least, she snapped me out of my daze.

My eyes come back into focus, but only for me to realize that they can't focus. Everything is still just a blob of color. I think back to what that crazy man on the bus said. *How did he know?* I shake it off momentarily, but then the thought creeps back and repeats itself. How *did* he know? Was what he said actually true? It couldn't be. But then...how does one explain *this*?

Closing my eyes shut and opening them again, in rapid succession at least four of five times, I figure something will shift and I'll start to see properly again. But it doesn't work. Without much else to do, I seek the nearest object on which I think I can appropriately sit, and I do just that. I rest my chin in my hands, my elbows on my knees, back arched in the worst possible form if I were about to perform a deadlift. I'd sure as hell pinch a nerve if I tried to pick up anything significantly heavy in this position.

I think back to the bus and then to my hotel. What hotel was I staying at again? What direction was it from here? Where *is* here?

I pad my hands around the pockets of my jeans, reassuring myself that my wallet and phone are still within my possession. I slide my phone out of my pocket, no small feat given the position my leg is in, and I wobble the phone in my palm to get the screen to turn on. *Fuck.* I can't see a damned thing on it. It looks like one big colorful nightlight sitting in the palm of my hand.

I sit on this—I don't even know what it is, maybe a bench—for longer than I think I've sat on anything other than a plane or car seat. I don't usually sit still for too long, but in this moment, I'm not sure what else I can do. I fumble around on my phone for a while, trying to navigate my calendar for details about where I'm staying. This is embarrassing. I usually have a great memory, certainly when it comes to travel details. But I simply cannot remember a thing about the hotel where I'm staying, though I have a lingering feeling that it's a real dump.

A few times, when it seems like someone is sitting near me, I ask if they would be so kind as to help me open up a website. No one replies. I'm starting to think that getting off that bus was a bad idea. Okay, I'm not *starting* to think it. I'm actively in denial about the decision I made. Eventually, some stranger walks up to me and asks me if I need help. I must have been sitting here for hours. I can only imagine how many other people considered doing the same, only to not do anything at all.

"Yes," I tell her. "I'd like to talk to my travel agency. The contact is saved in my phone. If you could just dial the number, I should be able to take it from there."

"A travel agency? Those still exist?"

I laugh.

"My company is a little behind the times. And yes, they exist. They should be thanking me every time I call, for keeping them in business, you know."

The woman doesn't say anything. I extend my phone in my hand and wait for her to take it.

"SEG Travel," I tell her.

She dials, and in short time it connects with a real, live person. I hold the phone off to the side of my face, and I thank the woman who helped me. I don't know if she's still there, but she doesn't respond. I return to the phone.

"How may I help you, sir?"

I think about it for a moment. I could ask her what hotel I booked, but what good would that do? I would then have to get back to that hotel, navigate its halls alone, navigate my room alone, all amidst a blurry set of blobs (assuming this shit doesn't improve before then). That hardly seems like an improved position.

"Uhh, hi."

"Hi, sir."

"I, uh, I'd like to..."

I slowly slide the phone from my ear and swat at the red blob of a circle on the screen.

Fuck.

Laurent

The wheels on the bus go round and round, round and round, yeah yeah yeah. Even the French version of this song sucks. I couldn't stand that my boy loved it so much. Why couldn't he have been smitten with a song by, I don't know, Manu Dibango? Or Donald Byrd? That would have been far superior. But I learned a long time ago that you can't change your kids. Quite the opposite, actually. Only your kids can change *you*. That's a mind fuck, but it doesn't affect everyone. Me, for instance...my kids didn't change me. When my little girl was born, and while Margot was still recovering from the Caesarian, I was out with some new girl. I couldn't help myself. Even when I was only getting two, maybe three hours of sleep per night, rocking her to sleep, battling through the colic, the acid reflux, the lingering jaundice...even when my eyes were sagging, my mood along with them. Even then, I had that drive, that *appetite*.

I never should have married. But it was too late, even back then. I had already made the plunge. So the only logical thing to do was to keep it as discreet as possible. I never bragged, never took them out, never kept very close in communication. It was very private. Margot knew of it, sure, but she didn't ask. She didn't want to know the details. She was a good woman.

I should have been better to her. I certainly had the chances. She was always there for me, steadfast, reassuring. When we had the boy, I told myself I was going to stop. And I believed it, I really did. I'd see an attractive girl in the coffee shop, and I'd tell myself, sometimes verbally if I had to, that I was a married man and that I had no business striking up a chat with her. Even still, sometimes my curiosity would get the best of me, and I'd lean in, ask what she was reading or whatever it was that the cute girl was doing at the time.

But then I'd stop myself. *No!* I'd say, inside, and I'd bid her adieu and leave the coffee shop, sometimes without even picking up my drink order. I'd walk down the street feeling regretful but stoic, and somewhat proud. I had conquered it, I thought. Anyone can get past anything if they try hard enough.

It didn't last. The boy proved to be a nightmare child to raise, making the girl seem like a cakewalk, and I hardly wanted to be home for that. It drove me out. *He* drove me out. But truly, I know it was just my instinct. It wasn't his fault. In fact, he was probably such a challenge *because* he was my son. I'm sure it was at least a majority my fault, if not entirely on me.

From then, I never stopped having something on the side. It hardly seemed fair that my prowess be contained to one woman, but in retrospect, life isn't fair, and no one forced me to commit myself to one woman. I chose that, and then I actively and repeatedly betrayed that. I sinned so often that I didn't even know how to talk about it when I went to confessional. I didn't know how to describe my behavior. It was bad, I knew it, and yet I continued to do it.

Perhaps this limbo here on this bus is my ultimate punishment. A universal karmic revenge that I can't escape. I can't say I don't deserve this. I deserve worse. I don't know what could possibly be worse, but I believe I deserve it. I really do. I was a piece of shit for so long, and so aware of it the entire time. And yet, I continued to stink up the place.

Yes, I deserve this. So as the wheels continue to roll and roll and roll and roll, so does my life, dwindling away one rotation of the axle at a time, counting down the days until I can no longer remove myself from the bus seat, and I die in place and eventually reduce to a heap of dust on this very seat. And then someone comes onto the bus, and they open the window. An innocent act, sure, but monumental with regards to my legacy. And then the bus takes off...and there goes my dust. All over everyone in the bus and all out the windows. It coats the seats with a thin, grey film, and it covers the ceiling in an ashy grey soot. The floor, it's covered in dust. A diaspora of me. Never again to be one being. There I go.

I sit here, pondering everything, knowing deep in my heart that this may very well be my ultimate end. I've made too many shitty decisions in my life, and this is my punishment. Perhaps I am already dead? The thought *has* crossed my mind. Is this the afterlife? Is it Hell? Is it limbo? Good lord, this isn't Heaven, right? It can't be.

Margot, I'm sorry. Wherever you are, I hope that you are happy. I hope that you can move on. I don't expect you to forgive me. I wouldn't. It's too much. *I've* been too much. I'm so sorry. If I could see you again, I'd tell you all of this. I really would. I'd be different this time. I *am* different now. But I don't think I'll be getting the chance to prove this to you or to myself or to anyone. I think this is all that I've got to look forward to.

"Glacière-Tolbiac..." the driver mumbles through the speakers overhead, a suggestive leading pause as though he's poised to say more. He doesn't.

People get on, and people get off. The bus rolls on.

Wendy

He's looking off into the room with his vapid stare. I think he's trying to conjure up words of encouragement, but he doesn't know what to say, and the result is him sitting there, suspended in motion, mouth agape.

"Yes?" I prod.

"What?" he returns.

Perhaps he was not trying to think of anything. That might just be his natural disposition. With Grant around, I always found Sam to be charmingly goofy. A fun, younger brother with whom you could enjoy yourself in almost any situation. Not reliable, but as long as your expectations were clear, he was a great guy to have around.

Without Grant, I don't see any of this. His goofiness is now just irritating. His seeming lack of concern for anything that resembles responsibility is a stinging reminder of how much he is *not* his brother. And how much I wish his brother were here.

"Nothing," I say, and then I head to the kitchen to refill my water.

I don't offer anything to him. If he wants something, he knows how to ask. After a few moments of pregnant silence, he offers a worthless comment that I already knew.

"Piper hasn't heard from him either."

"Yes. You said this."

He shrugs.

"What do we do? Should we call the police?"

"The police? Isn't that extreme?"

"I dunno," he mumbles. "Who do you think we should call then? Would anyone in the EU office know, maybe?"

"I texted Raji, and she said she hasn't heard from him either. If she hasn't, I doubt anyone else out there would have."

He nods. I want him to spring up into action, to pace around my apartment, to shove his hands in and out of his pockets, crossing his arms in anger and then shoving his hands in his pockets again. *That's* the look of real concern. But he just nods and sits on my couch like an immobile log of a human. No amount of me wanting anything can change this guy. He just is who he is.

I miss Grant so much.

"Hey," he says, looking me in the eyes for what I'm now realizing might be the first time since he got here. "We'll find him, okay? He's somewhere. I'm sure he's fine."

"How? How are we going to find him?"

"If—"

"And don't say the police, Sam. We're not calling the French police. Not yet, at least."

"I wasn't going to say the police. I was going to say that we should call his hotel. Do you know where he's staying?"

Finally, a productive idea from him. Albeit fruitless.

"No. I don't. Do...yeah, you don't either, I take it?"

"Grant never tells me adult things like that," he laughs. "But wait. Do you have access to his calendar? I bet he has it in his calendar. I remember when we were in Paris, he kept getting all these notifications for things that we were doing. I'm pretty sure he puts *everything* in his calendar. Like, *everything*."

"On his phone? Why would I have access to his calendar?"

"I dunno. Is that a thing? I figured that was a thing."

"If I was his assistant, sure. But I'm his..." I stop, and we both know why. I don't have a label. I'm just someone in Grant's orbit. I'm not his *anything*.

"Would you be able to guess his password? Maybe he booked on Expedia or something. We know his email, or at least could try a few of them. Right?"

He's onto something, and it fires a trigger in my head that races around my brain until it connects to the other triggers that simultaneously fired, all scattering around trying to find each other.

"We use a travel agency for business travel," I tell him. "We always use the same agency."

"Do you know the agency?" he asks.

"Yes, of course. I use them all the time!"

"Great! Great!"

Finally, Sam springs to his feet, though at this point I don't care about his urgency. We have somewhat of a plan. I wanted the urgency when we had nothing to go on.

"Good job, Sam," I commend him, even though I'm gritting my teeth as I say it.

"Sure thing, sis."

Grant

With each incorrect bus that passes by this bench, another brick of regret is laid atop the wall that is forming somewhere in the recesses of my brain. If this doesn't end soon, the wall just might explode out of my skull and expose all of my thoughts to the outside world around me. At this point, I'd give nearly anything to have not stepped off that bus. I should have just listened to that man. *Laurent.*

My bladder is on the verge of bursting, but until my vision comes back, I'm not confident that I could leave here and find my way back. I sit and wait, squirming, thinking of that scene in Magnolia with the boy on the game show. No, that won't be me.

"Excuse me?" I ask into the empty air around me, hoping someone replies.

Silence.

I try this again every few minutes until finally, a woman's voice responds.

"Can I help you?" she asks.

My skin flushes as I begin to speak. "Thank you for answering me. I've been sitting here quite some time." I spin my head to look in the direction where I heard her voice, but I can't be confident where she is or if I'm even looking in the right direction. "I'm blind," I blurt out, unsure what else to say.

"Do you need assistance?" she asks with a touch of care in her voice.

"I just need to find the nearest restroom," I tell her. "Would you be able to help me?"

Wendy

Do you know any French? I want to ask him. But I know he doesn't. It's not even worth asking. Besides, when you try to speak French to a Parisian, they get all uppity and act more upset than if you weren't to even try at all. I don't understand that reaction, but when it comes to cultural things, I usually judge but keep my judgement silent.

"Do you want me to call, or should you?" he asks.

I shake my head and sigh heavily through my nose.

"I'll call. What's the number?"

He hunches over his laptop and squints before reading the numbers to me. He forgets to tell me the "plus" part, and I forget to enter it too, so the first time I dial, it just immediately makes that *you messed up* noise. I try again with the correct format, and eventually it begins to ring. The rings are interminably long, like I'd wronged someone at the switchboard and now it was finally their time to get revenge.

"Just pick up already!" I shout.

Sam stiffens his neck and continues to stare forward at his laptop, trying to pretend—but failing—that he's not affected by my outburst.

"*Bonjour?*" a voice asks me, followed by a series of French words that I think might be in reference to the name of the hotel, but it was all so fast, I can't tell.

"Hi," I begin slowly.

"Hello," the person on the other end says, now in English. "How may I help you?"

"I'd like to reach a guest that's staying at the hotel."

"Most certainly. Do you know the room number?"

"I do not."

"Very well. What is your name?"

"*My* name? Why?"

The person on the other end pauses for a moment, likely to catch composure before responding. "So that I may know who is calling for one of our guests. It's standard process here at the hotel."

"What do you need to know that for?" I ask.

"It's standard process here at the hotel. Will this be a problem for you?"

"I just...no. It's fine. My name is Wendy."

"Very well. And what is the surname of the guest?"

I look over at Sam as I say it, seeing if his ears perk up at the mention of his name. They do, but ever so slightly. He remains still, fixated on his laptop screen. The person on the other end of the phone mumbles something before asking me to please hold. Bach's "Fugue in G Minor" fills the phone's speaker as I sit and wait. Lovely song. Not exactly a high-quality transmission, but a nice touch, nevertheless. You can tell they're at least trying.

Sam must feel me staring at him, but he refuses to shift even a millimeter out of position. His laptop fan kicks on and fills out the silence in the rest of the room. I didn't realize it was silent until it came on, and perhaps it wasn't. I was too distracted by the Bach melody as it filled my right ear. The music abruptly stops, and I snap into focus.

"Ma'am?"

"Yes."

"I tried ringing his room, but he did not answer. I'm afraid he must be out at the moment."

"Right." I look down at my watch, trying to calculate the time difference. "Well, of course. He's probably out."

"Sorry about that, ma'am. Perhaps you can try again later."

"Erhm...could you please, uh, could I leave a message?"

"I'm afraid our rooms do not have private answering machines. We discontinued that service last year. Usage was low..." the voice trails off, sadly. At this moment, I realize that I can't tell if it's a man or a woman. The more I think about it, the harder it is to pin down.

"I don't need to leave an answering machine message. I'd just like you to take a message and deliver it to him when he returns."

"I see. I suppose I could help with that. What would you like to say?"

I think for a moment, and at this point, I've probably been staring at the back of Sam's neck for the better part of three minutes.

"Say, *Grant.* Then, next line. *It's Sam. Please call me when you get this.*"

"Sam?"

"Yes, Sam."

Silence. Long, long silence.

"Ma'am, did you mislead me earlier?"

"Pardon?"

"When I asked you your name, you said it was Wendy. Now you are saying it is Sam? Which is it?"

I hate that I have to play nice here. I want to tell this person to go to heck and to get their manager on the phone on their way there.

"My name is Wendy. This is a message for the guest at your hotel, from his brother."

"His brother?"

"Yes. *Sam*," I seethe. "That's the name I want in the message. Okay? Sam. I am Wendy. Sam is the one he should call back. Got it?"

There's a long pause, a kind of pause that makes me wonder if this person is even going to do anything I'm asking them to do.

"Very well, ma'am."

"You'll take this message for him?" I confirm.

Another long pause.

"Certainly," the voice coos. "Just one thing."

"What?" I bark.

"What is the return number for this Sam?"

"You can just tell him to call Sam. He knows his number. It's his *brother*."

"Hotel policy, ma'am. I'll need a return number if I'm to take a message on his behalf."

I pull my mouth away from the phone, though not very far.

"Sam, what's your number?"

He finally snaps out of his stance and turns to look at me. He recites it to me; I recite it to the hotel person.

"Anything else?" I ask.

"That'll be all. Have a wonderful rest of your day," the voice states flatly, an empty comment that fools no one.

The phone clicks, and the room is again silent, lest for the whirring fan practically blasting Sam's laptop into a full hover over the table. He looks up at me and smiles.

"Left a message, did you?"

"Let me know as soon as he calls you back," I snap, storming toward the bathroom before I can even see his reaction.

Sam

It's late in the afternoon at this point, maybe four or five or maybe even later than that. I suck with time. I don't wear a watch. My phone is tucked in my back pocket. I've been doing this ever since Matt warned me about the dangers of phone radiation and my junk. I'd rather have a butt cheek tumor than a non-operational nut.

Anyway, phone's in pocket, watch is non-existent, time is...what is time? I've got to think about it for a little while, because I'm pretty sure that the last occasion I assessed it, time wasn't really real.

I fall asleep. There's something weird going on in my dream. There's two girls. One of them is Piper, but she's also not Piper. Because it's one of those kinds of dreams where it's accurate and also vague, yet also still somehow even the vagueness is plausible. The Piper girl is singing a melody I remember from when I was really young. She's singing to the other girl. That girl is riding my dick like a dirt bike, and I'm pretty sure she's a mogul or two away from snapping my boner in half. Nevertheless, it's working for me, at least for the brief time being.

The Piper girl keeps singing, softly and slowly, an odd juxtaposition against the girl thrashing against my hips. Her hair is whipping around almost in a counterclockwise swirl, rhythmically, fucking fantastically. I come, I think. I don't know. I come again, and this time I feel more confident that this is, in fact, what I just did. Piper turns into Marcy, a girl I dated after high school. Marcy stops singing. The dirt bike girl is gone, and all I have left to remember her by is the residue she left on the outer edge of the base of my dick. That, and the imbued image her writhing body impressed into my memory. That is, my dream memory.

I look at Marcy, and she's about to say something, but then a phone rings somewhere. I look for it. I keep looking for it. Where is it?

Something from the real world is reaching into my subconscious and grabbing me directly. It has made its way into my dream, but it is not *of* my dream, of this I am now fairly certain.

My eyes flutter open. I grope around for my phone along the seams of the couch. I feel it vibrating in my pocket, and I somehow manage to slide it out and answer the call, all in the same motion. Purely an accident, but it seems suave as hell to my just-coming-to-its-senses brain.

"Huh? Hello?"

"Monsieur?"

My eyes search the walls. I'm in my apartment. Whew. Now, who is calling me monsieur?

"Shawn?"

"I beg your pardon?" the voice asks, clearly not Shawn.

"Sorry, who's this?"

"Is this Mister, ahem..." There's a long pause. Then the man continues. "Mister Sam?"

I laugh.

"Yep, everyone calls me Mister Sam. That is I, *monsieur*."

"My name is Ferdinand. I am calling from Hotel Madeleine Haussmann."

I perk up.

"Grant's hotel?" I blurt.

It's now been, I don't know, maybe a week since anyone has heard from him? At least a few days since Wendy and I called the hotel and left a message. It's about fucking time he calls one of us back. Even Dad was wondering where he went. I pull my phone away from my ear and consider texting Wendy right away, but then I pull the phone back to my ear and catch the tail end of a sentence I was too distracted to hear the beginning of.

"Sorry," I interject. "Could you repeat what you just said? I was...incapacitated."

I look around the empty room and shrug. There's no one to call me on my lie.

"Yes, well...I was saying, we received your message just the other day. I'm afraid to tell you that your friend has not returned to his room, or to the hotel. We've been attempting to contact him, but his phone seems unreachable. We're wondering if you might be able to put us in touch with him."

"Me? You guys are the last ones who saw him. How would I know how to get in touch with him? I called *you* to find out where he was."

"So, you cannot help us locate Mister Grant," this Ferdinand guy says flatly.

I sit upright, and little stars begin to fill the corners of my vision. I shake it off.

"Why do you need to locate him?"

"He has not returned to the hotel, monsieur."

"Yeah?"

I don't get it.

"We have another guest who will be staying in his room the day after next. We need to remove his belongings, and of course, we need him to settle his bill with us."

"Wait, he just left his stuff there?"

"That is correct."

"At the front desk? Or, like, in his room?"

"His belongings are still in the room. He was due to check out today, but we've seen no activity with his room in quite a few days. Our housekeepers have reported that his belongings have not moved in as much time either. He's seemingly moved on to another place."

"Another place..." I mumble.

"Monsieur, I thank you for your time. That is all we will need."

"Wait!" I shout, then out of sheer instinct, I spring to my feet, as though my physical distress will change the situation at all. "What happens to his stuff?"

"We will hold it," Ferdinand says politely.

"How long? How much stuff is it?"

He's silent for a moment. I hear shuffling in the background, but nothing terribly discernable.

"One large bag, one small bag, and a laptop."

"Okay. How long will you keep it there?"

"Sir," he pleads. "You have to understand that this is a small hotel and that this is a highly unusual situation here. We do not have protocol, per se. We have never had a guest simply vanish and never return, leaving behind all of their belongings. As such, we will keep it as long as is practicable."

"Do you think he's all right?" I ask, beginning to realize the potential gravity of the situation.

Grant could be hurt, in a hospital somewhere, unable to find a way to get a hold of any of us. Or worse, he could be held captive somewhere. Although that seems somewhat unlikely, I can't shake the idea of a male version of *Taken* happening and him being the guy that gets nabbed. I haven't seen *Taken* in a while, though, so maybe I'm a little off.

"I wouldn't hazard a guess," he replies.

"I see."

"But," he continues. "If you are able to come here and help us sort this out, I think that might be most helpful."

I snort.

"Helpful? For who?"

Ferdinand pauses for a while, and I anticipate his next words, as they are the only words that could follow mine.

"Helpful for any of us," he replies.

Piper

Hey Grant,

I wanted to tell you some of this in person, but I don't know when that will be. You're off in Europe somewhere, and no one can get a hold of you. Are you alright? People are genuinely worried. I'm worried…

Look. I know you always say that I sound like a bitch when I text or email anything somewhat serious, but I don't know how else to get through to you. I have so many questions for you. Like, what happened to us? We used to be close. We were friends. GREAT friends. Sometimes we'd even say best friends. Now we've drifted apart, and you're…where are you? Like, seriously, where the hell did you go?

I also have something I need to tell you, and I really didn't want to do this over email. I've decided to move back to Cleveland. L.A. just didn't turn out how I thought it would…and I think going back home is the right move for me. I'll arrange all of the HR stuff, but I just wanted to let you know. This is not the way I wanted you to find out, but then again, you're the one who abandoned me!

I hope everything is okay. Please just let someone know you're alright and that we all can stop worrying. We can talk about all of this when you're back, if you want. I just…miss you, I guess. But I know I'll have to get used to that too.

- Piper

The email only says part of what I'm feeling, but Megan was right: writing something, *anything*, would give me some perspective I desperately need. Reading it over and over and over, I've wordsmithed this thing to death, and it's still marginal at best. I close my eyes and breathe out heavily through my nose. Then I click, my cursor already hovering over the SEND button. When I open my eyes, I'm staring at my inbox, and the email's gone.

"Here we go…" I say aloud to myself.

Watching in slow-motion as Grant receded from my life was a lot harder than I thought it would be. My emotions have gone through a number of phases in the past few weeks. First, I was angry, then I was in denial, then I was angry again…this was followed by grief, then followed by more grief in the form of alcohol-induced crying, and then followed by an extra dose of denial. I may have missed a phase in there, but now I'm just…sad.

It's not like I think about it all the time or that I can't go on with my life, but the guy *was* legitimately my best friend. I don't know how something that meaningful could dissolve so easily. It's a lot harder without context or feedback from him. It was just, like, one day he was my friend; and then suddenly, he wasn't just kind of distant…he was literally in another country.

Maybe this is how all relationships go, with one person more *into* it than the other, regardless of whether the relationship is romantic or platonic or whatever variations exist in between. There's still always one person who is more into it. That person is me, for us. Maybe it isn't that hard for Grant. But how could that be!? We were so close!

I pause and think about Sam, and my heart sinks down to the bottom of my ribcage as I consider the idea that perhaps this is karma for the way I've treated him. He was always more into me, and I took his feelings for granted. Meanwhile, his goddamned brother is taking *me* for granted, and I'm stuck here thinking about *him*, and he wasn't even the guy that I was in the romantic relationship with! Life's cruel jokes will get you one way or another.

If it's karma, I don't know what the lesson is here. I can't help it that I wasn't as into Sam as he was into me. That's just how it goes, right? I sigh again, and then I have a realization I don't particularly want to confront.

I *was* into Sam at first. We were equally into each other, and I thought he was the greatest thing to happen to me. The more I got to know him, the more comfortable we got, and it was great. But that was also when I started to realize who he really was and, more importantly, who he wasn't. He wasn't ambitious, or savvy, or determined. He was the antithesis of his brother, and for better or worse, I admired Grant and the way he went about his life. The discrepancy between the two of them drove a mental wedge into my life that I never really could get past. It was a large part of what drove me to break up with him, but I could never tell Sam that.

I close my laptop and rest my face in my hands as I slouch down to the counter. I feel tears forming in the corners of my eyes, and I resist the urge to hold them back, because in some way I know I deserve to feel like this.

Wendy

About an hour before we need to leave for LAX, there's a knock on my door. I'm not expecting anyone, so immediately my mind begins racing. I fear the worst. The worst what? I don't know. As I open the door, I might actually be wincing as it swings open. The door extends and reveals a neatly dressed Sam, his suitcase behind him, the rolling arm extended.

"Hi," he says plainly.

I'm a little shocked. A part of me was expecting him to forget to even show up, or if he did remember, he'd be so late that he'd have to meet me at the airport because I couldn't wait for him. But instead, he's here, an hour early. *I'm* not even ready yet.

"Did you have the wrong time in your calendar?"

"Calendar?" he asks, smiling. Then he indicates that he wants to walk inside, but he mostly stays stopped in place. "Wait, should we leave now?"

"Now? We don't need to leave for another hour."

He nods. Then he gives me a look like, *okay, so now what?*

"Come in," I tell him. "I'm still finishing packing."

He walks in behind me and leaves his suitcase by the door. As he's rolling up his sleeves, he sits down on the stool at the edge of the counter.

"Figured you didn't want to be late, so I made sure to get here extra early."

It's like something has come over him. I don't know how to process this. The Sam I know—admittedly, I don't know him all that well—he has to be dragged just to get moving. The guy that showed up on my door seems like an entirely different person.

I finish packing, and Sam calls an Uber. The ride is uneventful, and on the way, I start to wonder what the point of all this is.

"Do you think he's all right?" Sam asks, for maybe the twentieth time since we called the hotel.

"I was thinking the exact same thing right now," I tell him, even though it's not really true. But I was thinking about what we were doing, heading to catch a flight to Paris to go looking for Grant. For all I know, he might just be avoiding us, and we'll be wasting our time and money and whatever else this ends up costing us, physically or emotionally.

"I can't believe I'm going to Paris again," Sam mumbles. "Like, it feels like I just got back!"

I shrug.

Sam gets the extra pat down at security. It's probably because of his beard. Meanwhile, I pass through because I look sweet and little.

On the plane, Sam and I are a couple of rows apart. We booked separately from each other—again, because I didn't trust that he'd actually pull through on his end—and then rearranged our seats once they were assigned. Close-but-not-next-to-each-other is exactly the distance I'd like to be from Sam on this twelve-hour journey.

Walking up and down the aisle are beautifully appointed flight attendants, red uniforms with white accessories and fringe. No male flight attendants, as far as I can see. I prefer it that way. The men always seem to be a little too handsy, often creepy. Touching your lower back, lightly resting their hand on your shoulder as they sidle by. No, not for me. I'll take the ladies. They never do that, and when they do, it's not creepy; it's just helpful or kind.

I lean my head against the cushion behind me, and I stare out at the clouds drifting by the oval window. The sky is getting dark, and the sun has disappeared behind the line of the horizon. Sam is fuddling around with his headphones. The guy next to me is already fast asleep, thankfully silent. The flight attendant passing by me smiles, but she offers nothing.

I let out a loud sigh, muffled by the sound of the plane, but loud enough for me to realize how worried I actually am. *I hope he's okay*, I concentrate and say to myself, over and over. *I hope he's okay.*

Grant

"Fucking blind," I tell him.

"That's awful."

"Yeah. You're telling me. Just like that!"

I snap my fingers, but you can barely hear it over the hum of the city all around us. I only know who one part of the "us" is in this scenario. The other guy is just some random stranger sitting alongside me.

"The bus should be here soon," he offers, as though his vision offers him insight into something I can't see.

"Mmmhmm," I reply.

"Been here in Paris before?" he asks.

I nod.

"I love Paris. You from here?"

He doesn't reply. It's quiet for a while. I concentrate on my breathing as cars and trucks steadily make their way down the road in front of us. Brakes screech about a hundred feet to my left.

"My bus is arriving," the guy tells me. "Yours will probably be here soon."

I scoff.

"Last guy said the same thing."

"Well," he adds. "Best of luck, at least. I'm sure you'll be fine. You look...healthy."

"Thanks. I am healthy. Or, I was. I don't know what I am now."

"Fucking blind," he reminds me.

"Right," I laugh. "*Fucking blind.*"

Sam

Wendy looks like she had the best sleep of her life on that flight. If there's a trace of jet lag running through her system, it's undetectable. I feel like a truck ran over my eyelids and then parked on my throat.

"Kind of a shit hotel, for him. Right?" I ask her quietly.

Quietly because we're waiting in the lobby for the shift manager to come speak with us. Quietly because there's a family at the check-in counter, and I don't want to spoil their stay by ragging on their accommodations. But really. It's quite drab, even by my standards.

"Grant never really cared about the quality of the hotel," she says softly. "He would say, 'The stars don't mean anything'..."

Her look is something sad, but I can't place a word to it. Wistful? Longing? Something about the way she's talking about him, as though he doesn't exist anymore; it's morbid. For all we know, he's on some ten-day fuck bender with a bevy of French girls. Or guys. Who knows? It's Europe. At least I'm not thinking that he's dead. I think he's just off somewhere, ignoring all of us. Still, I get it. I feign a sad face as well. I think this is what I am supposed to do in this situation.

A surly-looking man emerges from behind a bookcase where apparently, the business office hides somehow.

"Monsieur Sam?" he asks, again with the ridiculous combination of the formal title plus the first name. This must just be their style here.

"That's me. And this..."

"I'm Wendy," she offers, extending her hand and giving him a brisk, tight handshake like the lady boss that she is.

"How were your travels?"

"Fine," she says. Then, "Look. What's the latest? Did he ever come back?"

He shakes his head.

"I'm afraid not. We have been unable to reach him, and thus far, he has not returned."

A feeling of regret washes over me, like we just spent all this money and time coming here only to find out what we already knew before we left. I mean, we didn't know this would be the outcome by the time we got here...but then again, if the outcome were different, couldn't we have figured it out from L.A.? What would be the difference?

I pause, trying to think where exactly we went wrong. I just got so wrapped up in it all...

"Can you show me his things?" Wendy snaps, seemingly frustrated, possibly for the exact reason I'm contemplating.

"Certainly, madam."

He leads us over toward the bookcase in the corner, a narrow hallway extending into a small room.

"My office," the shift manager mutters.

On the back wall, a doorway leading to yet another room has its door agape. It feels out of place, like a room tacked on to another room by some third-rate contractor who took the job even though he knew it made no architectural sense. It's too dark inside the room to properly see what else might be in there, but a standing rolling suitcase appears to be at the front, with some sort of large paper-wrapped package leaning behind it. As he wheels the suitcase out, I recognize it as Grant's.

"That's his!" I blurt out.

"Yes, monsieur. We know this much."

Oh yeah.

"Can we..."

Wendy reaches forward and grabs the suitcase by the top handle, flipping it onto its side. She unzips it lengthwise, dragging both zippers in opposite directions before turning the corners and opening the entire thing wide.

"...open it?" I mumble, intent on completing my sentence, even though she just barged ahead and did it anyway.

She rifles through a stack of neatly folded shirts, underwear, and socks. There's an errant tie that's rolled up and shoved in the corner of the bag.

"A tie?" I say aloud.

Wendy shrugs and keeps shuffling his clothes around. There's nothing interesting in here, no clues or suggestions that we can build off of. Just a bunch of clothes that you would expect to find in the suitcase of a man on a trip through Europe.

"Can we go up to his room?" she asks, still facing the suitcase and running her hands along everything inside.

"I'm afraid not. There are guests in there now."

"I see," she says. "So...so..."

Oh shit. I've seen that look.

"Yes?" the man asks, wearing a smile that I'm just bracing to see evaporate from his face in a few seconds.

"So what exactly do we do now?!" she snaps. Her tone is almost always one of the following: jovial, lightheartedness, or snapping. There's lots of snapping with this one.

"I'm sorry?" he asks, his smile vanishing as I predicted.

"We flew all the way out here. What do we do now?!"

The man looks around, seemingly assessing whether the guests in the drab lobby just outside his office might be able to overhear our conversation. He ushers us out to the lobby, where there aren't, in fact, any listeners. The family that was checking in has gone off somewhere. It's just the three of us and the sound of the wind whistling through the cracks of the revolving door.

"I would suggest filing a police report. Or simply visiting the police station would be an adequate start. They can help you further."

"Adequate," she snarls. "Yeah. That sounds freaking awesome. Thanks so much."

Grant

At least the bench is comfortable, as far as benches go.

Occasionally, I fear that the bus came and went and I tuned it out as white noise amidst the hum of the city around me. But it hasn't, or at least I'm telling myself this.

Like a man awaiting his last meal before execution, I'm more unsure about the next thing I'm about to do than anything I've ever done in my life. If this doesn't work, and when I finally get up, I get on the wrong bus...or even if I get on the right bus...if this doesn't work, and I can't get somewhat back to normal? Fuck this all. I don't even know what I'll do.

A dull roar of a diesel engine emanates from down the street. It slowly gets louder and louder. *Could this be it?* I never thought I'd be so excited, so anticipatory, over a fucking city bus. It zooms on by and doesn't come close to stopping where I sit. It might have just been a delivery truck.

I honestly don't know how long it's been since I've been here. That trip to the bathroom feels like it was literally days ago. The sun is still out, and it has been this entire time, but the passage of time is elusive right now.

Another loud engine comes to my attention, and this time the vehicle it is emanating from comes to a rolling stop directly in front of me. I hear the familiar hiss of the entry doors opening. As far as I know, there was no one else on the bench with me, so there's no one to tell me if this is going to be worth my time.

Now or never.

I stand up and approach where I think the door is. Unsure of how to proceed, I wave my arms around to try to signal the driver that I'm in need of help. No one tries to help me.

"Hello?" I shout.

"Back again?" an older man's voice replies, seemingly from inside the bus.

Again?

"Is this the 21 bus?" I scream, aware that I must sound like a lunatic but unsure how else to proceed. I don't want the din of all the noise around us to fuck this up.

"Indeed, it is," the voice responds. "Come on board, son."

Someone grabs me by the inside of my arm and begins to lead me toward what I'm hoping is the bus. I see blobs of white and blue, and for a moment, I can almost make out an advertisement on its side. My shin presses abruptly against something firm. I lift my leg up, bending my foot back to not hook it on the ledge I'm pressing against, and I step onto the first step.

After what feels like an excruciatingly long ten or fifteen seconds, I'm on board. Nothing has changed; I still can't see shit.

"Please have a seat," the older man requests gently.

I grope around and eventually find a seat that I think I can sit on. I slowly lower my hips until I'm fully seated. The doors hiss, and the bus lurches forward. I shake my head.

Then it happens. Slowly, and from the edges of my eyes that I'm suddenly and surprisingly now aware of, objects begin to come into focus.

First, the frames of the windows, then the glass on the windows, then the pattern on the seats, then the rows of buildings as the bus rolls past them. I sigh...full fucking relief oozing through my body. At least for now. A smile cracks my lips apart, and only now do I realize how tightly I was clenching my jaw. Smiling for what? I don't know. A life sentence on the fucking bus, maybe.

"I knew you'd be back," I hear a voice say as he walks from the rear and rests his warm hand on my shoulder.

I whip my head around, and sure enough, there he is. He looks a little more beleaguered, and I pause to consider that maybe time within the confines of this bus world is simply non-existent. Or extremely slow. Or something else nutty. I shake it off.

"I thought you were crazy," I tell him.

"But then you couldn't see shit, *oui*?"

"*Oui*."

"It's a bitch, I know. You sure made it back a lot faster than me, that's for certain."

"Is that right? How long did it take you? Actually...how long did it take *me*?"

"What is time?" Laurent asks with a slight curl of his lips. "It took me a few months of living in this hell before I connected the dots—sheer luck, mind you—and then I got back on this bus. Took you...? Two days?"

"Two days?! No way."

He shrugs.

"Like I said, 'what is time?'"

"I feel like I lost everything I knew," I murmur, unsure of exactly what I mean but unable to conjure up a more appropriate sentence.

"We lose, a lot, in life. This is no different. But this is no life. Not my life, no. Not yours, I believe. This is something else."

"Do you think we died?" I ask him, somehow able to elicit the words that I've been dreadfully rolling around in my head ever since I parked myself on that bus bench.

He shakes his head.

"Maybe. But I don't think this is it. I think something went wrong."

"Something definitely went wrong," I confirm. "It's like we fell into another world."

Laurent jerks his head toward me, and his eyes are wide and full of terror.

Laurent

"It must be true!" I shout, and the boy looks bewildered. Being cooped up on this bus for however long it has been has eroded my decency and manners.

"What's true?" he asks meekly.

"This world. We're in a different world. We must be. It's the world of that painting. That godforsaken painting...I told you this, didn't I? Do you believe me now, hmm?"

His expression is stern and pensive, and he's still for quite a while. Then he slowly begins to nod.

"How did you possibly figure this out?" he asks.

"I've figured nothing out. It's simply the only explanation that seems to fit with what I see around me, with what's happening to me...to us."

"But then what does that mean?"

I shrug.

"My boy, how the hell do you expect me to answer that question? I'm as lost as you. Only difference is I'm better looking, and I've had a lot longer to come to terms with all of this."

He smirks, no doubt assessing whether I am, in fact, better looking than he. But we both know it to be true. If nothing else, the flesh in this world is as objective as it is in any other.

He ignores my comment and asks, "So what can we do then? How can we find out where the hell we are? How we got here...and, more importantly, how we get the fuck out of here?"

"I have one idea, but it's somewhat of a stretch. And it will quite likely result in the blind leading the blind. And I don't even know where we will start."

"What's that?" he asks with a sigh.

"You and I were both drawn to this painting. I happened to be the one who bought it. You...I don't know your story. Don't care, to be honest. But you seemingly were drawn to it too, yes?"

"Like you wouldn't believe," he says, his lips trembling, full of emotion.

"I bought it to impress my mistress," I admit. "But on some level, we both felt a need to have this painting. *Oui?* I only owned it for, I don't know, a couple of days? Something like that. Then...this happened."

"Jesus," the boy begins. "A few days? It took me *months* to find it. Honestly, I can't believe I did."

He stares ahead, and I imagine he's realizing that his "success" is really nothing to be happy about. His life would have been very different had he just not pursued the painting, had he left it alone. But he didn't. Just like I didn't.

"I shouldn't have been so greedy," he adds.

I shrug.

"What's done is done. Yes?"

"I guess."

We sit in silence for a while, and the bus hums along like we're not even here. Then I snap out of it.

"So what's done is done, sure. But that doesn't mean we have to just sit on our behinds and do nothing."

"What do you propose?"

"We find the painter. I know...this is easier said than done. I don't even know his name. But if we can find him...or her...I think that is the key."

The boy looks up from whatever he was looking down at and connects his gaze with mine.

"Palmieri," he mumbles, as though he was a little unsure how to pronounce it and didn't want to say it too authoritatively.

"What's that?"

"Palmieri," he repeats. "Antonio Palmieri. That's his name."

I leap from my seat.

"Brilliant, my boy! How did you find this out?!"

He shakes his head like I'm a buffoon.

"You think I was able to find *you*, the guy who bought this painting, but I didn't know who actually *painted* it?"

I laugh. Sometimes the most obvious things are right in front of us, and we don't even realize it. Of course he would know, unearthing it somehow through his research. And of course I didn't. The fat man probably told me, but I didn't listen. I just bought it because Patrice wanted it, and I wanted her.

"Palmieri," I repeat, certainly pronouncing it better than he just did, though I don't expect him to take notice. "An Italian?" I ask to confirm, and he nods.

"Lives in France though. Some place, um. Fountain Blue? Is that a place you've heard of?"

"*Fontainebleau?*"

"Yeah. Fountain Blue." He sees the wild look in my eyes that I can feel myself. "Why? What is it? Good?"

"Fontainebleau is a mere sixty minutes outside of the city. We could be there in no time!"

He smiles.

"Great. So then...what's next?"

We both sit and stare at each other, saying nothing.

Wendy

The hotel manager was understanding of our situation, and he offered to give us a guest room for the night, free of charge. I don't want to stay here—this place is way below my standards—but on the chance that Grant comes back or some bit of information about him surfaces, it feels like the right place to be. I'll put aside my standards...

Sam offers to get his own room, but we agree that he can just sleep on a makeshift bed on the floor that we'll make from the pillows and extra blankets tucked away in the room's closet. He's out trying to get a croissant. I hope he takes a typical Sam amount of time.

I miss Grant. I hate to feel this way, to feel like I might not get to have what I had with him again. We don't know where he is or what he's doing. I don't know if he's thinking about me, or off with some other girl, or, I don't know...something worse.

I know this feeling right now. I've felt it before, sparingly. I felt this way when I was too harsh with Ashley and she ran away when we were in high school. I felt this way when I yelled at Umma for embarrassing me in front of my friends. I've felt this way countless times over the past couple of weeks. I don't even want to put it into words, an acknowledgment of my wrongdoing.

Regret.

On the ceiling above me, there are faint cracks that spread from the wall to the seam of the recessed lighting. They are barely discernable, but they're there; and the more I stare at them, the more obvious they become. I think about Grant and his flaws, his cracks. If I stare long enough, any one of them becomes glaring. But you can't stare at something you can't see, someone you don't interact with anymore. In those moments—like now—you don't see the cracks. You don't see anything. You just remember how nice it was to have a ceiling.

I wish I hadn't been so angry all the time. I wish I wasn't still so prone to getting mad. Grant pushed me to see someone about it, and it only made me madder, which is expected; even I can see that. It's hard to acknowledge our own shortcomings. In a polite way, I would say that I have them, that we all have them. And in a calm state of mind, I might even admit the truth about what those are. Most times, though, if pressed for a fault, I'll offer a superficial one. It's a coping mechanism. Admitting it means making it real. I don't know if I'm ready for that.

Please come back, Grant. Please find your way back to me. I know that in times like this, it's easy to promise change in order to get what you want. I see this. I see how wishful I'm being. But that doesn't mean that I can't change. I can try harder. If you come back, Grant, I'll try harder. I'll be gentler. I'll go talk to someone. Maybe you can come with me. Maybe we can make this work.

A tear rolls down my cheek, and I don't stop to wipe it. It flows down to my ear and tickles my earlobe as it slides by and onto the bed. I let out another sigh.

I close my eyes and imagine Grant, lying beside me. He's not perfect. I'm not perfect. But together, we're kind of perfect in some kind of terrible way.

Grant

Blind leading the blind. I wonder how many times in human history this has actually happened. Certainly less than the number of times it has been said as an analogy. Laurent tugs at the sleeve of my shirt, and I step up onto the train. He mutters something quickly to the attendant and then gives my sleeve another tug. We amble down the aisle until we find a pair of available seats.

"All right, my boy," he declares. "To Fontainebleau."

Whatever the hell this world is, it feels like a cruel joke. I can't help but smile.

"*Excusez-moi?*" a woman seated just ahead of us asks in a hushed tone.

"*Oui?*"

She and Laurent exchange words in French. It's all too fast for me to understand anything other than the occasional utterance of *Fontainebleau*. After a few moments of conversing, I nudge Laurent.

"English, please."

"Right!"

Then some more French. I roll my eyes.

"This boy here, he is my accomplice. My partner." I can hear him shift in place, the fabric of his shirt sliding against the seat as he turns toward me. "This fine young lady has offered to help guide us once we disembark the train. She lives in Fontainebleau. How fortunate, yes?"

"That's very fortunate. Thank you, madam," I say, genuinely appreciative. Whatever they say about the French, I think they can often be very friendly. You just have to find the right way to talk to them, particularly if you are American.

"My name is Estelle," she informs me. I nod.

The train pushes along, and Laurent continues conversing with the woman in French. While I can't see any details, I watch as lush blobs of green are gyrating on the periphery of my vision. I try to think about what time of year it is, and my head hurts. Maybe time really isn't real here. Even my head won't let me consider it without a fight.

The train slows a few times to let passengers off and on. On the fourth stop, Laurent stands up and pulls my arm to suggest that I do the same.

"We're here," he announces.

As we step out of the train, the air is remarkably fresh. Surely just a contrast to the stale recirculated air of the train, but nevertheless refreshing.

"Now, what was the name of the artist you said?" Estelle asks.

"Palmieri," Laurent announces. "Antonio Palmieri."

"Very well. I've not heard of him, but I am friends with a gallery owner in town! Surely, he'll know of him. If not, I have other friends who are art collectors. One of them will help us, I'm certain."

Estelle leads us along wobbly cobblestone sidewalks, explaining along the way the shops and landmarks that we pass. A patisserie here, a boulangerie there. I don't understand the nuance between the two, but I listen as best I can, using my other senses to try to pick up the difference. We stop at the site of some activist landmark, but I can't quite understand what she's describing. I'm trying to be patient as she slowly marches us down the road.

"My place is just up here on the left. Would you like to come in for some tea?" she asks.

I expect Laurent to reply, but he remains silent. I consider it for a moment.

"Sure. Tea sounds lovely."

We stop in at her place, and she apologizes for the mess. Her son leaves his things all over the place, she says. It all looks the same to me, a blurry smudge of a mess. It could be the cleanest house on the block, and I wouldn't know the difference.

Two cats are circling me as I sit on the couch, crawling up and down the sides and enclosing me like a shark with its prey. Hector and Bobby.

"Bobby?" I ask, amused.

"My son's idea," Estelle explains.

After she pours us our tea, she phones up her gallery owner friend. A rapid conversation unfolds, and I hear her set the phone down on the table. The room is silent for a few moments.

"My friends, we are in luck."

"Yes?!" Laurent exclaims excitedly. For an older guy, he certainly has a lot of vigor.

"My friend doesn't know Palmieri personally, but he knows where he lives. In fact, I know where he lives, it turns out. He's built a fantastic villa not too far from here. I remember when it was being constructed. I didn't realize it was the home of a painter..." she says with a touch of disgust in her voice, probably the result of her comparing the results of her efforts—in whatever it is that she does for work—with that of a mere *painter*. Or maybe I'm just reading into it and projecting my own biases on her. "I can take you there whenever you wish. It's a mere ten minutes away."

We finish our tea, and I feel a wad of anxiety forming in my gut. I don't know what happens next, but as we exit Estelle's house and make our way back to the sidewalk, the scent in the air has changed. A slight touch of acridity hits my nose, and I cringe, worried that something toxic is burning nearby. The smell passes, or maybe I just acclimate. We continue walking, with Estelle pointing out yet a few more landmarks and shops. She's very knowledgeable about her town.

We arrive, and she shakes my hand.

"Best of luck, young man."

Then she speaks in French to Laurent, and I watch as they seem to embrace, ever so slightly. She starts to walk away.

"Did this feel too easy?" I ask Laurent, verbalizing the question that had been on my mind for the last hour.

He laughs.

"When you're lucky, my boy, you've got to embrace it. Else you'll be left with no luck at all; just a heap of questions."

I think something was lost in translation, but I let it go. Laurent walks a few steps ahead and lets himself into the property via a wrought iron gate. I follow closely behind him, a looming structure filling my vision until it's all that I can see. On the front door, Laurent raps a few quick knocks.

Sam

I don't know how long she wants to be alone for, but I'm fine to just give her time. She was in a pretty rough state when we got up there. Time to herself seems like the right thing right now.

Getting a croissant. Whatever. She—they all—can think that I'm just some dimwit, content to go along with everyone else, with no original thoughts of my own. But I know me, and I know what I'm thinking. I know that I'm *actually* thinking, almost all the time, actually. I know that no one else would think of the sacrifice I make every day by playing this role in their lives. But I see it. I *live* it. Though, it's also a choice. It comes with benefits.

The truth is, I don't want a croissant. They're full of butter, and I've just been getting fatter ever since Piper and I split up. I don't need a croissant; I need a walk. And most of all, I need to find my brother.

I don't know if this will be the occasion where everybody realizes that he's not the only brother with a brain. Like, if I find him and he's in pretty bad shape and he looks to me and says, "Hey, thanks Sam!"

It might not be this time. But there will be a time. And then from that moment on, I guess I will be exposed, and I will no longer be Sam, the brother in the other brother's shadow. I'll just be me. Or, some new version of me that everyone will have to get used to. The me that's been hiding all this time.

I slide my phone from my pocket and scroll through Google Maps. It's late in the afternoon, though it doesn't matter. I'm looking for the closest hospital; they all should be open. Not that I need to go in there—I'm sure I could call instead—but if it's close enough, it's not like I've got anything else to do right now.

Nothing looks super close. Hospital Lariboisière Ap-Hp—whatever that means—seems like the nearest one. The street view of this thing is insane. If this is what a hospital is like in Europe, I hope I come down with something terminal. It's damned near a palace!

I look at my watch as I dial the number. A woman answers, saying something rapidly that I can't begin to understand.

"Hello?" I ask, hoping that's all I need to do to signify that I am an American. But she repeats whatever she said before as though she either had no idea or was just waiting for me to self-identify.

"Sorry. American? I am looking to see if a patient is there at your hospital."

The line is quiet for a while, and then a man's voice comes in.

"Name?"

"Who, the patient? Or me?"

"Are you the patient?" he barks.

"No, I am not."

"What is the patient's name," he states, not asks.

I tell him, and I hear a keyboard clattering.

"Nothing. Sorry."

"Thank you."

"Maybe try the police station," he suggests helpfully.

"Thanks."

I call a few other hospitals before I even consider calling the police. I know they're going to have me come in and fill out a bunch of paperwork, and while I think Wendy wants some time alone, I don't think she wants *that* much time alone. Also, she might want to be there for it. Instead, I head back to the hotel, feeling good about the progress I made. I didn't find Grant, but I found some places where he's not. That's not much, but it's more information than we had before.

I smile to myself, but then the smile slowly fades from my face as I realize that this proud feeling I'm having is at the expense of my brother. I don't want it to be this way. But it is.

Oh well. He'll turn up. And if I have something to do with it, then new Sam can emerge. And if I don't, six more weeks of winter...

Piper

I close Spotify. Stupid song. I survey my now-quiet apartment. I can't stand the thought of living through a moment of such cliché: all of my belongings are packed and stacked neatly along one wall, and here I am, playing some sappy song about moving on with your life.

My frustration over Grant's decision to disappear off to Europe has folded into guilt over the way I've handled this whole situation. That guilt has collapsed into regret. That regret has manifested as a strong sense of humility as I stand here, my meager pile of possessions gathered into one modest-sized stack. Yes, humility. I've not felt this way in a while, but I know it's probably a good thing, so I'm going to try and embrace it.

I've been a little too proud for too long. Too proud to live with Gary; no, I had to have my own apartment. Too proud to use dating apps after Sam and I broke up; no, I'm better than that…I don't need an app to find someone I connect with. Too proud to date Sam when I realized he wasn't perfect on paper. Too proud to reach out to Grant when I learned he was moving, and too proud to try to reach him with more than just a call and an email. I was even too proud to check in with Sam or, God forbid, with Wendy. Even with this realization, I'm still too proud to tell any of them that I'm leaving tomorrow; my brother's the only person who knows, unless Grant actually read my email.

Humility. All I can do is stare at my boxes and think about the moving truck that Gary will be loading them onto. They'll trek all the way across the country, across three time zones and two thousand miles. They won't know they've traveled, of course, and I will arrive there before them. They won't know that either.

Possessions aren't proud. They aren't humble either. They're inanimate, typically, and they somehow also strike the perfect balance that I've thus far struggled to even come close to. I'm not a possession though. I know I'm flawed. I sometimes put that façade up so that I don't have to defend myself, but deep down I know where the faults are.

I open Spotify again and search for my Pearl Jam playlist. Fuck this sappy, get-out-of-my-life music. I want *Vitalogy* or *Vs.* or *Ten*. Out the window, a fine mist is beginning to turn into light rain. I check my watch, then I call for my car.

I look around my apartment, then at the door, my suitcase neatly pressed against the frame. I think about everything that I'm about to leave behind. Everything I wish it could have been—when I came out here—in some ways, it was. And in some very clear ways, it wasn't. Sam was a good thing while it lasted. I liked the job. I liked being near Gary. Obviously, the weather (aside from today). And the shopping. And the food. But all of this isn't for me, and it probably never was. Like all those sad, once-hopeful souls that think they're being subversive by agreeing with the anti-L.A. rhetoric in overheard quotes that they scroll by on IG, I'm just a person who tried and failed to make it in this city. I don't even know why I came here in the first place, but I know why I'm leaving.

Laurent

A medium-sized woman answers the door, and unfortunately, this is the best description of her that my brain can conjure, given my present sensory limitations.

"Allo?" she asks.

"Hi, madam. I was told this is the home of Antonio Palmieri. Is that right?"

"Who are you?" she responds, justly.

"My name is Laurent. I am a big fan of your husband's work. I have a piece of his in my hotel, back in Paris."

"And who's this?" she returns, clearly unimpressed with my fandom.

"A friend of mine. Also a big fan. See, we're just in town visiting a friend, and—"

"He's not in right now. Can you come back another time?"

It looks like she's still got her hand on the door, likely waiting to close it as soon as she can. I don't know if he gets lots of fans coming up to his door, but if that were me, I'd not have even answered it in the first place if I didn't know the people on the other side.

"I'm afraid we cannot," the boy says, and I wince. "I've traveled here from Los Angeles. I was hoping to speak to him. It's very important."

"As I said, he's not in. I can't make him appear, understand? He's not here right now."

"Can we wait? When will he be back? You know, approximately?"

I interrupt before she can respond, interjecting my silver tongue right into the middle of the conversation.

"Madam, if I may. Please. We are both visually impaired. The boy, he's just impatient. He's been traveling a long while, and as someone suffering from blindness, this is quite the challenge. I, too, am blind. We are just hoping to speak with Mr. Palmieri while we are in town. Would that be all right?"

She sighs.

"He never tells me when he's coming back," she mutters, and I see her hand slide down the frame of the door. "Tell me...blind? How did you get here then?"

"A very kind lady led us here. She lives in town."

"Is this someone I know? Does she know Antonio?"

"Her name is Estelle."

"I don't believe I know an Estelle," she remarks.

"Very well. She is friends with a gallery owner who sent us this way."
I pause for a beat, and she remains quiet. "We don't mean any trouble.
We'd just like to meet him if we could."

"Just to ask a few questions," the boy chimes in, though I wish he
would just leave it to me.

A few moments pass before the woman takes my hand in hers and
leads me into the house.

"My name is Sofia. Antonio is my husband. I'm sorry for your
condition and the way that I reacted. We don't get a lot of *normal* people
coming to our door. I'm sure you understand."

I tip my head to show my appreciation. The boy shuffles in behind me.

"There's a parlor over here. You boys can sit and relax, at least for a
little while, get your energy back. I don't know when he'll be returning, I
truly don't. Sometimes he goes off for days..."

We're led into the parlor and take seats on the couch. I rub my eyes
and let out a big yawn. I don't know what time it is, but I'm exhausted.

"Laurent," the boy whispers. "Is your..."

As he starts to say it, I notice it too.

"Can this be?" I say aloud.

As my vision comes back into focus, I get the same feeling as when I
first board the bus. It's like my head was just under a murky puddle of water
and someone lifted me out by the back of my hair. Like life anew has
washed over me.

"I can see again!" the boy cries, still in a hushed tone.

"This Palmieri is the key," I confirm. "He must be."

The boy leans closer to me and maintains his quiet voice.

"How long do you think she'll let us wait?"

I push myself back into the couch, trying to examine how supple its
cushions are. If she had to try to pry me out of here, could she do it? Or
could I sink myself in and hold on tight? I decide that she'd have to call a

man larger than me to get me out of here. But that hardly seems like the right course of action.

"Can I get either of you anything?" she asks as her feet *pitter-patter* down a long-sounding hallway. She appears in the doorway to the parlor.

"I think we're okay," I tell her.

She nods.

"Care to visit his studio?" she asks with a smile. "Again, I'm terribly sorry for how I treated you when you first arrived. I do hope you forgive me."

Where this charm and personality has come from is beyond me, but I won't question it.

"Surely, that would be fantastic!"

Sofia leads us down the hallway—it's somehow longer than it sounded, with not a single piece of décor adorning the tall, white walls—and back to a small door at the very end of the corridor. She swings the door open wide, and the doorknob slams into whatever is on the other side of it.

Inside is, in fact, an art studio. It's not very large, compared to the footprint of this enormous villa, but it is large enough to store at least a few dozen completed works, not to mention all of the supplies in use. In the center of the room is a large easel with a half-finished seascape. Nearby is a small easel with a close-up of a boat, and then leaning neatly along the perimeter walls are numerous paintings, all facing inward and creating a kaleidoscope of colors that, for a moment, send me back into a blind tizzy. A strange-looking stand holds another dozen or so finished works, seemingly to keep the paintings from touching each other.

"He's prolific," I comment.

"Antonio loves to paint. His *worlds*, they are unique and his own. He loves them very much. Every piece, he says. He loves each one like it's one of his children."

The boy begins thumbing through the stack in the stand.

"Lots of boats," he remarks. "Oh, and a horse race. And another boat. And...another boat."

"Wait just a moment..." she begins. "I thought you said that you cannot see?"

I look over at the boy and cock my head to the side in anticipation of his response.

"*Functionally* blind," he says, with a touch of sadness. "But I can still see the colors and shapes."

She nods understandingly, and I let out a quiet sigh.

"So, when do you expect him?" I ask again, hoping to divert her attention before she asks any more specifics.

"Laurent," the boy interrupts. "Hey, Laurent!"

I smile at Sofia and turn to look at him.

"I'm talking to the lady of the house," I affirm, with as much manners as I can muster.

"No, *Laurent*..." he repeats.

I can't hide the disgust on my face. She sees this and waves me on, suggesting it's fine. I walk over to him.

"I said, we're talking."

He's standing there at the stand, about three paintings from the edge of the stack.

"Did you see this one?" he asks.

I shrug.

"No." I turn and face Sofia for a moment, smiling a fake smile of interest. "I was planning on it, but..."

"Laurent, *look*."

I sigh forcefully through my nose and bring myself alongside him to look at whatever it is he's looking at. Thankfully, it's not another painting of a bus.

"What is it?" I ask him. "An old man? So?"

"Doesn't he look familiar?" he whispers under his breath.

I squint. Sofia walks over and examines the piece we're both eyeing.

"Oh, this? That's just a silly self-portrait. I'd asked him to paint something other than a boat. Something I could hang in my powder room. He took it upon himself to have some fun. He knew I wouldn't ever dare hang a picture of *him* in his own house. How ostentatious!"

I shrug. I'd consider doing it. It doesn't sound that bad. And it's a nice painting, albeit somewhat boring.

"This is him?!" the boy shouts, and Sofia jumps, taken aback.

"Yes. Why? What is the matter?"

"Laurent!" he shouts, and I have to press my hand on his shoulder to stop whatever vocal eruption will burst from his mouth next.

"Boy, what is it? Have you gone mad?"

"Laurent," he repeats, saying my name for nearly the tenth time in the span of a minute. "That's the bus driver!"

I squint again and tilt my head.

"My lord," I mutter. "You're right. You're right!"

Sofia is perplexed as we sprint toward the door, down the hall, and out into the courtyard. I can't even stop to thank her for her hospitality. We're on a mission now, this much is certain. We must get back to that bus!

Grant

I'm huffing and puffing. The staggering of my steps as I stumble across the uneven roads are making it look like I'm either raging drunk or coming off a gnarly ankle injury. Laurent is somewhere trailing me, but that's an unfair characterization since I did take off before him. For all I know, he could be a faster runner than me.

When we reach what I think is Estelle's house, I start shouting her name. Someone—not Estelle—comes out from a door a few feet away from me and kindly points me in the right direction. I yell her name again, and after a few moments, she appears.

"Can you get us back to the train?"

My words are nearly vomit in my mouth. I'm all out of sorts. Laurent catches up and rests his hand in between my shoulder blades.

"Back so soon?" she asks.

"There's no time to explain," I tell her. "Can we go?" She obliges. We walk, me upping the tempo with a hurried pace that I'm hoping she can match. The train station eventually makes its way into the blurry mess of my vision. I've begun to get used to this, and I almost feel like I can see through all of the smudges. Or it's just the adrenaline. I don't know what I'm feeling other than a swelling pit at the bottom of my stomach.

"Thank you!" I yell as the train hisses and the doors open.

We board, and off we go. For twenty minutes, Laurent and I sit in silence. He's the one to break it first.

"What's our plan?"

I breathe in deeply and let it all out through my nose.

"Get back on that bus and hope to all holy hell that he's driving it."

"And then?"

I shrug.

"And then ask him what the fuck is going on? I don't know. You have a better plan?"

"Nonsense. How could I?"

We sit in silence for the remainder of the ride. There's no tension between us, but the conversation resonates in my head and rattles around as though there is. I'm on the verge of apologizing when the train conductor announces our stop.

Miraculously, we find our way back to what I believe to be the same exact bus bench that I'd been sitting on for what feels like a nonzero part of an eternity. Laurent sits alongside me, stoic and silent. I think we're both thinking the same thing. We don't need to say it though. And we don't need to know.

Laurent

The boy rises from his seat at the sound of every diesel engine that approaches. Amazingly, when the bus actually does arrive, he stays seated. I rode the thing for so long, I know its sound like the voice of my *Maman*. Unmistakable, indelibly etched into my brain.

"This is it," I tell him.

He springs to his feet with true purpose. The doors open, and a crowd of passengers disembark. Then we slowly ascend the stairs. The boy is in front of me, and he pauses when he reaches the top step. Then he shuffles back into the bus, no doubt aware that this will all be easier when his vision comes back into focus.

We sit down and wait for whatever magic trick brings the world back to normal. It happens, thank God, and then we turn to lock eyes. Without saying a word, we stare at each other for the better part of ten seconds, closing in on forever. I stand up and march to the front of the bus. The driver is staring straight ahead.

"*Excusez-moi?*"

He doesn't turn to look at me and, instead, raises a single finger as if to tell me to hold on. I see nothing remarkable ahead, but I wait regardless.

"So now you know," he says, slowly and deliberately.

The boy is standing right behind me. I look down at my feet, and they are extending beyond the painted yellow safety line. I examine his face. It's certainly the man from the painting.

"Palmieri?" I ask, defying whatever it is that he thinks I *know*. I need to really *know*.

"Pleasure," he responds. "How was Sofia?"

The boy lets out a loud sigh.

"What's going on?" he blurts. "Hmm? What is this?!"

"She was lovely," I let Palmieri know. "Very hospitable."

He chuckles.

"Got her on a good day, I suppose."

"Hey!" the boy yells. "Enough of this shit. What's going on? We need to know. What is this? What *is* all of this?"

I place my hand on his shoulder and shake my head. The young have no patience. I didn't, when I was young. They all lack it, like our genetics simply don't allow for it until we're too old to care about getting worked up. I suppose for some, it never goes away. They must die young.

"My friend here is just anxious," I explain coolly. "We'd like to understand what has happened here. We believe you are the key to our understanding. Is this right?"

Palmieri turns to look at me briefly and then refocuses his gaze on the road ahead. The boy relaxes and stays silent, thankfully.

"What do *you* think this is?" he posits.

"Afterlife?"

He shakes his head.

"After what, exactly? What is *life*?"

Under other circumstances, I could entertain the existentiality of this question for quite a while. But I know this will cause the boy's head to explode, so I tuck it away and take it at face value.

"Still trying to figure that out," I admit. "I thought I had a life. Then I ended up...here."

The bus slows to a halt as we wait behind a line of Peugeots and Mercedes and Fiats, all lined up behind a red light.

"You were always here," Palmieri mumbles, just loud enough for me to catch him.

"I don't follow."

"Never you mind," he says abruptly. "Here you are. You're not alone. There are others here too." He pauses, collecting his thoughts. "But that is irrelevant. What is it that you would like me to do for you?"

"I'd like to go back," the boy announces. If nothing else, he's direct. I've got to appreciate that.

"Back where?"

"To my regular life," he replies. "The one I was living before I got sucked into this painting. That *is* what happened, right?"

"Like I said, you were always here," Palmieri repeats. "But if it's easier for you to reconcile it that way, I understand."

"How do we get back?" I interject, hoping to stem an argument. We need this man to help us, not to berate him for things we still are yet to even understand. The bus stops, and a handful of passengers get off. No one gets on. Palmieri keeps his hands on the wheel and stares straight ahead as the doors close.

"Let me ask you, Laurent. Why are you here?"

Though I'm unsurprised that he knows my name, it still gives me somewhat of a shock to hear him say it. Clearly, this man is more involved in my fate than I'd have ever expected a stranger to be.

"How are we supposed to know that?!" the boy shouts. Again, I give him a look to try to keep him calm.

"I have an idea why," I suggest. "As you know, I've been here quite a while."

"Indeed," Palmieri confirms.

"This is for my indiscretions. Right?"

"What indiscretions are those?" he asks with a hint of innocence, though I know better than to believe it is genuine.

"My penchant for women. Me going out on Margot. The affairs. The girls in the shops. The ones I took to the hotel. All of them. This is punishment, right? Time to pay for my transgressions?"

He shrugs.

"Your sins are your sins. It's not my place to judge."

I raise my eyebrows.

"But that *is* why I'm here, isn't it?"

He turns and stares directly into my eyes with no regard for the road. I instinctively trust that he has this under control, so I don't worry about what's ahead.

"Think of it this way," he begins. "Every day is a lesson. Every scene in life is an opportunity to grow. To learn something about yourself, to perform an act of kindness, to improve the world. But at the same time, each scene is also an opportunity to destroy. To take what's not meant to be yours, to hurt others, to cause damage to another person who is also just trying to live through their daily lesson. Do you see?"

I contemplate what he says as he continues.

"You're here because you were contributing too much to the destruction," he finally states. "And now, here...you can't. Do you see? This is a place where you can't be who you were, and that is good for the scenes you've left behind. It's good for everyone. You must learn."

You must learn. The boy is trembling with either anger or confusion, and I can feel it vibrate in the air.

"Are you God?" he utters, almost as a single syllable.

"I'm a painter," Palmieri states unemotionally.

"But are they mutually exclusive?"

Palmieri shrugs and changes the subject.

"Young man, do you know why *you're* here?" he asks.

Grant

I search the catalog of my brain for all of my transgressions, conjuring memories of Catholic confessional, my unfortunately strict upbringing, making up sins I didn't commit just to get through the service.

"I'm no cheater," I say, though I know that's not always been the case.

"There are plenty of ways to destroy," Palmieri offers.

I think about it for a moment. The moment turns into many moments. The bus chugs along. Laurent appears to be frozen in time. I don't know how many stops come and go, and now I feel frozen too. Finally, my lips part, and the words seem to just fall out and onto the bus floor.

"I'm never content with what I have."

At this, Palmieri nods and smiles.

"It takes some longer than others," he assures me.

I turn around, and the bus is entirely empty. Then I realize that we're not moving and, instead, we're parked alongside the side of the road.

"Are we destined to stay here forever?" Laurent asks, a note of acceptance baked into his words.

"How long you stay is entirely up to you," Palmieri says. "You can leave now if that's what should be. Everyone moves at a different pace."

"How do we do that?" I ask. "We already got off the bus. It's a blurry hell out there."

He remains silent for a while, and the deadened sound of traffic passing by is all that fills my ears.

"It's actually quite simple," he finally states. "You are to ask yourself: Will you be a better person if you're able to go back? Will you stop contributing to the destruction? Will you be different?"

"Yes," Laurent recites. "Very much yes."

"And you?" he asks, facing me.

"I'd like to be. I don't want to be a *destroyer*."

"No one does. It sometimes just happens to us. There's nothing we can do but be aware and try to correct it."

He's starting to lose me, but I'm trying to keep it all together.

"I know," he adds.

For a moment, the notion that he can read my mind is all that I can consider. So, I don't say anything, and I instead just think about all of the things that my greed has displaced in my life. Wendy wanders into the frame of my mind's eye first. Ahh...*Wendy*. My heart flutters every time I think of her, like she's a novel concept and I've never experienced her before. I'd give anything to get back to her.

I'd give anything just to be back home, in fact, with my whole life that I put to the side as I pursued this damned painting. Sam, who was always there for me even when I wasn't paying attention to him. Piper...*shit*. I feel terrible about the way I discarded our friendship. I don't even know if I realized I was doing it. If I ever get back to my old life, I'll treat them all so differently. They deserve a genuine version of me that cares about them as much as they care about me, not some destructive bastard who only cares about himself. I don't know how that was the man I became, but it won't be the man I am for even another goddamned second.

Palmieri turns his attention back to the road and waves his right hand in front of Laurent's chest.

"Perhaps it is time to go. Let's see," he says calmly, then slams his foot on the accelerator.

The bus lurches forward, its engine screaming and whining as the vehicle picks up speed and barrels ahead down the road. I stumble backward, and Laurent does as well. He falls harder than me, but I can't get up to help him; the velocity of the bus is pinning me to the floor. I crane my neck up and look out the window. Ahead is a bridge, crossing the Seine. The bus charges up the hill, and as we climb higher over the surface of the water, I see a string of sailboats crossing under the bridge.

I pull myself up using all of my strength, and at the moment I'm nearly upright, the bus jerks sharply to the right, its wheels slamming violently into the sidewalk, the front fender crushing through the railing. The bus careens over the edge of the bridge and enters a brief free fall. My body is flung high in the air, floating for a moment, and then I see the water approaching fast...

Wendy

His snoring wakes me up. Through blurry eyes, I stare over at the makeshift bed on the floor and spot Sam lying there, hands behind his head, mouth agape. The tiny blanket that he chose is barely long enough to cover him from chest to toe. As my eyes focus, I see one foot protruding awkwardly into the air, a glow from the streetlight outside illuminating his pinky toe.

I look out at the window, and dawn is approaching. I pull the covers over my eyes and try to fall back asleep. Maybe I do. I think I do. But then I think I don't. I wake up again. The room is bright now. Sam's still snoring, but now it's louder. It's like there's Sam, and then there's Sam in full 5.1 surround, and whoever set up the sound system here chose the latter.

Why is it so *loud?*

I grab the water bottle from the nightstand, and I throw it in his direction, hoping to startle him but not make contact. It lands squarely in his belly, and he curls inward upon impact.

"What the..."

I laugh inside.

"Sorry, buddy. You were snoring."

He shifts around and rolls his head across the pillow to look in my direction.

"The hell I was. *You* were snoring. It woke *me* up."

Now I laugh outside.

"I don't snore! Don't try to blame me!"

Sam has a look on his face like he's about to get up and do something erratic. I've never seen this look. I'm taken aback for a moment, and then

I hear the snoring again. My head swivels to the left, and that's when I see him. Mouth agape, just like his brother, his black t-shirt draped over his eyes. I know it's him without even the sight of almost any of him.

"Grant!" I shriek, pure joy resonating in my voice. I haven't heard myself this happy in...maybe ever.

He stirs and snatches the shirt from his face, then gasps for breath.

"Where am I?"

Sam is standing, looking over the two of us as we lie here together unexpectedly in this bed.

"Where *were* you?" Sam modifies and asks in return.

Grant sits up and looks at his hands. Then he runs them through his hair, pushing it back from his forehead. Then he gasps a few more breaths.

"Is this...for real, where am I?"

I try to orient him with specifics.

"We're at the Madeleine Haussmann hotel in Paris."

He looks around and seems to remember it by the décor.

"Here? Why did you choose to stay *here?*"

"I didn't choose this," I tell him. "You did."

He ignores me.

"Which painting is this?"

I look around the room, and there are no paintings anywhere. He glances at Sam and then connects his gaze with me.

"Is this *real?*" he asks, his eyes full of fear.

"Yes," I say assuredly, though I'm unaware of what he's afraid of, so I don't know that it's a fantastic answer to his question.

"Are *you* for real?" Sam asks, still standing awkwardly over the bed. He's been helpful, but I kind of wish he wasn't here right now. "Where have you been, dude? We came all the way to Paris to try to find you! How did you get back here? Why did you just climb in bed? Why didn't you wake us up? How did you even get in? Don't they change the keys when you check out? I mean, I guess you didn't check out…"

I look over at Grant, and he's smiling, his brother's rambling string of largely unnecessary questions probably amusing him more than it ever will again.

"You guys wouldn't even believe me if I told you," he says.

"Try me," I tell him.

He looks into my eyes and throws his arms around me.

"I missed you so much," he says, and I melt in time.

And so, we're back. I can already tell. At least for now.

Laurent

"Dad!" the boy yells.

The boy?

I spring up to my feet. *Merde!*

I take the steps two at a time, almost tumbling midway but regaining my composure, and I leap into the living room. No one is here.

"Dad!" he yells again. This time I locate his voice more clearly. I rush to the back door.

Margot is lounging on the chaise, sunglasses on, a book resting on her lap. The boy is fiddling with the wheels on a model train.

At my presence, Margot lowers her glasses and connects her eyes with mine.

"I told you he was here!" the boy exclaims, his long hair swinging down in front of his eyes. "I heard him upstairs."

"Been off a while? *Business?*" Margot asks snidely, and I know what she's thinking.

"It's not like that," I begin, but then I relent. "It's hard to explain. But…I'm back now. And I'm never leaving."

She raises her sunglasses back and rests her head back against the seat.

"If you say so."

"Laurent!" I hear Ettie call out from over the wall. "Is that you?"

Margot will have to wait a moment. Besides, it's a private conversation. The boy shouldn't have to hear a word of it.

"It's me."

"Hey, have you heard from Armond?" he asks.

I look at Margot, then at the boy, and neither are looking at me. I roll my eyes for posterity.

"I have not."

He lets out a *hmmmph*, and then his sliding door whooshes shut, as though nothing from the past few months had even happened. I walk over to Margot and sit down on the edge of the chaise. The boy is fixated on his model, so I take the opportunity while I can and kiss her on the cheek.

"I promise. On my life."

She lowers her glasses again, and this time, there's a glint of joy in her eyes, something I haven't seen in a long time.

"I don't believe you, but I'm glad you're back."

She smiles. It feels genuine, even if it's nothing more than a formality, a micro-gesture of goodwill for a man undeserving.

"You'll see," I tell her, a maniacal smile erupting across my face.

I'm back. By God, I'm back! I will not take this for granted.

"You'll see, my love," I repeat. "You'll see."

Grant

I'm clutching my knees with the inside of my elbows, the point of my tailbone teetering on the stone step. Every now and then, she budges from her position and I rock in response, my precarious perch susceptible to even the slightest nudge. The view from up here never gets old. Wendy has her hands wrapped around my arm, her face half-buried into my shoulder. She's clinging to me like it's much colder than it is. I smile.

"Tell me," she says quietly, staring off at the city as the lights begin to twinkle on all the tops of the buildings. "Did you find it?"

I shake my head.

"Find what?"

"What you were looking for," she explains. "Did you find it?"

I sigh and think for a moment. I want to give her a thoughtful answer. There's no reason to rush. That's one thing I've learned with all that's just gone on. Everything can wait. It's all up to you.

"Yes," I say, and then I pause. "And yes. But in two totally different ways."

We say nothing for a moment as an errant balloon floats diagonally across the sky above us.

"I don't get it," she admits.

"I don't either. But I'm different now because of it."

"Different *good?*"

I look around and inspect the people around us, hoping that maybe the sight of one of them will inspire a poignant answer. There are a few solo travelers, one large group, and other than that, it's just a bunch of couples. *They're probably no different than us,* I think. Then I instinctively start to size them up. One guy has an attractive piece of arm candy clung to his side, her fur-lined boots whisking against his legs as they stroll in front of the fence. Another guy is wearing a Saint Laurent jacket that looks like it's just my size. In the street on the far side of the church, there's a Ferrari steadily humming as its engine idles.

There's something that catches my eye everywhere I look...but then I turn my head back to Wendy, and I see her inquisitive, sweet doe eyes just looking up at me with more affection than I've ever had directed at me in my life. There isn't a possession in the world that compares to this feeling right now, and I know this deep in my heart. I close my eyes and let out a soft breath of air through my parted lips.

"Yes. Different *good.*"

Sam

While they're off exploring the city, their first time as a couple, I'm off exploring it as well, my first time alone. The juxtaposition makes sense on the surface, but it also feels a little odd. Out on my own...perhaps new Sam has already begun to emerge?

At a coffee shop just off of Champs-Élysées, I unlock my phone and check Instagram. Nothing interesting. Also, it takes forever to load on the free Wi-Fi. I search for Piper, scrolling back through her pictures. She doesn't post a lot, so in a few scrolls, I'm back at a point in time when we were together.

I put my phone down, and a strong feeling overcomes me. If only life could be so easy as to travel back in time with a couple of swipes. I'd live in that world. I'd take the volatility if it meant getting to be back with Piper. Sure, she could probably swipe away too, but at least we could give it another shot.

I zone out for a little while, deep in contemplation. Then I come back to this reality. *But is it too late?* I think to myself. Maybe it's not. Maybe we could still make it work.

I think about texting her, but then I get inside my own head. I don't even know what I'd say. I'm always rambling in messages; I'm never effective. This message will be better delivered in person. It's an important one. That's the right way to do it.

Antonio

My brush scrapes across the canvas as it always does, the palette knife in my other hand chopping up the paint as I spread it. Cityscapes and vessels are well-suited for this style. Portraits are not. But why let that stop me? I'm a *creator*. I've told Sofia as much, but she seems to have misheard me, or otherwise demands a better answer.

"Antonio!" she yells out, her voice echoing down the empty hall.

Her footsteps approach me—*pitter-patter, pitter-patter*—until she's practically on top of me. I don't turn around. She knows that I can hear her. The rest of the place is as silent as a tomb.

"Antonio," she repeats. "What did you say?"

I shake my head.

"I was creating," I try to tell her. "I need space. Can't you see? I need space to create. This is what I do. I am a *creator*."

"You have space," she tells me. "You have all this space!"

It feels like we've had this argument before. I pause and recollect myself, knowing there's got to be a better exit to this conversation than what otherwise could be about to happen.

"You're right, my love."

She smiles.

"See?" She nudges my arm and nods her head at the canvas. "When you paint something *other* than the boats and the buses, you see how much happier you are?"

I let out a deep breath.

"You're right again, my love."

I set the brush and the knife down on the palette, and I turn to look at her. She's staring ahead at my work.

"Lovely-looking girl," she marvels. "Truly astonishing."

"Thank you."

"But, tell me. Where is a pretty girl like that going in the rain? And with a suitcase, no less?"

I shrug.

"Where she goes is up to her," I respond. "That's always been how it works."

CPSIA information can be obtained
at www.ICGtesting.com
Printed in the USA
LVHW091910020320
648717LV00007B/288/J

9 780999 374382